Praise fo

I devoured *Scare Away the Dark*....had to *make* myself put it down. I was totally drawn in by page three... the heart-stopping plot twists and turns just kept unfolding. Complex, believable characters, ... lush locations in British Columbia's lower mainland and Calabria, Italy. I may never recover from the ending, which literally took my breath away. Can hardly wait for book three!

—Bonnie Hutchinson, *Transitions: Pathways to the Life and World Your Soul Desires*

Scare Away the Dark...from the moment I picked up the book, to the last sentence - which had me jumping up out of my seat - I was hooked. Karen takes you on a journey filled with terror, suspense, action, intrigue, beauty and romance...twists and turns that will keep you turning the pages, even after you say, "just one more chapter and then I'm going to sleep."...a great sequel to Deadly Switch...can't wait for the third book in the Stone Suspense series!

—Linda LeQuesne

Scare Away the Dark draws the reader into the twisting maze of events that occur as Jordan Stone searches for truth. Superbly written descriptors and eloquent writing places you in each moment as if you were there yourself. Complicated friendships, kidnapping, murders and international spy rings are all interwoven through each chapter. You become so involved that you think you have found the solution for Jordan only to turn the page to find another surprise awaits.

—Briar Ballou

I loved the building of suspense in Karen's Dodd's second book. It was less laced with non-stop action, and for me, that made the suspense more delicious and the inevitable moments of action, more believable and vivid. It was an irresistible ride!

—Gail Muise

Scare Away the Dark... I had to force myself to put the book down. What an exciting mix of mystery, adventure and love. ... lots of twists and turns ...Being myself a Sicilian, I wanted to remain in Sicily with Jordan a little longer...I want to know that this story will continue, because let me tell you, it is far from being over!!!

—Lucy Traini

I enjoyed Deadly Switch but *Scare Away the Dark* is even better... careful scene descriptions and relatable characters grabbed me... starts off with a bang, then an unlikely partnership emerges and pulls us through the unpredictable story. Romance, travel, intrigue, all carefully woven into a great thriller, spanning BC, Italy, and California. A page-turner that's good till the last drop.

—Rod Baker, *Um, where is Belize*

Karen Dodd's latest suspense thriller, *Scare Away the Dark*...wrought with cagey characters, raw emotion and vile villains...you'll be closing the curtains, locking the doors and looking over your shoulder. You won't see the end coming!

—Penelope J. McDonald, *The Emerald Collar*

Scare Away the Dark is an extremely well written page-turner! This second book in the Stone Suspense Series is every bit as addictive as the first... fast-paced, gritty, real, exciting... characters are well drawn, memorable and alive in the imagination. The writing is at every turn, superb - clever, witty and masterful. The ending strikes the perfect balance of being extremely satisfying while leaving you craving more!

—Angela Greville

Scare Away the Dark...I have just put it down and I am breathless, wrung out and emotionally raw with empathy for the main character, Jordan Stone...a carousel of mystery and danger! This second novel of Karen Dodd's takes you away like you are holding on for dear life to the tail of a kite and never lets you touch your feet to the ground...

—Karen Sanderson

SCARE AWAY THE DARK

KAREN DODD

SCARE AWAY THE DARK
A Stone Suspense
KAREN DODD

Published by
Pegasus Press

Cover design by **Sharon Brownlie, Aspire Covers**

Formatting and layout provided by **Aspire Covers**
http://aspirecovers.com

For Nina,

Also by Karen Dodd

DEADLY SWITCH: A Stone Suspense

With gratitude

Karen Dodd.

For Glen, for your unwavering support and patience.
For being there to nurse me through the challenges
as well as celebrate the joys!

Chapter One

Jordan Stone gazed desolately out her office window high above Vancouver's slick gray sidewalks. With virtual certainty, one could forecast that Halloween would be ushered in by vicious winds driving monsoon-like rain horizontally across the downtown's darkening streets. This year's celebration of ghosts and goblins was to be no exception. Except, this time it fell on a Friday.

The press room that housed the crime beat reporters thrummed with activity. Jordan's research assistant, Rachel Sommers, was busy rounding up her fellow staffers and herding them toward the elevator so they'd be in time to cadge the first happy hour drinks at the pub across the street. Always up for anything that involved costumes, the quirkier the better, she was dressed in a vintage Wonder Woman costume she'd originally bought for Jordan. She had tried unsuccessfully to convince her friend and boss that with her height, naturally streaked chestnut hair, and a figure "thousands would die for," it would be perfect. Now, as Jordan watched the last of the stragglers clear out for a night of unrestrained revelry, she lagged behind telling them she would finish up and join them soon. *I promise*, she silently mouthed across the room to Rachel, who glared at her from beneath impossibly arched jet-black eyebrows. Jordan's conscience pricked at her a little, knowing all the while, as soon as everyone was gone, she would begin the hour-plus drive through pelting rain to the area known as the Fraser Valley.

Having risen—fought, would be more accurate—to the status of being the youngest senior crime reporter on staff at one of Canada's leading newspapers, Jordan had more than paid her dues. It was the end of a long week and having worked her typical twelve-hour day, she would have been justified in sending a junior reporter out to follow up the anonymous tip. Half the time it was just some schmuck who called in hoping for their fifteen minutes of fame and to make a few bucks. The solid leads almost always came from tirelessly working her virtual Rolodex of confidential informants, not from a call the latest temp receptionist misrouted to her office. Albeit Jordan was a self-professed workaholic, there was something about this particular lead that compelled her to head out on a vicious, blustery evening without telling either her editor or her assistant. Secrets, she thought. You're keeping too many secrets, Jordan.

Despite the usual Friday night rush hour traffic and the tension of straining to see through the inky darkness and blowing rain, she eventually reached the address she'd been given on the phone—an all-night diner—and parked her car. She reached for her umbrella and pushed open the car door only to have it snatched from her hand by the howling wind. She tossed the umbrella back in the car, grabbed a small flashlight and dashed through icy sheets of rain. Cautiously, she made her way on foot across a gravel parking lot, head down, focusing on avoiding ankle-deep water-filled potholes. Someone called her name. She pushed back the hood of her raincoat, then peered through the torrential downpour to see a hand beckoning her from the open window of a van.

"Hey, are you Jordan Stone?" he called. "I'm the guy who…"

The downpour pummeled her face as she stepped closer to hear what he was saying. Then, as if someone had shut off the lights, her world plunged into darkness.

Chapter Two

She heard the unmistakable sound of a rat scratching a zigzag path through the dust and debris in the abandoned shipping container. This time it chose a route *around* the filthy mattress where she lay, rather than skittering across her prone body. On her back, with all four limbs shackled to bolts on the metal floor, she could either look up to the rough-hewn wood ceiling or turn her head toward the rusted insides of the rail car. A dingy bulb that was programmed to come on automatically, cast a faint yellow hue in her prison, expanding her view. To one side was an ever-growing cache of discarded cigarette butts, to the other was a web being methodically spun by a spider to trap its supper or maybe its breakfast. In the far-right corner, through the delicate filigree of the web, she counted the marks scratched into the metal walls that surrounded her. Did each stroke represent the number of days another pathetic soul had been buried alive? Unlike her, they must have had their hands free. With a ragged sigh, she closed her eyes and tried to sleep.

A hazy image floated through the soupy fog of

her brain. She focused on taking deep, slow breaths. As she'd done so many times during her captivity, she struggled to remember. Each day, as she lay shivering in the dark, the same theme repeated itself. People in ghoulish costumes taunted her. She knew them. And then she didn't. She saw herself driving through blinding rain, but she couldn't put the pieces of the puzzle together. Now, as she gave up all hope of being rescued, her clenched jaw ached from concentration. Images of ghostly faces danced in the darkness. They were laughing and begging her to come along with them. *Come on, Jordan, don't be such a bore. It's Halloween!*

Fifteen Days Later
Somewhere in the Fraser Valley, British
Columbia, Canada

Abruptly, Jordan's cocoon of darkness ruptured. The hinged trap door above her opened with a slow, menacing creak. Familiar tentacles of terror wrapped themselves around her gut. The light of a dull gray sky pierced her eyes, sending a searing bolt of pain through her head.

He was back.

Peering through scrunched-up, watering eyes she was barely able to make out his outline. He looked down to where she lay in the twenty-foot converted freight container he had buried ten feet below ground. For this "special occasion," he'd said. But this wasn't the creature with limp, greasy hair and pale skin that reeked of a life lived underground—the animal who had visited her regularly for an indeterminate period of time. This man was taller, bulkier. *Oh god, he has an accomplice.*

In the beginning, when she thought each visit counted as a day, she methodically kept track of how many times he entered the box that had become her home. But then his visits came closer together, sometimes within what seemed like hours of each other. Frustrated, she lost count of the days. Had she been there a few weeks, or was it months? Did it really matter?

A sudden infusion of fresh air snaked down the makeshift wooden staircase, raising every hair on her bruised and battered body. Was she shivering from the cold, or was it the sheer terror that overcame her each time she heard the door open? She could no longer tell the difference. There was no sound of rain above, but her nose prickled with the unmistakable smell of fresh moisture mixed with the sharp muskiness of the earth. *Petrichor.* It was something her father had taught her as a little girl when they used to hike through the woods hand-in-hand on Annabelle Island. As the rain cleared and the sun's rays spread through the lacy canopy of leaves, she would lean so far back to see the top of the western red cedars that she toppled backward. But her father was always there to catch her. He'd wrap his arms around her and she felt the warmth of his body as he held her close. Feeling safe and content, she would lean against him in the old-growth forest and listen, fascinated, as he patiently explained how the reaction of plants secreting oils into the air combined with bacteria produced by the soil. *Petrichor.* The memory brought fresh tears, but it provided a dim ember of hope that her mind still worked. And she was relieved that the essence of fresh rain helped cover the putrid stench in the pit.

Whoever this accomplice was, he wasn't alone. Blurred faces surrounded the tall stranger and now several new pairs of eyes peered down into the hole. She wanted to cover herself, but she could only tug impotently at her restraints. A beam from a high-powered flashlight hit her face, making her twist her head violently to one side. Her heart pounded, and her breath caught at the base of her throat. The primal scream she'd repressed for so long began to push its way out like water through a compromised dam. Her high-pitched voice echoed through the rail car.

Even after twenty-five years in the Royal Canadian Mounted Police, Inspector J.J. Quinn would never get used to the visceral screams. They reverberated in his own head. Echoed in his own voice. They permeated every cell of his body, where they remained long after rescues and cases were successfully concluded. While each victim was unique, their expressions of agony were not. It was as if the universe absorbed every tortured soul's pain and then one day, unable to bear one more assault, she let loose with an agonized collective wail. To this day, Quinn couldn't bear to see images of the famous Edward Munch painting, The Scream. It reminded him too much of victims, many of whom had died with their screams frozen on their faces.

But this one had survived. "Get that light out of her face," he shouted. "Stand back, everyone! King, get over here. Now."

Faces were just beginning to come into focus when suddenly they disappeared from her line of sight. *No, don't leave me.* Then a woman appeared; she crouched and peered down into the bunker. In silhouette, she appeared to have long, wavy hair. "Jordan. Are you Jordan Stone?" the woman called down the shaft.

Her screams turned to gulping sobs and all she could do was nod her head. Her tongue felt woolly and thick, words refusing to form on her parched lips as she struggled to say something. Anything. If she didn't answer, they might leave.

"It's all right, Jordan." The woman stepped tentatively onto the first wooden stair that led down to where Jordan lay shackled. "I'm Sergeant Stella King and this is Inspector Quinn. It's over, Jordan. We're here to get you out."

"*No…*" Her cry came out thin and reedy, not with the urgency she intended. "B…bomb!"

The officer froze. She removed her foot quickly, but with the grace of a ballerina. "Where?"

Jordan yanked harder at the chains that bound her hands and feet. "He…he told me he arms it every time he leaves…" She sucked in huge breaths of air, which brought on a coughing fit. She was afraid she would choke. Tears ran in rivulets down her filthy cheeks. "Please. Please don't leave me."

This time it was the man who called down to her. "Jordan, we're not going to leave you. We'll get you out of there just as soon as we can." He shone the flashlight around her prison. "But I have to talk with my team, so we can do it safely. Sergeant King...Stella...she's going to stay right here with you, where you can see her, okay?"

On her knees again, the policewoman leaned further into the stairwell. "Jordan, you're safe. We're going to get you out. It will just take a little while to get some special people and equipment down here. I need you to take some deep breaths with me and we'll get through this together. Can you do that?"

Through a film of tears, she struggled to put a face to Stella's warm, velvety voice.

Chapter Three

Inspector Quinn beckoned to his second-in-command, Theo Rollins. "Our victim told King there's a bomb rigged under the stairs going down into the bunker. I want a bomb squad out here, stat." Having dispatched the officer, Quinn then marched to the makeshift communications center and waved over the dog handler whose canine had located the twenty-by-eight-foot underground metal box. "Can we get Fido here to tell us anything? Have him sniff around the opening for explosives?"

"Inspector Quinn," said the petite, blond handler. She rolled her eyes and sighed. "Kayla is highly trained as a trailing or area search dog." She gently ruffled the German shepherd's ears. "As I've already told you, I chose her specifically for this assignment because she's also been cross-trained in the location of dead bodies." She signaled her charge to stand and follow her away from the scene. "Our job here is done," she said, turning her back to Quinn.

"Kayla isn't a jack-of-all-trades," Quinn heard her mutter. "She doesn't do explosives, for god's sake."

You moron, he suspected she wanted to add.

Rollins returned to his superior's side. "Inspector, the bomb squad's ETA is sixteen hundred hours. Ambulance is already here. Forensics are on their way."

At least this time they needed an ambulance and not a coroner's wagon, Quinn thought as he turned back toward the scene. After two weeks underground, it was a miracle the victim was still alive. Although, from what he'd seen so far, she might live to wish she wasn't.

Unknown to her, Jordan Stone had just become the newest member of an exclusive club that no one in their right mind would aspire to. Welcome to my world, Quinn lamented silently.

Media trucks already lined both sides of the narrow gravel road leading to the derelict farm, their giant white satellite dishes standing against the angry gray sky like futuristic temples making offerings to the gods. A couple of individuals in civilian clothing, neither press nor police, attempted to climb onto a beaten down fence for a better look. One gawker managed to stand atop a section that lay almost horizontal against a treacherous looking thicket of blackberry bushes and decaying leaves, until his weight caused him to tumble backward off the heap of underbrush and slip from view.

Serves you right, Quinn thought as he looked at the sky and pulled his collar up against the late afternoon drizzle. "Shit, we're already losing the daylight. Set up all the floodlights," he instructed Rollins. "And get me a bigger tent over the entire entrance area there." He pointed to the bunker's hinged trap door that lay open against the moist earth. "The press and rubberneckers are gathering like vultures. Why the hell isn't the highway patrol holding them back at the entrance to the road?" A news helicopter buzzed overhead, and he had to shout to be heard above the noise. "Clear them out of here now," he said with a broad sweep of his arm. "All of 'em. Jesus Christ, this is turning into a goddamned circus."

Chapter Four

Jordan's skin itched as she imagined insects crawling over her body, feasting on raw flesh. Open sores left by the chains that chafed her wrists and ankles had made her into carrion. Something threaded a path through her matted hair as if seeking shelter from the sudden freshness of the air. She could only raise her head high enough off the mattress to determine that she was wearing some clothes, but she wasn't sure what condition they were in or how much of her they covered. All she knew for sure was that she was freezing.

Stella had apologized for not being able to come down or even drop a blanket over her. They couldn't do anything until the bomb squad got through doing whatever it was they did. Then forensics still had to take photographs. Various pieces of equipment were intermittently lowered through the entrance and Jordan heard a dog barking and people yelling above. She had waited so long to be found, but now that she had been, it all seemed to take an eternity.

"Jordan, I'm just going to stand up for a minute," Stella said as she rose from her crouched position above the opening in the earth. "They're updating us on whether they've found any explosives, but I'll just be off to the side, all right?"

Jordan was used to enduring long stretches of immobility, but she worried that Stella must be stiff and cold from kneeling all this time. Even with all fours chained, Jordan learned that she could raise her butt off the bed and stretch, as she did in Pilates classes. At least she *used* to be able to do that for a while after her capture. Now, her quads weren't even strong enough to support her dwindling weight.

She was trying to figure out how long her stamina had been declining when Stella scrambled down the stairs, saying the bomb squad had cleared them to enter the shaft. He had lied to her, that son of a bitch. But then he always lied, saying if she was good for just one more day, he'd let her go unharmed. Unharmed. It was much too late for that.

At once, Stella was at her side. Jordan felt a flush of embarrassment creep up her neck, aware of the stench that emanated from her. "I'm sorry." She gazed into the policewoman's deep brown eyes. "He would only let me use the toilet whenever he came and sometimes I couldn't hold it."

"Ssh," Stella soothed. "Nothing to worry about. You're doing great, Jordan."

A male officer followed behind Stella, and with a mini-grinder, he began to cut Jordan free from the irons on the floor. Stella put a hand on his forearm to stop him. "Where the hell is my photographer?" she shouted up to the surface, then turned back to the officer. "We can't touch her until we get photos."

She had explained to Jordan the need for them to

take photographs before they could move her or cover her up. "We'll be able to get you warm very soon." She smiled with beautiful white teeth against her tawny skin. The three of them watched as a woman came down the stairs, camera in hand.

Startled, Jordan jumped at the noise and brightness of the camera's flash. Taking another deep breath, she willed herself to be calm. After a few minutes, Stella tapped the photographer on the shoulder. "Okay, Bobbie, you've got enough. Go on up so we can get a stretcher down here, now."

The three of them jockeyed for space in the minuscule enclosure. Jordan held her breath as one by one, the officer cut through the chains. Once done, a paramedic came down backward, followed by another, each holding one end of a stretcher. Space was so tight that Stella had to step onto the edge of the mattress so the medics could squeeze past. They wore blue Nitrile gloves and Jordan's skin tingled when one of them touched her. Stella had gloves on when she came down the hole but took them off when she approached. Jordan was grateful that her first human touch of her rescue was from a woman. She savored the smooth warmth of Stella's bare hand gently clasping her forearm.

"Hi Jordan, I'm Brian and this is Victoria," the paramedic smiled and looked directly into her eyes. "Can you slide over toward us a little bit, so we can lift you onto the stretcher?" Stella remained beside her, crouched on her heels on top of the foul, stained mattress.

Jordan focused on putting every ounce of energy she could muster into shimmying toward the edge.

"You're doing great, Jordan. Okay, here we go. Good job," Brian encouraged. He covered her with a clean-smelling flannel sheet, then a blanket, and gently secured her on the gurney. "We're going to have you on quite an incline going up those stairs, but we've got you, so just relax."

Instead of relief at finally leaving her hellhole, Jordan felt an overwhelming surge of panic. "Stella. Where's Stella?" she cried out as they started up the stairwell.

"I'm right behind you, Jordan." Stella reached past the paramedic and touched her feet through the sheet. "I'll be with you all the way. In the ambulance, too. I won't leave you, I promise."

Jordan felt her heartbeat and breathing slow. When they finally reached the top, fat raindrops splatted against the blue tarpaulin above. It was like an irregular little drum roll announcing her arrival back to the surface. Enormous lights on stanchions flooded the area and assaulted her eyes. She squinted into the infinite darkness beyond—a hollow blackness she had become accustomed to.

Chapter Five

"Okay guys, hold up for a minute," Jordan heard a male voice upon her arrival on the surface. The tall man, whom she'd first seen when the trap-door opened, stood beside her stretcher. "Jordan, I'm Inspector Quinn." She looked into tired, blood-shot eyes sunken into a weathered, craggy face.

"I understand Stella's been taking really good care of you. Look, I know you've been through a lot, but it's important that you try to answer her questions on the ride to the hospital. While things are fresh in your mind. Can you do that?"

She looked at Stella, suddenly feeling like a timid child who needed reassuring. The policewoman looked her straight in the eye and gave a single nod. "Yes, all right," Jordan replied, not taking her eyes away from Stella's.

"Excellent. You're clear to go," Quinn said to the paramedics. "Jordan, I'll see you at the hospital just as soon as I wrap things up here."

She wondered what hospital they were going to. "Where…where am I?"

Stella and Inspector Quinn exchanged looks. "You're in Chilliwack, Jordan. On an abandoned farm. Looks like it might have been a marijuana grow-op, about ten miles off Old Yale Road. Stella will fill you in on everything you want to know." He turned to the sergeant. "I'll get things wrapped up here and see you at the General."

Chilliwack. Old Yale Road. That overwhelming skunky odor. She would never forget that smell. It clung to him when he came for his "visits," and smothered her like a shroud, as she lay numb and broken after each new assault.

Jordan was loaded into a waiting ambulance which slowly headed down what felt like a rough and potholed road, then with sirens blaring they hit the highway. The paramedic who rode in the back with her and Stella thoroughly checked Jordan's vitals.

"How's she doing?" Stella asked.

"Given the circumstances she's in fairly decent shape." He adjusted Jordan's saline drip. "Dehydrated," he added, "but her breathing is good. Blood pressure's a little low." Then he finally addressed his patient. "How are you feeling, Jordan? Do you have pain anywhere?"

"My back and bum feel tender." *Damn, too much information.* She didn't want to be punished for sounding whiny.

"That's to be expected," he reassured her. "You've got a few bed sores there that need treating, so that's what you're feeling."

"How…how long was I there?"

The paramedic looked questioningly at Stella and she took over. "You were reported missing fifteen days ago, Jordan. Do you remember what happened, or if you were taken somewhere else first?"

Fresh tears stung Jordan's eyes and she sucked in short gulps of air, struggling to answer.

"Jordan, you're hyperventilating," the paramedic cautioned. "I'm going to put this oxygen mask on you for a few minutes to help slow it down. Just take nice deep breaths." She saw him shake his head at Stella, as if sending her a silent admonishment before he checked Jordan's pulse again and jotted something on his clipboard.

A cell phone rang. Jordan jumped. "King," Stella answered, and listened for a few seconds, watching Jordan out of the corner of her eye. "No, nothing yet," she told the caller. "Think we'll give it a little time...until we get to the hospital. I'll keep you posted."

Once they reached the hospital, the paramedics wheeled Jordan into a treatment room, where she requested Stella stay with her as long as possible. Several hours later, after the most intrusive tests were done, the sergeant asked Jordan if she'd be okay while she stepped outside to make a couple of phone calls. "I promise I'll just be around the corner. Let one of the nurses know if you need me and I'll come running." She managed to elicit a small smile from Jordan.

Stella emerged to see Quinn pacing the patients' lounge, which he had sequestered at the end of the corridor. He gulped down his coffee, then crushed the cup and tossed it in the trash. She knew he had to be dying for a smoke.

"I don't have to ask if you ran a rape kit," he said when he saw her.

Suddenly exhausted, Stella chose the closest seat. Perched on the edge of a faded yellow plastic chair, her muscles were coiled so tight she thought they might snap. She leaned her elbows on her thighs and hung her head in her hands. "You're right, you don't."

"What were the results?" Quinn asked.

"What do you think?" Her look dared him to press for more details. They had worked together long enough for him to know she would have been present when the RCMP's Integrated Forensic Identification Services unit photographed the injuries on Jordan Stone's body, as well as when DNA was collected. Stella had gone to great lengths to round up all female technicians to do the more intimate procedures. Now, all they could do was wait.

"You get any kind of description of the piece of shit who…of her abductor?" Quinn asked.

"Not much. Slight build, skinny. Skanky. What did you find out at your end? Did the door-to-door produce anything?"

"Nah. The closest neighbor is over a mile away. Obviously, whoever kidnapped her chose the location for that reason. A few drive-bys we interviewed said they suspected the property was a grow-op, but nobody really gives a rat's ass." Quinn ran his fingers through his thick gray-peppered hair. "Farmers, drug dealers, and rednecks. It's a different crowd out there if you know what I mean."

"Tell me about it. You forget, that's where I

started out as a nineteen-year-old rookie."

Without acknowledging her comment, Quinn continued. "IFIS lifted multiple tire and boot tracks from the road leading to the property. The techs are still processing the bunker but unless he has a record, we're not going to come up with a match." He leveled his gaze at Stella, jerking his head toward Jordan's hospital room. "So, I need to ask you, based on what you saw in there, is it likely he'll be in the system as a sex offender?"

Silently, Sergeant Stella King thought of the revulsion she'd felt inside the private room where the forensics team examined Jordan. Revulsion that she shouldn't feel after all these years of being a cop. But as a woman she could smell the victim's shame and visceral fear from across the room. It was as palpable today as it was eleven years ago. Only this time, Stella wasn't the victim.

"King?" Quinn's gravelly voice jolted her back to the present. "Is he likely to be in the system?"

She stood to face him. "I would say that's a distinct possibility, yes."

He kicked the waste can into the corner and yanked open the door. "That's the first bit of good news I've had all goddamned day. Let's go light a fire under the criminal sketch artist. I want to see what this piece of shit looks like."

Chapter Six

Quinn paced back and forth across the floor of Jordan's private hospital room. In truth, the room was too small to actually pace but to Jordan it felt like a palace. The inspector took a few steps before reaching the window, then pivoted on his heels yet again. Jordan was getting dizzy just watching him. Stella sat quietly in the corner, taking notes.

"Just so I have this straight," Quinn said on his return trip past the foot of Jordan's bed, "you were working on an investigative piece about some of our friends in the Italian underworld when you were abducted. But you were on your way to meet an informant about a marijuana grow-op?" His fleeting eye-contact with Stella didn't escape Jordan.

"In my world those two things don't go together," Quinn said. "It's usually the gangs and low-lifes on the food chain who control the grow-ops. Why meet with that kind of informant?"

"It wasn't just any informant," Jordan replied. "He was one of my first sources when I covered the city desk at the local rag I started with right out of university. I trust him." Even as the words left her lips, she knew that using the words *trust* and *informant* in the same sentence was highly questionable.

"So, what was so important that you drove all the way out to meet him on Halloween?"

"Before that night, he had told me he knew a guy who was a key player in constructing underground bunker systems that housed huge grow operations. Called himself the Lego Man."

Stella's pen froze on her notebook. Quinn's head snapped sideways.

"And you don't think there's a connection between him and your abduction?" Quinn all but spat.

Undeterred, Jordan continued. "Some of them have five, six shipping containers all joined together like one long tunnel. Their own generators, everything."

"Are you *kidding* me? There is nothing I don't know about sophisticated systems used in grow ops. For god's sake, you were held in an underground bunker. You didn't think it was important to tell us there was a connection?" This time, he included Stella in his withering glare.

"I'm telling you now," Jordan retaliated.

Over the last two days, with nothing to do but lie in a hospital bed, she had scoured her brain until it hurt. The call had definitely come in from her long-time informant. She'd been working with him on the Mafia story for months but after that, something had gone awry.

"My source told me Lego Man had been contracted by a higher-up in one of the Italian crime families," Jordan said.

"One of those posing as a clean-living citizen right under the noses of us incompetent authorities? Are you telling me they're now getting their hands dirty working grow-ops?"

Jordan shook her head, ignoring Quinn's sarcastic reference to a quote attributed to her about the police's laissez-faire attitude toward Italian criminals living in Canada. "No, something much bigger than that. My informant claimed to have seen Lego Man's detailed blueprints for building an underground house somewhere in the Fraser Valley."

Noting the look of confusion on Quinn's face, she explained. "In Calabria and Sicily, several notorious Mafia kingpins stayed for months at a time in subterranean bunkers, sometimes right under their own homes. One guy lived beneath an old abandoned farmhouse for an entire year without ever coming out. He had everything he needed to live a quasi-opulent life, complete with gilded paintings on the walls and brocade-covered wing-back chairs."

Quinn stopped at the foot of her bed and stared at her. At least she'd captured his attention enough to put an end to his pacing. "And you think that someone was planning something like that here?"

"That's what I was aiming to find out that night I drove out to the valley." Jordan shivered at the recollection. "Except, I was either double-crossed by my informant or someone else met me in his place. I was knocked out before I saw who was in the van."

Quinn seemed to be considering his next question when Jordan tried unsuccessfully to stifle a jaw-separating yawn. Stella looked up from the corner and suggested it might be time to wrap things up. She winked at Jordan, who returned the gesture with a quiet smile.

"Okay, but we're not done here," Quinn said. "King will be back first thing in the morning. In the meantime, I suggest you think about anything else of significance you might have neglected to tell us."

Stella winced. Jordan would be forever grateful to her for conducting the first post-rescue interview on her own, without Quinn. With no one present but the two of them—except for the constant reminder of the red light of the recording device—Jordan had divulged every abhorrent detail of her fifteen days underground. When her voice frequently cracked, and she looked away ashamed, Stella's firm but gentle coaxing gave her the strength to tell her everything she could that might help with the investigation. It was only days since her rescue but still, the police had no leads on her abductor. And now, Quinn was clearly pissed.

Jordan's nurse performed her usual night-time ritual and after checking that her patient was comfortable, she turned down the lights in the room and closed the door behind her. Jordan lifted her head from the pillow and looked around for the white and blue plastic bag patients were given for their personal belongings. The police had finished with her work cell phone and returned it, almost out of power. One of the nurses had found a charger she could use, but what Jordan really wanted was her personal cell phone.

Rachel, and Ash Courtland, whom Jordan had referred to as Uncle Ash since childhood, had made the drive out to Chilliwack General as soon as they were notified of Jordan's rescue. By then, it was late into the night and she had endured what seemed like hours of endless forensic tests. Further insults to her bruised body and battered psyche. When at last she was wheeled into a permanent room for the night, she had barely been able to keep her eyes open while Rachel fussed and fluffed pillows, and Ash had pulled a chair up to her bedside.

"I thought we'd never see you again, Jordan," Rachel had said, her eyes full of tears. Ash nodded in agreement and he clasped Jordan's hand tighter. It was the first time she'd seen him at a loss for words. She couldn't remember saying goodnight to them before falling into a deep sleep from which she didn't emerge for twelve hours. When she awoke, the nursing staff had changed over, and the darkness outside her room had turned an optimistic, deep cobalt blue. She needed to get home or at the very least, get back in touch with the outside world.

As if her thoughts had summoned a genie, the door to her hospital room swung open and in walked Rachel. Jordan couldn't see her face behind the enormous vase of flowers she carried, but she would have known her friend's quirky mismatching tights anywhere. Each leg had completely different patterns: one, hot pink with orange stripes, the other, polka dots. Her feet were encased in heavy, black-patent Doc Martins.

With a flurry, she plunked down the vase of flowers on the windowsill, then turned and kissed Jordan on the lips. She tasted Rachel's familiar Peppermint Patty lip gloss.

~ 26 ~

"They're gorgeous, Rachel, you shouldn't have." She really wanted to ask if her friend had remembered to bring her phone and laptop computer, but she didn't want to seem insensitive.

As if reading her thoughts, Rachel pulled both items from her backpack. "Ta-da," she sang. "Like Ash, I don't think you need a computer right now, but this is me being your unwaveringly loyal, bestest bestie in the world." Rachel's irascible enthusiasm brought a smile to Jordan's lips.

"And, I even remembered your chargers. You can thank me later."

"Thank you, now," Jordan replied as she reached up for a hug.

It took Jordan every ounce of patience she could muster to remain engaged in mindless conversation with Rachel before seeing the door close behind her. She reached for her cell and laptop. Surely, one of them would hold the key as to why she'd really gone out to the valley that night.

Chapter Seven

The one good thing about having a cabin on a remote private island in the Southern Strait of Georgia, was there were few distractions. No Wi-Fi or television. Cell phone coverage was spotty at best, depending on where you stood. Jordan's father used to keep a short-wave radio in the storage area built into the rock under the house, for emergencies, but it was long ago rendered useless, eroded by the sea air. Without that, she could choose to remain blissfully out of touch with the world. Everything she needed for the next few days, she had downloaded before she left the mainland.

She poured herself a glass of wine. After all, it was five o'clock somewhere in the world. Lethargically, she shuffled to the couch and shoved a pile of books to one side of the coffee table to make room for her glass and laptop. Sadly, she couldn't remember when she had last read *one* novel, much less stacks of them. When she and her parents spent carefree summers on the island, her mother would have to dismantle a fortress of books from her daughter's bed before tucking her in for the night.

Jordan's childhood books had shiny covers depicting flying white horses, and bears whose heads got stuck in honeypots. Even though her reading tastes matured as she did, the hefty works that now perched precariously on the edge of the living room table hardly qualified as scholarly tomes. Although many were mysteries and thrillers, it was the true-crime stories that were worn and dog-eared. She had known since adolescence that she wanted to be an investigative crime reporter. Now, as she fired up her laptop, she prayed the years of experience she had under her belt before her abduction would pay off big-time.

The island was the only place she could spend a few days in anonymity, where she'd be alone with her thoughts and do the research she needed to formulate a plan. When the water taxi dropped her off two days ago, the overly friendly driver tried valiantly to obtain her cell phone number. "Just in case of an emergency," he'd said. *What, like a tsunami?* She'd gracefully declined. Okay, not gracefully. It irked her that even one person knew she was there. Thankfully, the old-timer who was a friend of her parents, no longer owned the taxi service. Even after all these years, she was sure he would have recognized her in an instant.

The island had no restaurant or cozy little gathering place like a neighborhood pub because there were no others to gather with unless one was trespassing. Nobody could pop in unannounced, so Jordan hadn't even bothered with her pre-abduction daily ritual of showering, washing her hair, or putting on makeup. It wasn't that she had consciously decided to liberate herself from the daily minutiae of being female. She had simply stopped looking in the mirror. With no shops on the island, she had brought enough food to sustain her for a week, doubling up on provisions of wine and liquor, neither of which she was supposed to touch. At least that's what her doctor had said. As did the caution labels on the medications she'd been prescribed for anxiety.

She rose from the couch to top up her wine glass and reluctantly considered making something to eat before she tackled the files on her computer. Truth was, since her rescue and subsequent outpatient treatment, Jordan had very little appetite. Her clothes fit almost as loosely as they had after her two-week abduction. However, she suspected she was in for a long night and reached for the refrigerator door. As she did, her cell phone vibrated across the granite kitchen counter, where she stared stupidly as if it were a fish marooned at low tide. The caller I.D. flashed on the screen. *Not again!* That brought the total number of times Inspector J.J. Quinn had called to an even dozen. So much for lousy cell phone reception on the island. The first call was a quarter to one in the morning. Was Quinn, like her, plagued with insomnia?

After listening to his first message and hearing the police had made no headway in the investigation, Jordan hadn't bothered to check his subsequent ones. She knew she was just being cantankerous but until her kidnapper was found, she saw no reason to speak with the cop from the Serious Crimes Unit again. In the off chance he was simply checking on her welfare, she wasn't going to give him the satisfaction of knowing she had sought psychological counseling through the Force's victims' services department. That's when psychologist, Dr. Diana Danforth had entered her life. She too had called, no doubt wondering why Jordan had missed her last appointment.

She couldn't remember why she'd gone into the kitchen, so she returned to the couch and clicked on the last file she had been working on before she was kidnapped; it seemed as good a place to start as any. After attaining a certain level at the newspaper, Jordan no longer did her own research, which is why she'd hired her intrepid friend, Rachel. But she still had a nose for peeling away the intricate layers of criminal activity which would have rivaled a truffle-smelling dog's. The genesis of her "ordeal," as she euphemistically referred to her abduction, was that she had stumbled onto a case that seemed destined to be her journalistic swan song. At least that was Quinn's opinion, which he revisited annoyingly often while trying to talk her out of returning to her job at the paper.

To say Jordan Stone's professional relationship with the cop, who was an integral part of the RCMP Serious Crimes Unit had degraded somewhat, would be a gross understatement. Even through her foggy consciousness at the crime scene in Chilliwack, there was something vaguely familiar about Quinn. It wasn't until he was pacing her room at the hospital that night and he'd made the sarcastic remark about a snipe she'd taken at his department, that it dawned on her who he was.

A couple of years back, when asked to comment

on information contained in an investigative piece she had written for her syndicated crime column, he had called her a "sensationalistic sadist." Of course, in her mind, that not only proved he was ignorant, but also illiterate. After her ordeal, however, the senior member of the task force appeared to have softened. Even when both realized they knew each other, Jordan steadfastly continued to ignore Quinn's pleas to get out of her high-risk line of work in favor of something "more tame."

He had taken her to the café in the RCMP headquarters building, where civilians were allowed. "For god's sake, Jordan," he had bristled as he yanked his hands through his hair and rolled his eyes toward the ceiling of the busy restaurant. She remembered the frustration etched on his face as he tried in vain to get her to quit her job—her *life*— as one of only a handful of award-winning female crime reporters.

"Which part of going off the grid do you not understand? Hasn't this taught you *anything?* We haven't got the guy who did this to you and there are hundreds more pieces of shit out there, just like him." He'd steepled his hands together, index fingers touching his top lip, and let out a tortured sigh.

"You're a damned fine journalist. That's the problem, you're now a moving target. You can't possibly be serious about going back to the newspaper."

"Of course I'm going back. What else would I do?" The café had suddenly become hot and the room threatened to swallow her whole. She was afraid she was going to be sick right there at the table. "I just need a little time to get past this and I'll be fine."

"Are you *kidding* me?" A couple of diners cast furtive glances in their direction. Quinn leaned in and lowered his voice. "Jordan, this isn't something you just *get over*, like the flu. For Christ's sake, you haven't had any counseling since you left the hospital." He rubbed his two-day beard. "Geez, as a cop and part of the team that found you, I have to bloody well go through counseling!"

She threw her napkin on the table and pushed back her chair. "Quinn, I'm sorry but I have to go." His vociferous protests followed her as she nearly knocked someone over in her desperation to flee. Out on the street she spotted a waiting taxi, and with her heart pounding, she slipped into the rear seat of the cab and forced herself not to look back.

While Jordan was in the hospital, Sergeant Stella King had conducted most of the interviews. At the time, she'd had a sense that Stella was running interference between the bombastic inspector and herself. Later, when she asked Quinn why Stella had disappeared and was no longer part of her case, he seemed evasive, mumbling something about being needed on a high-priority investigation. What, hers wasn't high enough?

A few days following their lunch debacle, he had demanded that she "get herself into the station" to answer further questions about her captor. As she walked into the security entrance of the RCMP headquarters, the sun was suddenly eclipsed by a threatening black cloud. Looking back on it later, the ominous weather change should have warned her of things to come.

After receiving a visitor's pass and being directed to the correct floor, Quinn met and escorted her down the hall to a small boardroom. This time though, instead of a friendly conversation, he immediately jumped in, interrogating her relentlessly. As he grilled her about a particularly horrific part of her ordeal, her answers became more hostile. His impatience rose, and then, out of the blue he seemed to rein himself in and suggested taking a break for coffee.

Even now, she could recall the feeling of her body thrumming with the unrelenting pressure of what felt like a herd of charging bulls running riot through her gut. But as emotionally charged as the session was, her natural curiosity had kicked in. "So, what does *J.J.* stand for?"

He poured Jordan a coffee, and then one for himself. "Jesse James," he replied, simultaneously tearing the tops off three packets of sugar and dumping them in his coffee. He mixed in the contents and licked his stir stick.

She suppressed a grin as they walked back into the meeting room and took their seats. "You're kidding, right?" It felt good to focus, however briefly, on the ridiculous.

"Unfortunately not." He'd downed most of the lukewarm liquid in one gulp and then turned the tape recorder back on.

The cabin's fire crackled through the window of the wood stove. Jordan twirled her long-stemmed goblet in front of the flames as if watching a distorted retrospective of her life through a warped crystal screen.

What life? Her life as she had known it, was over but she'd be damned if it would be in vain. All she had to do now was lay low enough to formulate a plan. At least her island hideaway assured her of that opportunity.

Chapter Eight

It was after three in the morning when Jordan had finally fallen asleep, and even then, she slept fitfully, drifting in and out of the same dream. The recurring nightmares started while she was in the hospital. She was banging on the inside of the door of an underground room trying desperately to get out. Images of her abductor's thin, straggly hair and eyes devoid of emotion penetrated her brain. She smelled the stench of his greasy white flesh. Now, Jordan realized the loud ruckus was coming not from her dream, but from outside, and she fought to break through her grogginess.

Someone banged several more times. "Jordan, open the door!"

It was daylight. *It's not a dream. I'm on a remote island, how could anyone be at my door?* Grabbing her robe, she pulled back the curtain. At the end of the dock she saw the guy who had taxied her to the island. He stood with one leg on his boat and the other on the wooden dock. The wind blew his long blond hair over his eyes as he tried to look cool balancing on the choppy water.

"Hey, don't leave until she answers," Jordan heard someone yell.

He nodded.

"Could she have left on her own? Does she have a boat?"

Jordan recognized that voice.

"Nope, no boat. Trust me, I'd know if she left," the young skipper shouted back. "I tried to get a phone number from her, but no dice."

"Yeah, well it wouldn't have made any difference, pal. She's not answering her phone. I've been trying since yesterday. Jordan, open the goddamned door. Or I'll break it down!"

"Hey man, are you a cop or something? Can you really do that?" the skipper yelled into the wind.

Jordan opened the bedroom window and briefly considered dropping a pot of mummified geraniums on his head. Instead, she stuck her head out. "Quinn, what the hell are you doing here?" The icy wind coming off the water drove her back inside. What are *either* of you doing here, she groused.

Confused as to where the voice was coming from, Quinn looked around, then up. "There you are! You know I've been phoning you day and night?"

She stuck her head out again. "Yes, I know that."

"Hey, dude, can I go now? Gotta pick up some early morning customers. Give me a call when you want a ride back, okay?"

"Yeah, okay. Thanks." He looked up at Jordan. "Would you *please* come down and open the door? It's bloody freezing out here!"

Shirking off her robe, Jordan struggled into a pair of torn sweatpants and a fleecy sweatshirt she'd discarded on the floor the previous night. Hopping on one leg, then the other, she pulled on a pair of her dad's old hockey socks. Running down the stairs from the loft, she could see him through the etched glass windows on either side of the front door. Sure enough, there was Inspector J.J. Quinn, larger than life, standing on her porch. Hands jammed into his pockets, he was stamping his feet. She cracked the door open as far as the security chain allowed. "What do you want?"

"What I want is to get out of this goddamned freezing weather, for starters. Come on, Jordan. Open the door. If you don't talk to me, you'll be talking to the higher-ups handling your investigation. And trust me, you'd rather be talking to me right now."

"Oh, really? Why is that?"

"Geez, Jordan, you've been a victim of—"

She sighed and opened her mouth to make a retort.

Quinn shook his head. "You've been a victim of an abduction. You can't just run off and not tell anyone. What the hell do you think the police thought when you suddenly disappeared off the face of the earth? Again." He blew into his cupped hands to warm them up. "And as a victim of a violent crime you *need* to get some counseling. But there's something more pressing we need to talk about."

"First of all," she said through the barely open door, "I am *not* a victim. Secondly, you should be out there catching the scumbag who did this, not lecturing me to get counseling."

"Jordan, please. Gimme a break. I've been up forty-eight hours straight. I hate the water, I'm freezing cold, and the least you could do is offer me a coffee."

She closed the door. Pulling back the chain, she opened the door.

He eyed her up and down. "Jesus, you look awful. Are you okay?"

"Nice to see you too, Inspector. How did you find me?"

"The surfer dude." He jerked his head in the direction of the retreating boat. "One of your colleagues at the paper thought you might be here, so I went down to the docks and just started asking around. Can I come in?"

Jordan stepped aside, turning her back on him as she walked into the living room. He closed the door but remained standing just inside the entranceway.

"Do you have any coffee?"

"There's some in the coffee maker," she pointed toward the kitchen. "Help yourself."

"O-*kay*," he stretched the word out slowly. "You want one?"

"No, thanks."

He looked around the house. "Isn't summer usually a better time of year to come here?"

He headed into the kitchen. "This coffee has an oil slick on it," he called out. "Do you have something a little fresher?"

Jordan joined him in the kitchen, reached into the cupboard for a canister of coffee, and plunked it down on the counter in front of him.

"Okay then," he said, sounding falsely cheerful. "Let's see if this ex-cop can still make a cup of coffee you could stand a spoon in. Looks like you could use one yourself."

Suddenly, Jordan was a bit more interested. "What do you mean *ex*-cop? Aren't you still with the Force?"

"No, and I can't afford to retire on half pension. However, the powers that be strongly suggested I might want to move on. Voluntarily, of course. It's kind of like an honorable discharge." He shoveled several heaping scoops of coffee into the coffee maker."

"So, you *retired*?" Jordan asked, unable to keep the shock out of her voice. "I thought when you took early retirement you could still go back casual, or part-time or something."

"Yeah, well, some do, but my invitation apparently got lost in the mail." He fumbled with the cord and looked around for a wall socket. "I don't golf, so I'm not sure what the hell I'm supposed to do with myself at the ripe old age of forty-four."

She thought for sure he was in his mid- to late-fifties. "So, what are you going to do?"

He rubbed his arms briskly, not answering her question. "Do you have any heat in this place? Can I build a fire?"

"I'll throw some more logs in the stove. It's probably still going from last night. Are you hungry? Do you want some toast or something?"

He arched one eyebrow. "Will I have to scrape any mold off it?"

The gurgling coffee was starting to smell good and Jordan felt a smile coming on in spite of herself. "No, there's some cinnamon buns in the fridge. Got them at the convenience store on the mainland.

They've got enough preservatives in them to last forever."

"In that case I'll have two. Do you have any butter?"

"On cinnamon buns? Really?" She wondered if he still smoked.

Quinn looked around at the state of the kitchen, apparently ready to make a retort, then appeared to think better of it. They carried their coffees back to the living room, taking a seat on couches opposite each other. Jordan watched in amazement as he wolfed down two cinnamon rolls in the space of a few minutes, then eyed hers that she hadn't touched.

"You going to eat that?" he asked before swallowing the last bite of his own. He must have noticed her incredulous look. "Sorry," he said sheepishly, "I don't remember when I last ate."

She shook her head. "You can have it. Do you want some more coffee?"

"Thanks." He brushed the crumbs off his pants, putting his plate aside. "I feel almost human again."

Jordan brought two fresh mugs of coffee from the kitchen and set one down beside him. For a moment, they sat in awkward silence.

"So. Any new leads on my kidnapper?" It sounded as if she were merely inquiring about the weather rather than the person responsible for her abduction, attempted murder, and other things she still couldn't bear to put words to.

Quinn cleared his throat awkwardly. "Believe me, they're doing everything they can, but..." He chewed his lip and looked down at the floor.

"What?" She felt her heart doing cartwheels. "What aren't you telling me?"

"Well, to start with, the reason I've been up forty-eight hours—thanks for asking, by the way—is that the shit hit the fan when you just up and disappeared without telling anyone."

Jordan opened her mouth to argue. She had actually told Rachel but had sworn her to secrecy.

"Don't interrupt me. Anyone with half a brain would know that's a colossally stupid thing to do when you've already been abducted."

Jordan thrust out her chin. "For god's sake, Quinn, I just needed some time to think after I got out of the hospital. What happened to being a free citizen?"

"I hate to tell you this, but you don't have that luxury anymore." He held her gaze. "And you won't in the foreseeable future if you don't cooperate."

She swallowed a reply.

"Before I left the Force and was part of the investigating team, I knew we needed more specifics about the time you were in captivity. Like remembering certain things he may have said or done to you. Things that might have been unique, only to him."

She wondered if he could hear her racing pulse. The coffee lurched around in her cup, which she clutched with shaking hands. "What do you mean? I told you and Stella everything I could. How can I tell them what I don't remember?" And by the way, why did Stella suddenly take a powder? she wanted to ask.

Quinn's eyes bored into hers, completely unnerving her. He took a deep breath. "Look, Jordan,

I'm no longer involved in the investigation but…"

"But what?"

"They think you may be suppressing things that are too painful for you to recall. They want you to undergo hypnosis."

"Hypnosis? Who are *they* and what are you, their lap dog? You can't be serious." A coil of nausea snaked its way up her throat. "Excuse me," Jordan stammered, racing for the bathroom.

She knew Quinn could hear her retching violently into the toilet. She hated these raw emotions that lurked so close to the surface. In her old life, she could have played poker with the devil himself.

After she was sure she had gotten everything out of her stomach, she ran a washcloth under warm water. With it halfway to her face, she froze at the reflection of the stranger who appeared in the mirror. *Who is this deathly pale, painfully thin woman looking back at me?* Hands shaking, she wiped her face, unlocked the door, and ventured back into the living room. Quinn stood with his back to her, adding more logs to the fire.

"Feeling better?" he inquired, without turning around.

"I've told you everything. I want him caught. Why would I hold anything back?"

He turned to face her. "It's not about you consciously holding anything back, Jordan. This is a common phenomenon with crime vic…uh, individuals who have experienced a traumatic event. You *know* this. You've written some of your most powerful articles about the impact of these types of crimes."

She felt herself sliding over the edge. "Really? Were those the same articles that prompted you to call me a voyeuristic parasite on victims and their families?" Like a paint bomb that had found its target, blood-red rage exploded and splashed across her brain. Any possibility of keeping her emotions in check was over. Paralyzed and rooted to the spot, she heard someone screaming. It was her, and she couldn't stop. Quinn's face was frozen in shock as she sprinted past him and bolted out the front door.

"Jordan," he yelled. "You don't have any shoes on."

She tore blindly across the half-frozen, sodden grass, stumbling over rocks and tree roots.

"Jordan, stop!"

His voice was getting louder, and she could feel him closing in on her. *Run like your life depends on it. It does! You can't let him get you again.*

"Jordan, it's me, Quinn." He lunged for her, only to be left holding a handful of fabric from her sweatshirt. She struggled and tugged, then quickly twisted sideways. He must have slipped or caught his boot on a rock, because he went down hard, taking her with him. The air expelled from her lungs as she hit the ground on her back and he landed on top of her. He smelled of coffee and sweat.

Sweat. She was back in the pit with that deranged animal with the sweaty, greasy skin. She should have fought back harder. He was a lunatic, but she could have outsmarted him. Instead, she'd been pathetically weak and had given in. Well, not this time.

The air came back into her lungs and she heard the pulse thunder in her ears. Frantically trying to free herself from Quinn's iron grip, she turned her head and sank her teeth into one of his hands that pinned her to the ground.

"Ouch! What the fuck?"

"Get off me, you bastard! I should have...I could have..." Enraged, she choked back tears. "Don't you ever put your filthy hands on me again or I swear to god I'll kill you." She managed to pull one leg free and nailed his back with her heel.

"Jordan, it's me, J.J. I'm not him!" He held her in a bear hug. "You're safe. I'm not going to hurt you." Then he rolled off her, panting. "Jesus, I'm sorry."

Gasping for air, she looked at him. He stared at her, his face ashen. She stopped struggling and for a moment their faces hovered over each other's. Quinn got up, reached out his hand and she let him pull her upright. They stood eying each other, both covered in mud and slush and decayed bits of leaves.

"Jordan, come back inside, *please*. I'm sorry I came, I just thought you'd be willing to do whatever it takes after what he did to you. I didn't have that option when my wife and kid died."

The pain she saw in his eyes registered for a split second, but then disappeared from her consciousness.

"You're shaking. Let's get you inside."

Numb, with all the fight gone, she let him lead her back to the house.

"Here, give me your socks."

Jordan put a hand on his shoulder for support as he bent down and peeled them off her frozen feet the way her father used to do at the end of figure skating lessons.

"Go sit in front of the fire and I'll bring you some hot coffee."

She shook her head. "No more coffee. I don't think I can keep it down."

"Okay, how about some weak tea? Have you got tea?"

She nodded, temporarily distracted by the licking flames of the fire. They seemed to reach out and pull her into their center. "Could you put some milk and honey in it?"

His tight expression turned into a smile. "Yeah, I can do that. But you have to promise me you won't run off again. Do I need to nail the door shut?" She jumped when he smacked his forehead. "Geez, I'm sorry, I didn't mean it that way."

"It's okay." She gave him a weak smile. "And yes, I promise."

After an hour-long debate with Quinn telling her all the reasons why she should go back to the mainland, and her arguments to the contrary, Jordan finally gave in and agreed to go with him. As she packed, she could hear him downstairs speaking in hushed tones to someone on his cell phone. Was it a former colleague on the Force? Or perhaps it was a woman, someone he was going home to. She wondered how his wife and son had died, and if he now had a whole new family.

Chapter Nine

Sixty miles away from civilization, I watched a giant osprey circle over the gray stretch of water known as the Strait of Georgia. With laser focus, the raptor folded its wings and plunged fifty feet towards its prey. Sharp talons snatched a fish as it skimmed the surface, then swooped back into the air. I yearned to follow as the osprey carried the spoils of its hunt high into the trees close to its rudimentary shelter. I watched and envisioned the bird's unfettered satisfaction in ripping its helpless victim to shreds.

It had taken days of meticulous planning, followed by mind-numbing boredom. I shivered, wet and cold on the outskirts of the dense bush, not a hundred feet from what Jordan Stone euphemistically referred to as a cabin. I was so close I could see her walk back and forth in front of the giant picture windows. I pulled my hood up against the bitter cold; all I had to do now was wait for darkness to fall and it would all be over. At last.

The wind howling through the trees sounded like the guttural cries of an animal in distress. The sea was a cauldron of angry gray waves crowned by white foamy tips. As I finalized the plan in my head, I heard voices coming from the direction of the cabin. My heart sank when I saw them. Jordan and the cop. I ducked back into the wooded covering I had hidden in earlier when he'd chased her across the mossy rocks and tackled her to the ground. What had changed to make her accompany him to the dock, luggage in hand?

The same water taxi that delivered the cop to the island was idling alongside, its skipper deftly fending off each time a wave slammed it against the jetty. I watched the cop toss a bag to him, then he and Jordan jumped into the boat and they took off.

No! That spoiled, undeserving bitch had been within reach. My fingers twitched as I imagined them clutched around her warm throat while her eyes bulged with recognition. But it was too late. Paralyzed, I stood frozen in place as the small craft became a tiny speck on the horizon.

Chapter Ten

It was a tense crossing via water taxi back to the mainland. The wind was coming in from the southeast, gusting to forty miles an hour. If it hit fifty, the ferries would be canceled. Jordan's sour stomach lurched each time they crested another towering wave and then dropped with a shuddering crash into the cavernous hollow scooped out by the sea. It gave her perverse pleasure to see Quinn's face turn from pea green to ash gray.

She was relieved that the sound of the engine straining against the maddened sea prevented her from having to answer the water taxi pilot's nosy questions. None too soon, they pulled up to the government dock in Horseshoe Bay and Quinn scrambled off the boat before the skipper had fully secured the lines. As Jordan reached out to take his hand, she glanced at Ashton Courtland standing at the far end of the dock, looking oddly out of place in full business attire.

After a few words between the two men, Jordan got the distinct impression Quinn was greatly relieved to be passing her off to family, or at least the closest thing to family she had left.

"Are you going to be all right, my dear?" Ash asked, enveloping her in a robust hug. "You know you gave us all another scare."

Jordan leaned in and returned his warm embrace. The sleeve of his navy-blue cashmere coat felt comforting against her cheek. It smelled the way a garden did after a fresh rain. A lump in her throat rose out of nowhere and she bit her lip, afraid she might cry, and then not be able to stop. She hadn't seen him since he had faithfully visited her daily in hospital. She felt guilty she hadn't told him where she was going. "You're sweet, Uncle Ash, but I'm fine. Really. I just needed some time alone to figure out where to go from here."

"I understand. But are you sure you should be alone tonight? I tend to agree with the Inspector. Going back to your house by yourself might not be the best idea, under the circumstances."

Obviously, Quinn had filled Ash in prior to their arrival. That must have been who he was speaking to on the phone. Quinn cleared his throat as if to remind them he was still there. Then, he quickly took his leave but not before exacting a promise from Ash that he would drive Jordan straight to her psychologist's office. In a weak moment back on the island, she had told Quinn she had started therapy.

Indignant, she started to protest, until she thought she saw the same pain in the inspector's eyes that she'd glimpsed during their outdoor chase. Why couldn't Stella have been here? Jordan was sick of men telling her what to do.

During the ten-minute drive, Ash made a few

stabs at small talk, but getting little response from Jordan, he remained quiet until they arrived at Dr. Danforth's office in the tony West Vancouver neighborhood. "Take all the time you need," he said. "I'll be here to pick you up when you're done." Like a little kid being dropped off at school, she felt him watching her until she disappeared through the office door.

Jordan estimated the psychologist to be in her mid-fifties. With high cheekbones and an aquiline nose, none of her features were classically beautiful, but somehow taken in their totality, she was almost handsome. She wore her fine blond hair pinned back, and as she poured them each a cup of herbal tea, Jordan observed how long and elegant her fingers were.

"You've come back to see me." Dr. Danforth put her cup on the table between them, picked up a pad of paper and a pen, and sat down. "Post-traumatic stress disorder is not something that should go untreated. Do you think perhaps you took a break from our sessions a bit too soon?"

In her head, Jordan heard Quinn saying the same thing. She could only nod as hot tears filled her eyes.

"In the past, you've told me that you're having disturbing memories and thoughts about your experience. That you had trouble falling or staying asleep, and that you were having recurring nightmares. Is that still the case?"

"Yes, the nightmares are getting worse. And recently, I had the same feelings of panic with a…a friend." Jordan's voice broke as she recalled the episode with Quinn on the island. "My heart felt like it would pound out of my chest and I couldn't breathe."

"It's a good sign that you were aware of that." The doctor made a note on her pad. "What would you like for yourself today, Jordan? What should we work on?"

"I don't know. I just feel...trapped."

Dr. Danforth nodded. "What else?"

"Weak. Guilty." The dam broke, and the tears fell in fat droplets onto her lap. "I should have fought harder." She looked up at the ceiling and tried to hold back the torrent that had been building. "It doesn't matter what I do, I can't seem to move forward. It's as if I'm paralyzed. I keep reliving what he did to me. I was terrified, thinking I was going to die in that underground tomb and nobody would ever know." She shrugged. "It's hard to explain."

"You're doing a good job. I'm sure it was terrifying. And it's stopping you from moving forward? These visions create feelings that leave you completely disempowered."

"Yes, that's it. Disempowered and no energy. I feel like a ragdoll. Like I've had the stuffing knocked out of me. It's as if I have no control and can't take care of myself the way I used to." Jordan shook herself as if it might push away the memories.

"Have you ever in your life felt like that before?"

"No."

"You never felt disempowered?"

"I don't think so, not like this."

"What about at school or at work? Any bullies?"

"Well, when we were kids, Rachel—she's now

my research assistant—and I were crazy about Wonder Woman comics. When I started getting bullied in grade school, on our lunch hour, we would draw Wonder Woman zooming down from the sky with her arm outstretched and her fist clenched. She always took out the girl who was the lead bully, of course."

"Of course." Dr. Danforth smiled. "Were you ever bullied in your job?"

"Well yes, now you mention it, but as a woman in my line of work that's par for the course. When I was first promoted to the crime beat at the newspaper I had this editor. A woman, ironically. She would set me up for a fall and then expose my mistakes in front of my peers at our Monday morning meetings."

Dr. Danforth nodded. "You were well respected in your field. I'm wondering how you coped."

Jordan blushed and shook her head. "I feel stupid telling you about it."

"It's your choice of course, but I'm interested."

"Rachel and I would reminisce about doing the same thing we did to the school bully to Debbie Downer—the editor's real name was Deborah—we laughed about making Debbie explode into tiny pieces in a flash of white light and disappear off the face of the earth." Jordan gave a little smile. "Juvenile I know, but it was very satisfying. And I was less scared of her after that."

Dr. Danforth chuckled. "Because you went back to something that you were familiar with, so then as an adult, you found a way to cope. It helped with the fear." She took off her glasses and reached into a basket under the coffee table. "Jordan, would you be willing to try something I've done with some of my younger patients?"

"Sure, I guess."

"Just so I understand, could you draw Wonder Woman zooming down from the sky with her fist outstretched, so I get the picture?" She passed Jordan a pad of paper and a handful of colored felt pens.

"I feel like a child doing this, but okay." Jordan reached for them. "Shall I draw Debbie?"

"I'm thinking you might draw your captor."

Jordan dropped the pens as if they had suddenly ignited in her hand. "I can't…I can't do that."

"I understand, but they're just felt pens. You said it yourself, you and Rachel liked to draw on your lunch hour."

Jordan tugged at a dead piece of skin on her thumb and it started to bleed.

The doctor passed her a tissue. "Could you just draw a little bit of him? Your captor."

Jordan reached out a shaky hand and chose the black pen. She felt the therapist's eyes on her, but she said nothing.

"This feels weird." Jordan drew a rudimentary figure.

"What happens when Wonder Woman hits him?

Jordan grabbed the red pen and scribbled over the image of her perpetrator until he was hidden. Her blouse was stuck to her back, her underarms bathed in sweat. At the same time, she felt a sense of perverse satisfaction.

"You've destroyed the perpetrator," the doctor said.

"No," Jordan corrected her. "He's still there

underneath. Not gone."

"Okay, so what could you do to finish him off?"

"Chop him up into little pieces." If only, Jordan thought.

Out of the basket, the psychologist pulled a pair of scissors. "Chop him up, just leave Wonder Woman."

Carefully, Jordan cut around Wonder Woman, then with fine, fast movements she chopped up the scribbled-out perpetrator.

"What should we do now?" the doctor asked.

"Well, I'd like to burn him, but I don't imagine we can do that here." Jordan grinned.

Dr. Danforth got up and pulled a metal waste basket over to where they were seated. "Of course we can. Would you like to do the honors?" She handed Jordan a lighter.

She reached down and deposited the chopped-up bits of paper into the basket, then flicked the butane lighter. What was left of her captor disappeared in seconds, leaving only a trace of ash at the bottom.

"How are you feeling now?"

"Weird. Different, but oddly, better. I don't know, it's like I've got some power back."

"You *took* your power back, Jordan."

Jordan swallowed the lump in her throat and nodded.

"It was your idea we used. I'm glad it worked, and the good news is you can do that any time you want. A bit like medication except it's free and there are no side effects."

Jordan smiled, the hint about the medication and her complaints about the adverse effects not lost on her. "Thank you, that was amazing. It feels like…like I'm equipped somehow. Like I have a weapon to fight back."

"Well done, Jordan. You used your own ideas to fight this thing. To bring yourself back into the light and reclaim your power. Great work." The doctor looked at her watch. "Our time is winding to a close. Would you like to talk again next week?"

Out on the sidewalk, Jordan pulled up her collar and opened her umbrella. The same one she'd tossed back in the car that Halloween night. She shivered as she made her way to Ash's waiting car. Dr. Danforth was wrong; no matter how many times she'd said she hadn't been responsible for her own abduction, Jordan alone knew the truth. She *had* brought this on herself. Just as surely as her informant had mentioned those fateful words that had compelled her to drive out to the valley that night.

"I know where your father is," he'd said on the phone. "But I don't know how long he'll be alive."

Chapter Eleven

In the early light of dawn, Jordan awoke exhausted, having seen almost every hour change on the digital clock beside her bed. She couldn't get her informant's words out of her head: He claimed to know where her father, Gavin Stone was but not whether he would remain alive. And there was no mention of her mother, Kathryn.

It had taken every iota of self-control not to go in search of her informant after Ash had dropped her home the night before. Mickey—not his real name—had lured her out to the valley that night with one hundred percent certainty she would come. But why, after years of being her most valuable C.I., would he suddenly betray her? It didn't make sense. It wouldn't have been him calling to her from the van in the blinding rain, asking if she was Jordan Stone; he knew her. Either it was a person other than Mickey, or someone had put him up to it.

She snatched her phone off the bedside table and scrolled through every number she'd ever saved from his incoming calls. Although she knew it would be fruitless, she dialed each one of them, just as she'd done when Rachel had brought her personal phone and laptop to the hospital. That first night following her rescue, she'd almost been relieved she couldn't contact Mickey, but now, the quiet sense of power and control lingered from her session with Dr. Danforth. She'd be goddamned if she'd be cowed again.

Of course, all her informant's calls would have come from burner phones. She'd never find him that way. She looked at the date and time on her cell. As early as it was for suburbanites, the daily grind of the downtown eastside would just be swinging into full gear. After all, it was welfare Wednesday.

Jordan rolled down the window of her red and black Mini Cooper as the car crawled alongside the broken curb in front of Pioneer Square, otherwise known as Pigeon Park. Unlike the addicted and mentally ill denizens of the area, her informant did not live on the streets or on park benches. Not anymore. But it was always somewhere in these few city blocks that he had chosen for their meets. They'd go for a walk in the park or, in addition to what he referred to as his "fee," he'd hit her up for breakfast at one of the locale's more colorful diners. No longer an addict himself, Jordan knew him to volunteer at the local men's shelter. It was his way of giving back, he'd said. How he made a steady income, Jordan hesitated to guess, but she was sure he was no longer dealing.

She jumped as an anorexically thin woman with dull, unfocused eyes stumbled into her almost stationary car. The lineup across the street of people waiting for their welfare checks snaked all the way around the block. With one last look at the scene of abject poverty and the seemingly bottomless pit of hopelessness, Jordan drove away. Could she really be that certain of anything anymore? *Dammit, Mickey, where are you?*

With barely half an hour to spare before Quinn was due to pick her up, Jordan threw the jeans and ratty sweatshirt she'd been wearing into the laundry hamper and took a quick shower. All the while, she cursed herself for having agreed to go to RCMP headquarters for an appointment with the Force's hypnotherapist. When Quinn had arrived unannounced at her cabin on the island, Jordan eventually wheedled it out of him why he was staying close to the investigation even though he had retired. As he had stood on the front porch, freezing his ass off, he'd lectured her on why victims of violent crimes needed to get psychological counseling.

"What the hell do *you* care? You're not even on the Force anymore?" she'd asked.

"I fucking care because…" he'd shot back before stopping himself. "I'm sorry, I care because your stubborn lack of cooperation is causing the now head of the investigation to wonder why you're not more motivated to solve your case."

"What do you mean by 'my stubborn lack of cooperation'? I've been poked, prodded and questioned ad nauseum. Jeez, Quinn, I've told them everything I know."

He'd raked his hands through his hair and shook his head. "You don't get it, do you?"

"What do you mean?"

"I *mean*, we know this guy did things to you, Jordan. Awful things. Unspeakable things."

She remembered clenching her hands as the hot rage had bubbled up inside her. It had been like trying to tamp down a volcano before it erupted.

"You had to know I've read King's case notes from your interview." His voice was so soft she'd had to strain to hear him. "Jordan, I've worked with hypnotherapists on other cases like yours."

He'd put up a hand to stop her from interrupting. "It's not uncommon for survivors to block out things that could help in investigations. Like little things he said or did that might help nail this bastard. We're getting nowhere from the crime artist's sketch."

She didn't know if it was the fear that her kidnapper was still out there, or the tormented expression on Quinn's face that day, but his comments had cut close to the bone. Whatever it was, she'd reluctantly agreed to go through hypnosis. But now, all she could think about was finding Mickey.

She pulled on a grey cashmere turtleneck over black pants. From her bedroom window, she caught a glimpse of a small sailboat making its way into port. The rain had eased to what the locals referred to as a Scotch mist, and the sky boasted a lighter shade of grey: two concessions to an otherwise unpromising day.

While she waited for Quinn, she perched on the side of her unmade bed and looked discerningly around her bedroom. Decorated in soft, muted shades of cream and beige, it was here she had spent countless hours creating a refuge, a sanctuary in which to hole up after reuniting with her father the year before.

At sixteen, she had washed her hands of Gavin Stone when he left her mother and her for another woman. Following their ten-year estrangement, a motivation that to this day Jordan couldn't fathom, propelled her halfway around the world in a quest to find him. Although she told herself she didn't give a damn about him as a father, the previous year, she had used her considerable investigative skills to eventually locate him in a tiny town in Calabria, Italy. That simple act of recklessness had proven to be the proverbial case of kicking over a hornet's nest.

And out of that nest emerged the vilest of creatures, Vittorio Constantine. A former Mafia kingpin in his glory days, toward the end of his life he was disowned by his own crime clan. Even the mob followed a code of ethics: one of the most sacred rules was that silence and secrecy—a term referred to as *omerta*—must be adhered to always. Constantine, with his blustering megalomania, had loose lips. Under the N'arangeta clan's code of conduct, a cross was given to each member inducted into the 'family,' which bore the phrase, "I swear to be faithful to N'arangeta. If I should betray it, my flesh must burn, just as this image burns." Having long ago ostracized Constantine from the fold, the N'arangeta didn't get the pleasure of carrying out the burning part. Shortly after, in a moment of poetic justice the outcast gangster burned to death in a shootout that turned everything around him into an inferno.

In the final moments before the explosion, Constantine's henchman, Salvatore Castellano, was seen sprinting behind a wall of flames heading toward the entrance of an underground tunnel. Though the Caribinieri, the federal police of Italy, were certain Castellano couldn't have survived the ensuing blast, Interpol was reluctant to close the case. They couldn't establish if there were more of Constantine's people out there who might still pose a threat to witnesses whose testimony could put any remaining members away for good.

Two of those witnesses were Jordan's father, Gavin Stone, and her biological mother, Kathryn. For their safety, her parents were forced to enter protective custody. She had a painfully brief reunion with them before they were whisked away under heavy security, and she returned to Vancouver alone, with a gaping hole in her heart.

The days following her return turned into blurry weeks and agonizingly long months. Desperate to pull her out of her depression, Uncle Ash had proposed she move from the trendy condo she'd been renting in Deer Ridge and buy a forlorn-looking beach house adjacent to the West Vancouver seawall. She got a steal on the property because although it afforded an unobstructed view of the Lions Gate Bridge and the outer harbor, the house itself was in sad shape. However, with the amount she was able to put down, the monthly mortgage payments were the same as she'd been paying in rent. And as Ash pointed out, she was building equity. Thanks to his business acumen, as her trustee, he encouraged Jordan to take the interest from the money her father had put into a living trust for her and use it to pay for some much-needed renovations and furnishings. That's when she'd taken her first leave of absence from her job at the newspaper and the renovations distracted her from the cavernous void left by the absence of her parents.

She looked out her window and counted the ships in the harbor waiting to load up with grain. No matter how dreary a day it was, the sights and sounds of living within spitting distance of the sea felt like the only thing keeping her sane. Sane, but no longer safe.

The tension was palpable as Quinn drove along the Upper Levels Highway, heading toward the Lions Gate Bridge. "You're doing the right thing, Jordan."

"Oh yeah, and what would that be?" She felt her spine tighten as she took another sip of the take-out coffee Quinn had brought to drink in the car.

"Agreeing to see a hypnotherapist. I've seen people recall deeply buried memories after they've gone through the kind of ordeal you have." Jordan noticed his tactfulness in not referring to her as a victim. But the coffee still tasted like a bribe.

"Whoever did this to me is an evil son of a bitch, Quinn. I want him caught, but there's another part of me that just wants to forget it ever happened."

Without taking his eyes off the road, Quinn fumbled through the gas receipts in the Honda's console for a packet of Juicy Fruit gum, unwrapped a stick, and stuffed it in his mouth. He *had* stopped smoking, but Jordan wasn't going to give him the satisfaction of acknowledging it.

"I understand why you don't want to put yourself through it again," he said. "It *is* kind of ironic though."

"What?"

"Just that you were like a pit-bull when it came

to hunting down the bad guys as an investigative reporter. A pretty good one, I hear."

Jordan turned to look at him. "Really? That's not what you *used* to think of me. Is this you using reverse psychology?"

Keeping his eyes trained on the road, he ignored the jibe. "Have you thought any more of what we talked about back at the cabin?" He chuckled as he asked the question. He had told her that what she referred to as a rustic cabin would be considered a country mansion in his circles.

"No," Jordan replied, thinking back to the last conversation they had before leaving the island. "I've been a bit busy in case you hadn't noticed."

"No need to be sarcastic." Quinn chewed his gum vigorously. "I just thought seeing as I'm unemployed and you're an experienced investigative reporter, that we might make a good team. As a former member of the RCMP, I'm not required to take any more training to be a PI, you know."

"How nice for you. So why do you need me?"

"Because I hate writing reports and I thought that might be something you could help me with, so you don't have to go back to the paper."

"What, be your secretary? Thanks, but no thanks."

Quinn sighed as he drove into the underground lot and pulled into one of the parking spots allotted for RCMP members. Interesting, Jordan thought, he still had his pass.

"Could you just get it through your head that I'm on your side? I can't afford to retire at forty-four on half pension. I get it that you don't want to give up what you're good at, but you're not thinking this through. Someone held you prisoner for fifteen days and for some perverse reason didn't kill you. And he's still at large." He took his hands off the wheel and bumped it gently with the heel of his palm. "Would you at least think about it? Maybe you could keep writing articles but do it freelance. And switch from crime reporting."

Jordan finally looked over at him. There was little use in pointing out that she'd built her reputation on writing about crime. She'd won awards for several crime investigative series. Now *he* didn't get it. What was she to write about, recipes and restaurant openings?

"I'm sorry, J.J., you've been really kind to me. Although my ribs still hurt from when you tackled me to the ground." She tried not to give him a smile, but she could feel it breaking through anyway. She hated that since the abduction, her emotions lay so exposed, raw and just beneath the surface.

"Well, you didn't leave me much choice. You fought like a goddamned wildcat."

Jordan opened her car door, signaling she was ready to go upstairs. Side by side, they walked to the elevator. "Yes, I will think about it but I'm not making any promises. Let's just get through this first."

"Fair enough." Quinn thrust out a business card.

She turned it over in her hand. "What's this?"

"Where you can reach me from now on. You can get me on my cell twenty-four-seven."

She looked up as the elevator door opened.

"Call me for any reason, no matter what time it

is." He punched the button for the eleventh floor.

Funny, that's what Giancarlo had said when she saw him off at Vancouver airport just a few months ago. "Call me anytime, cara." The former Italian Special Prosecutor had cupped her chin in his hand and she had felt herself free-falling into his liquid chocolate eyes.

Then he'd simply vanished.

Chapter Twelve

The phone was ringing as Jordan let herself into the house. Somehow, she had survived the session with the RCMP hypnotherapist. Even after he'd patiently gone over everything with her, she wondered if anything she'd said would increase the likelihood of catching the bastard. Her biggest fear was she may have divulged the real reason she'd gone out to the valley that night. If she had, the therapist hadn't said anything.

She closed the door quickly and punched in the code to the new alarm system Quinn insisted she have installed. Damn, she'd missed the phone. As almost no one called her at home she figured it was probably just Ash checking in. Then it rang again. She glanced at the caller I.D. and her heart raced when she saw it was an international call. Silently, she prayed it would be Giancarlo. "Hello?"

"Jordan?" It was Simon Grenville calling from Italy.

"Yes, hi," she replied, trying to conceal her disappointment as she held the phone between her ear and shoulder and unbuttoned her coat.

"Where have you been? I've been calling you here and on your mobile. I've left messages. Why haven't you returned my calls?"

"I know, I'm sorry," Jordan stammered.

"I've been worried sick about you. I even tried calling Inspector Quinn but he's not with the RCMP anymore."

Simon's initially warm tone turned officious and scolding. In contrast, Jordan thought wistfully of Giancarlo's softly accented whispers as they had made love the night before he returned to Italy. She shook off the memory and wriggled out of her coat. Glancing out the kitchen window she paused, momentarily distracted by the blood-red sun setting over the ocean. Just a few months ago, she was encased underground, certain she would never witness that splendor again.

"Jordan, are you there?"

"Yes, I'm here. Why are you calling?" Then she caught herself, remembering that delicious English accent and the long nights they had put in together when they were both in London. A story they were mutually investigating, though from vastly different angles, led her to the impossibly charming Interpol agent. Although nothing had ever happened between them, there had been an unmistakable crackle of sexual tension whenever they were together. But that was before she met Giancarlo Vicente.

"Sorry, I didn't mean it that way. You sound anxious. What's up?"

"We've got some new intelligence." There was a long pause. "On Salvatore Castellano."

The mere mention of the gangster's name made

Jordan's pulse quicken. Her stomach did a little flip flop. Although Interpol hesitated to pronounce the case closed, everyone had been adamant that the henchman who worked for the 'Ndrangheta, one of Italy's most powerful crime syndicates, was dead. Everyone, that was, but Jordan. Before she left Tropea, she knew in her gut that something about his supposed death wasn't right. She just couldn't prove it. Not at the time, anyway. But intuition told her she was getting incredibly close before she was abducted that rainy night in Chilliwack. She had been working her informants for an investigative piece she was writing that began in Italy and had far-reaching tentacles all over the world. In the past, her long-time informant, Mickey, had always provided her with solid leads. Following her rescue from the bunker she'd berated herself for letting her journalistic greed seduce her into going to a remote location for the meet. In her heart, she knew it was only when he'd told her he knew her father's whereabouts, that she'd thrown caution to the wind.

"Dammit Jordan, are you there? I said Castellano is definitely still alive."

"Yes, I'm here." A sense of foreboding washed over her. Simultaneously, she felt that little flutter of excitement; the same feeling she always got before she broke a new story. Now Simon was telling her Castellano was alive. Jordan wiped her sweaty hands down her pants. "Where is he? Do you know?" Silence. "Simon?"

"Yes, we have it on good authority that he's in the US Pacific Northwest, near the Canadian border. We're running an analysis on some surveillance footage, but I'm pretty sure it'll come back confirmed." The *we* Simon referred to was the UK Interpol office, where he headed up the IRT, or Incident Response Team, for the international agency. Her knees buckled, and she put a hand out to steady herself before perching on the edge of a kitchen barstool.

Simon's voice faded into the distance like a foghorn's warning lost in the mist. She was unsure if it was a poor phone connection, or if she was still buried alive, hearing her own voice echoing off the rusted metal walls of her underground prison. Confirmation that Castellano was indeed still alive, and on this side of the Atlantic, unleashed an icy chill down her spine.

Now Simon was telling her that not only was Castellano likely alive, but he was somewhere just south of her. Her instincts said she should sit this one out and let the authorities do their job. But her gut told her she'd be a coward if she didn't do everything she could to locate the piece of human garbage who was responsible for her being separated from her family. Ever since her father abandoned Jordan's mother and her, she'd told herself she could live without him again. After all, she'd stubbornly refused to see him before eventually locating him in Italy. The significant difference this time, was that when she had finally found him, she got two for one. She was also introduced to her biological mother, Kathryn, the woman he had left them for. The woman who was Jordan's mirror image.

With sudden clarity, Jordan came to the only logical conclusion possible: to get to Castellano before the police or Interpol did, then to make sure he didn't live long enough to put everyone through a long, expensive trial. A trial that wouldn't guarantee the outcome she obsessed about, day and night.

Chapter Thirteen

It was hard to imagine that just a few weeks ago Jordan was adamant about not heeding Quinn's advice to quit her job at the newspaper. Even after using part of her trust fund for the renovations, her savings plus the money from her parents' trust were doing well in investments. She could afford to take another leave of absence for at least a year and consider her next career move without cutting into the capital. Maybe now was the time for the book Rachel had been urging her to write. As a crime reporter, Jordan had certainly seen enough horror to write a compelling tale. But seeing and experiencing that horror first-hand was a whole other story; one she could not possibly bring herself to write about.

As usual, Jordan's best friend and former colleague, Rachel Sommers, was having trouble containing her exuberance when she and Jordan met for their weekly Martini Monday. "God, Jordan I'd give anything—*any*thing—to be a fly on the wall in some of your investigative interviews. You've got at *least* one book in you."

As the conversation developed, it became evident

Rachel's motive for encouraging Jordan to leave the paper to write her book was not entirely selfless. "You know," she continued, "you could share an office with Quinn, help him out with a few reports here and there, and write."

As Jordan's former research assistant, Rachel was intimately familiar with her work. The reporter who was brought in to replace Jordan while she was on medical leave, turned out to be a brash obsessive-compulsive type whom Rachel loathed. "Think of the Devil Wears Prada as a nursery rhyme," she described her new boss.

"I have to get out of there, Jordan, the woman is sucking the soul right out of my body. But I can't afford to." Rachel had always been given to dramatics, even when she and Jordan were in grade school, then eventually at the same university. They both went in for journalism but while Jordan exceled, Rachel's professors essentially gave her the choice of failing or switching programs. As it was so far into the first term, the only seat she could get was in computer programming. Rachel was devastated, but as one door closed another opened, and she finished with the highest marks in her class. They were both hired right out of school; Jordan to a tiny, fledgling local paper, Rachel to a leading security company.

"Are you even listening to me, Jordan? I have to get out of there or I swear I'll lose my mind. You and Quinn could share office space to save money and I could work for both of you part-time. You'll still need someone to do your research, whether for your freelance pieces or your book." She winked at Jordan. "What do you think?"

"I think you're crazy, my sweet friend. Why would I want to share an office with Quinn? And I don't know what or even *if* we could pay you."

"Why don't you let me worry about that, just until you get up and running? I've managed to squirrel away a bit of savings and it's not as if I live high on the hog. It's just Sassafras and me in my tiny apartment." Sassafras was Rachel's overweight, laid-back, Bengal tabby cat. If the truth were known, the cat was the only roommate Jordan's adorable, but unusual friend had been able to maintain for more than a few months. But aside from being eccentric and quirky in the extreme, Rachel had packed a wide scope of invaluable experience into her young life.

When Jordan worked with her at the newspaper, Rachel was unsurpassed as the most tenacious researcher there. At their peril, several senior staffers made the mistake of equating her intelligence with her unique fashion statements. Before coming to the paper, she had been a "legitimate" hacker for one of the country's top security firms. Her job was to find holes in their clients' security systems, thus allowing them to beef up their online security against more dangerous impostors. For Jordan, Rachel's former job skills brought a measure of apprehension, thus she had long ago stopped asking where her research assistant acquired her information. All she knew was that with Rachel's resources and tenacity, their symbiotic relationship resulted in Jordan cracking some of the top crime stories of all time. She could still see the staffers' collective jaws lying heavily on the floor each time she and Rachel broke a new investigative series.

"Earth to Jordan, come in please. As I was saying, you could consider me as a volunteer until Quinn's P.I. business and your freelancing takes off. That way I could quit working for dragon lady."

Jordan turned her attention back to her friend. "That's so sweet of you, but I don't know if Quinn even *has* a business, Rache. And I really can't get my head around sharing an office with him. My god, he's kind of a Neanderthal." She chuckled, as the waiter brought another martini for Rachel and cranberry and soda for her. Staying true to her word, Jordan was on her meds and off the booze.

Rachel arched one perfectly drawn, coal-black eyebrow as she trained her sights on Jordan, and they clinked glasses in a toast. "It seems to me that Inspector Quinn had your back when you were in a pretty grim place," she said. "Although, I will admit we have some work to do on his bedside manner."

"And his hygiene and diet." Jordan laughed, relaxing a little.

"That too," Rachel conceded, then turned serious. "But you know, he has a lot of experience. I don't think you'd be making a mistake hitching your horse to his wagon." Like Rachel's other tastes, her vernacular was often vintage.

Jordan had enormous respect and love for Rachel, having learned long ago to trust her and her instincts. The truth was she'd come to rely heavily on Rachel to provide her with the quality of research that earned her the professional recognition, not to mention awards for journalism that Jordan had amassed. She wasn't sure she could continue to pull off those articles without her. But it wasn't fair to

Rachel.

"Rache, you know I would love to have you but since my abduction, I've—" Jordan shook her head.

"You've lost your confidence," Rachel finished her sentence. Jordan's eyes filled with tears.

"Is the counseling helping?" Rachel put a hand on Jordan's arm.

"Yes and no." Jordan hadn't told her about the appointment with the hypnotherapist, but she knew she was seeing Dr. Danforth. "I hate reliving the memories. Honestly, I'd rather just try to block it out." The next words stuck in her throat. "And I don't want what happened to Angelina to happen to you." She reached in her purse for a tissue.

Rachel cocked her head. "The interpreter you hired in Italy? Jordan, Angelina's murder wasn't your fault. Why would you even think that?"

"She wasn't just my interpreter, Rache. She did research for me, like you do. That's how she unearthed Castellano and his boss's relationship to my father. It was the very next morning that her mother found her in her bedroom, strangled to death." She stared at Rachel. "How could that not be my fault?"

"Oh, sweetie," Rachel reached across the table and took Jordan's hand. "Are you afraid that something like that could happen to me? You're home now, Jordan. You're safe. *We're* safe."

Rachel might not have said that if she'd known Salvatore Castellano was possibly three to six hours south of them.

In spite of her reservations about spending more time

with Quinn, by the end of the evening with Rachel, Jordan had to admit she found the possibilities of a freelance career exhilarating. She hadn't admitted it to anyone, but since Simon's phone call, she had been unable to think of anything other than finding a way to flush out Castellano. With Rachel's research acumen and Quinn's experience in the RCMP, particularly the Serious and Organized Crime units, Jordan suspected they'd both be invaluable in locating the gangster. If Quinn believed Castellano was behind her kidnapping, surely, he'd be willing to help.

A few days after her conversation with Rachel, Jordan was supervising the setup of her office furniture directly across the open reception area from what was to be Quinn's workspace. She jumped at the whine of an automatic drill, her mind reeling back to the mini-grinder the police had used to cut her free from her restraints. But it was just the handyman Jordan had hired from her old apartment, putting the finishing touches on her workstation.

"I think that should do it. That baby is as solid as a rock." Harold tilted his head toward Quinn's office. Jordan followed his gaze to the small room filled with boxes, a beaten up old wooden desk and god knows what else.

"Want me to put anything together in there before I go?" Harold asked.

"I would, but I think you'd better come back when he's unpacked." *If he unpacks*. "I'd be afraid to venture in there if I were you, Harold. But I really appreciate what you've done. How much do I owe you?"

"No worries. Just give me a call and I'll collect from you when your bookshelves arrive. By then your partner might be organized. Do you think?"

"Let's hope," Jordan rolled her eyes. Quinn was *not* her partner. But he could certainly come in handy about now. Before her case went cold.

Chapter Fourteen

"How can you eat those things?" Jordan asked as Quinn stuffed the better part of a chocolate donut in his mouth and washed it down with a gulp of coffee.

"Don't get so high and mighty," he retorted. "All I ever see you ingesting are those expensive triple-shot trendy coffees. Don't you ever eat anything solid?"

"Now children, play nice," Rachel admonished, as she handed Quinn two manila folders. "We need to go over these case files now if you want Jordan to write the reports."

"Wow, two cases," Quinn exclaimed. "That should help pay the Starbucks bill."

"Would you two just quit?" Rachel scowled. "I can assure you Jordan's coffees don't come out of the firm. I'm assuming you can say the same about the donuts."

Jordan shot him a smug "gotcha" look.

"All right, I think we're ready to wrap everything up and send our final bill on the Hoffman affair," Rachel said. "Oops, no pun intended!" she giggled. Quinn frowned; they all knew he loathed working cheating spouse cases, but for now, they helped pay the bills.

"I'll have the final report on your desk by five." Jordan got up to refill her coffee and turned to leave but Rachel stopped her.

"I'm not sure what I should be doing to open up this new file, Jordan. I can do the research but it's going to be tricky as it's a cross-border situation. Do you have anything more solid than just the surveillance footage on your guy?"

Damn! Jordan lowered her eyes and took a sip of her coffee. She'd have to have a word with Rachel about not discussing their work in front of Quinn. She intended to talk to him and enlist his help, but not like this.

"Cross-border. What guy?" he asked, spitting bits of his donut into the air.

"Inspector Quinn, this is Jordan's freelance piece. Do you have a problem?"

"He's not an inspector anymore," Jordan pointed out peevishly.

"You're goddamned right I have a problem." Quinn glared at Jordan. "Since when are you involved with surveillance in the US?" He grabbed the file from Rachel and flipped through its contents. "Who the hell is Salvatore Castellano?" he asked, glaring at them both.

Jordan took a deep breath and snatched her file back. "I'm finishing my series on known Mafia members living here in Canada. What's the big deal?"

Rachel and Quinn's heads snapped up simultaneously. They stared at Jordan across the conference room table.

"Who is Salvatore Castellano?" Quinn repeated. "And what the hell are you thinking? I thought you quit the paper to get away from these guys, at least one of whom could be responsible for your abduction."

Rachel looked at him and then back to Jordan. "I think that's a reasonable point Inspector...uh, Quinn brings up." She tilted her head questioningly.

Jordan toyed with the fruit salad Rachel had put in front of her after noticing she had consumed, as Quinn stated quite correctly, a triple-shot Americano on an empty stomach. Old habits from the newspaper business died hard. Any decent journalist worth their salt knew they would have time to eat and sleep after the story was filed.

"Well?" Quinn leaned his chair back, balancing on its two legs and stared Jordan down. She hoped it would slide right out from under him.

"Okay, it's not exactly part of my investigative series," Jordan admitted. "Castellano is a former member of the 'Ndrangheta." In truth, she knew there was no such thing as a former member. When it came to the Calabrian Mafia, one was with them until death, which more often than not didn't occur by natural causes.

Quinn abruptly righted his chair. "The same guy Interpol has been trying to nail? Wasn't he one of the wiseguys you were researching before your kidnapping?"

When she didn't reply Quinn banged his hand on the table. "Are you fucking kidding me? What the hell were you thinking? I thought your boyfriend, Simon whatever-his-name-is with Interpol had taken over the investigation. This is why you quit the newspaper business, remember?"

"Agent Simon Grenville." Jordan glared at Quinn, feeling her face flush. "He did, but his people lost Castellano a few weeks ago and I thought maybe I could get a leg up on him."

"For Christ's sake, Jordan. This isn't our bailiwick. And you're not working for the damned paper anymore."

"I haven't quit the paper. I've only extended my leave in case this doesn't work out." Which was looking more likely every day, she thought.

"Whatever. Let him handle this. Haven't you been through enough?"

"It's not that simple, Quinn. Castellano disappeared from Italy and now they have intelligence that he is possibly somewhere in the States."

"Jesus, Jordan, I'm trying to keep your case from going onto the RCMP's back burner. You should have talked to me about this first."

"We're talking about it now." She pushed her chair back from the table so quickly it threatened to topple over. "I knew I couldn't work in the same office with him," she said to Rachel.

"Will both of you calm down? Let's just discuss this like…" Rachel began, but it was too late. Jordan snatched up her jacket on the way out of the tiny conference room, leaving Rachel and Quinn watching the metal coat rack spinning like a dervish.

Jordan was beyond exhausted when she finally got home from the office in the late afternoon, but she forced herself to go for a run along the seawall to clear her head. Physically, she was still in that place where she appreciated the freedom she had so recently been deprived of. So, she ran even though she didn't feel like it. Emotionally, everything else sat in her brain like an enormous tangled ball of multi-colored wool. Red-hot anger lay in wait just beneath the surface. Brown for the filth she endured imprisoned in that underground bunker for fifteen days. Yellow was the nausea she felt each time the trapdoor in the earth opened and she knew what was about to happen at the hands of that twisted, evil piece of garbage.

After returning home from her run and taking a hot shower, she made herself a decaf espresso. While she waited for the machine to warm up, she flipped open her laptop and clicked on the file that held reams of painstakingly detailed research. She had bookmarked several websites that dealt with people who entered the Canadian and US federal witness protection programs. Except for the few who left voluntarily, not one of them had been harmed.

But what about Gavin and Kathryn Stone who had gone into an international protection program? They had been living in Italy at the time they witnessed the crimes the late Vittorio Constantine and Salvatore Castellano were accused of. Her parents could be anywhere in Europe, possibly still in Italy. They might have one official "handler"—two at best—who would know their exact whereabouts. Jordan knew from sources she'd interviewed how technology presented new challenges to keeping the identities of witnesses, secret. Thanks to social media and smart phones, several protectees had ended up dead, by unusually grisly means.

Exhausted, she snapped her laptop closed and drained her cup. One thing she knew for sure: staying in Vancouver, under Quinn's abject scrutiny wasn't going to get her any closer to finding her family.

Chapter Fifteen

Arriving at the office just moments before their morning meeting, Jordan did a double take when she saw Rachel's cat, Sassafras, lying in a bed on top of the reception desk. With a cumbersome white plastic Elizabethan collar tied around her neck, the tabby acknowledged her with an embarrassed look.

"Oh dear, Sassy, what happened to you?" she asked, fondly scratching the feline's ears. The cat purred and pushed her nose into Jordan's hand.

"Does it bite?" Quinn asked Rachel, as they both emerged from the coffee room.

"Only people *she* doesn't like." Quinn reached out his hand, Sassafras hissed, and he snatched it back.

The three of them settled themselves around the small conference room table. Quinn had already polished off his first chocolate croissant when Sassy jumped from her perch and self-consciously bumped and scraped her way over to lick the buttery flakes off the floor beneath his chair.

"How long will she be staying?" he asked, peering down.

"Until her bottom...er, her abscess, heals. I can't leave her alone while she has the stent in. Somehow, she manages to get that darned collar off. She's already pulled it out once." Rachel looked at Jordan. "Is it a problem? I would have asked you, but it was so late when I got her home from the emergency vet last night that I didn't want to call."

"Of course, it's all right." Jordan sneezed. She looked at Quinn and dared him to disagree.

"Oh my god, Jordan, I forgot you're allergic!" Rachel said. "I'll try to find somewhere to board her, but it won't be until tomorrow."

"It's fine, Rachel, really. I can just take an...*achoo!*" Jordan groped in her purse for a tissue. "...an antihistamine." Three more sneezes escaped despite her best effort to stifle them.

"This is ridiculous," Quinn said. "We can't have a goddamned cat in here. It's a place of business, not a vet, for god's sake. Clients come in here."

"*When?*" Jordan and Rachel asked simultaneously.

Jordan felt the sting of mascara as her eyes streamed. She put her hand up to rub them, then thought better of it as she'd already touched the cat. "When was the last time a client came in here?" Or, the *first* time, she thought. "Rachel is not going to pay to board Sassafras when we're barely paying her to work here, Quinn." She put a tissue to her nose as another sneeze came.

He nodded. "Okay, as long as she doesn't shit anywhere."

"Sassafras would never do that." Rachel looked indignant. "I've put her litter box in the copy room and she'll use it."

As competent as she was eccentric, Rachel's Monday morning attire painted her as a contradiction in terms. Sometime over the weekend, she had dyed blue a patch of her short, jet-black hair. She wore a black and white polka-dot dress and teetered on impossibly high red platform heels as she bustled around the conference room filling coffee cups for the three of them. After insisting Jordan and Quinn have one of her fresh baked Morning Glory muffins, she pulled a manila folder from the small pile in front of her.

"All right, now that we're all sufficiently fortified, let's take another run at this." She eyed Quinn. "First off, I'm going to ask you to refrain from your usual colorful language and to listen to Jordan's entire explanation before responding." She looked to her left. "Jordan, I want a commitment from you that you will be fully present for this discussion and not rush off in a huff if things get heated between you two." Rachel fixed them both with a non-negotiable, expectant look. "Do we have a deal?"

"Okay by me." Quinn warily eyed the Smurf pen Rachel pointed at him.

"Jordan?"

"Yes. And for what it's worth, I apologized to Quinn for taking off the other day." She directed her best conciliatory look at them both. "It won't happen again." Interestingly, neither of them seemed to question that their woefully underpaid assistant was in charge. "Jordan, can you fill us in on what more you know about this Castellano character? Like Quinn, I worry this is something you shouldn't be involved in."

While silently cursing Rachel for throwing her under the bus, Jordan took a deep breath. She had been awake half the night rehearsing what she was going to tell Quinn. "At our last meeting," she said, "I told you that Salvatore Castellano appears to have surfaced in the States. Surveillance pictures have confirmed his identity."

"Am I missing something here?" Quinn interjected. "It's not our job to find him. Besides, your boyfriend, Simon, has more resources at his fingertips than we could ever hope to have."

Before Jordan could react, Rachel held up her hands in a gesture of equanimity. "Let's not make this personal. As far as I know, Agent Grenville and Jordan have a working relationship. The rest of the story, if there even is one, is none of your business. Or mine. That said, Jordan, has Simon's office explicitly asked you to get involved?"

Jordan tried to keep her hands steady as she reached for her coffee. "No, they haven't. However, it's no longer as simple as it might have been."

"Oh yeah, why's that?" Quinn bit down on his stir stick.

Jordan wasn't sure which annoyed her more, his previous habit of smoking, or currently, his constant gerbil-like chewing. "Because the last intelligence chatter on him is that he's been spotted in Washington," she answered.

"So? Let the authorities back east deal with it. I would have thought that helping investigators to find your kidnapper might have been your top priority," Quinn volleyed back.

Jordan swallowed another sigh and ignored the jibe. "Not Washington DC. He's been spotted in Seattle, Washington."

Once Quinn had blown off some steam, he agreed to put out a few feelers, thanks in large part to Rachel's intervention. He said he had a contact high up in "one of the US federal agencies," as he vaguely put it, and was confident they would be able to get a line on Castellano. However, he drove a hard bargain, making Jordan promise she would not get personally involved.

"Let my guy do it and don't even think about going down south," Quinn warned as he poured himself a coffee and took it back to his office. "The whole idea of you taking a leave from your job at the newspaper was that you'd quit putting yourself at risk from the whack jobs you used to write about."

Jordan followed him, stopping in the doorway of his office. She had one chance to get this right, so she measured her words carefully. "Quinn, I can't just sit around waiting for the police to come up with a lead in my case. Don't you see? I have to do something and writing investigative pieces is all I know."

Quinn turned and looked at her with weary eyes. "Jordan, I'm not going to insult your intelligence by telling you how close you came to dying before we rescued you. But I will say this: if you think you are going to put all of us through that again, I for one will not be a part of it."

He turned his coffee mug around and around on his desk. "We got lucky. It was only because of one fluke of a lead that we were able to locate you. If the drug enforcement guys hadn't been out there looking for a meth lab, you would likely never have been found." He stopped playing with his cup and looked her squarely in the eye. "Look, I know what it's like to be too late to save someone from the twisted minds that are out there." He squeezed his eyes shut as if trying to block out a persistent memory. "I've been there, Jordan, and I can't do it again. Not even for you."

Chapter Sixteen

Rachel seemed in a playful mood when she stuck her head into Jordan's office near the lunch hour. "Want to try the new restaurant downstairs? It's called the Amorous Oyster. It might get you in the mood."

"For what, exactly?" The last thing on Jordan's mind was *that*. In fact since her abduction she couldn't even think of that without feeling nauseated. She cast an evil eye in Rachel's direction.

"Okay, well how about just going for their great clam chowder. I was there the other day with Quinn and it was delicious."

Though sadly underpaid, Rachel had left the newspaper and was now with them full-time. She and Quinn seemed to have found their respective comfort zones; he had even come to terms with Sassafras who, while completely recovered, had stayed on and seemed to have become their office mascot. As for Jordan, she popped an antihistamine each morning and seemed to be fine.

"He actually asked the waitress what all was in it—the chowder I mean—so he could make it at home. Men who can cook are sexy, don't you think?"

"Quinn, sexy? You can't be serious!"

"No, not him in particular. Just men who can cook, generally." She reached over to the side of Jordan's computer monitor and switched it off. "Come on, let's go before the place fills up."

If anyone other than Rachel had done that, Jordan would have scratched their eyes out, but back on their old footing, she found it endearing. "Okay, but you're buying."

"Hey, you're back," the waitress said to Rachel. "You must have liked the chowder." She looked pointedly in Jordan's direction.

"Oh, this is Jordan. We work together. I was just telling her how the chowder was to die for. Just the same, I had to pry her fingers off the keyboard and drag her down here. All the while, she was kicking and screaming. So, don't make me look bad." Rachel grinned.

"Really?" The waitress's name badge said she was Callie.

Jordan rolled her eyes and smiled. "No, not really. As you might have noticed, Rachel has a flair for the dramatic. You look really familiar. Have we met before?"

Callie nodded. "We might have, I was the hostess up at the Deer Ridge Country Club. But I'm taking some night courses, so I had to give it up for daytime hours."

"Ah," Jordan nodded. "That's where I must have seen you. My uncle's a member there. Ash Courtland. Maybe you know him."

"Can't say that I do, but there are a lot of

members."

"There are." Jordan closed the menu, deciding to take Rachel up on her glowing endorsement of the seafood chowder.

"It's nice to meet you, Jordan," Callie said. I'll bring you ladies some water and your soups will be out in a jiffy."

Regardless of what she'd said about Rachel buying, Jordan grabbed the check when Callie reappeared. While she fished in her bag for her wallet, Rachel piped up, "So, what are you taking at college, Callie?"

"I'm just starting with a basic communications course, and business writing." She seemed embarrassed. "I'm actually hoping to get into journalism, but I don't know…"

"Oh my gosh, that's what Jordan does." Rachel volunteered. She's an award-winning journalist. Actually, she's won multiple awards for—"

"Rachel, don't bore this poor woman to death," Jordan admonished.

"No, really, I'd love to hear more about what you do," Callie said, handing Jordan's credit card back.

"Uh-oh, I think your boss is giving you the look," Jordan said. "But you're welcome to come up to our office anytime. We're on the seventh floor. Quinn Investigative Services."

"Really? That would be amazing!" Callie looked over her shoulder. "But you're right, I'd better get back to work. I sure as heck can't afford to get fired."

Chapter Seventeen

Jordan was a bundle of raw, jumping nerves as she paced her beach house waiting for Simon's call. He'd sent a text earlier in the day to let her know he would ring her once she was home from the office. It would be midnight his time, and she could only imagine what he might be doing. Normally, a run would have been in order, but afraid of missing his call, she turned on all the lights—a new habit that developed after her abduction—and instead, poured herself a glass of wine. *Sorry, Doc.* Taking a seat in front of the floor-to-ceiling living room windows, she distracted herself by flipping open her laptop and googling former RCMP Inspector, J.J. Quinn.

After his warning to stay away from the case, she was more determined than ever to find out what had happened to his family six years ago. Rachel could have found out in a heartbeat, but Jordan didn't want to involve her. There wasn't much on the internet, but as a journalist she had several research links at her disposal that allowed her to drill down at a much deeper level. Using her old login from the newspaper, she held her breath and prayed she still had access.

Bingo. Apparently, The Devil Who Wore Prada wasn't that efficient after all. In rapid succession, Jordan hunted down several threads, all of which led nowhere other than to describe Inspector Quinn's meteoric rise through the RCMP ranks, and various cases with which he'd been associated.

Then, the bold headline screamed, "Undercover Cop's Family Incinerated in Suspected Gang Retaliation." She clicked on the link and up popped a full-color photograph of firemen attempting to extinguish a burning car. Scrolling down to the story beneath, Jordan scanned the contents of the article. Captivated, she read that Quinn's wife, Karyn, and their 9-year old son, Tyler, were returning from the boy's baseball practice. Though it was early evening, Inspector Jesse Quinn, who at the time was working undercover narcotics, was home in bed. He awoke to the sound of an explosion and when he looked out the bedroom window, he saw a car fully engulfed in flames in front of his house. The article reported that he rushed outside with a fire extinguisher to help.

Jordan covered her mouth as she read on. When Quinn got outside, he discovered it was the family SUV with his wife and son inside the burning vehicle. Autopsy results showed they had both been shot in the head before the car was set on fire. Stunned, she sat in silence. She scanned to the end, where several links provided updates on the original story. Citing undisclosed developments in the case, authorities eventually confirmed that Quinn's wife and son were the victims of a targeted execution. Inspector Quinn, it was reported, subsequently took an extended leave of absence from the Force.

So, this unimaginable tragedy was the reason for Quinn's perpetually brusque nature. She couldn't imagine how he had the fortitude to get up day after day and put one foot in front of the other. Now she understood why he said he couldn't go through it again. What was wrong with her that she had lied to him and was willing to put herself in danger in order to get Castellano?

Was it because like Quinn, she no longer had anything precious to lose?

Chapter Eighteen

Special Agent Nate Jackson coughed loudly into Quinn's ear, causing him to hold the phone at a distance. "I'm looking at the surveillance footage right now and I'm telling you this guy matches your description," he said. "But there's been no sign of him since it was taken. You sure he's still here in the States?"

"Reasonably sure, based on a confirmed sighting of him in Seattle," Quinn said. He rounded his desk and closed his office door. "What I'm really interested in is how you came to catch this guy on surveillance."

"You know I can't tell you that, my friend," Jackson replied. "But, I can tell you this is one bad dude with even worse connections."

"Speak." Quinn sat down and absently flipped through the mail, mostly bills, on his desk.

"Jesus, I shouldn't be telling you this..."

"Cut the crap, Nate," Quinn replied, good-naturedly. "You owe me, and you know it."

"Okay, okay," Nate sighed. "The guy we've been watching goes back to 2008. We also got two of his compadres back then, but he himself pleaded not guilty. The judge sent him home with an ankle bracelet and eventually the charges were dropped. Not enough evidence. Had to let him leave the country."

"To where?"

"British Columbia. Vancouver."

Quinn dropped the pile of bills onto his desk and sat bolt upright. "You're shittin' me."

"Wish I was. But at least it's given us a second chance. I'm not retiring until I get this bastard," Jackson groused. "Now it would appear that he's somehow connected to the 'Ndrangheta clan if I understand you correctly."

"Not just connected. My guy is Italian. I mean like real, just-off-the-boat Italian." Quinn pronounced Italian with a long *I*. "How could he be a suspect in drug running since '08?"

"Hey, it's a smorgasbord now. Asians, Colombians, bikers—you name it—we got 'em all. It's like the United Nations down here. You need a play book to keep track of their comings and goings."

"Tell me about it." Quinn crooked the phone between his shoulder and ear while he typed *Castellano* into his browser search bar.

"You know *dick* up there," Nate scoffed. "Wish I could come back and work in your cozy little neck of the woods."

"Yeah, yeah," Quinn cut him off, having grown weary of his former colleague's jibes about him living in lotus land. He heard a signal indicating another call was coming in, but let it go to voice mail.

"Listen," Nate said. "I gotta go, but why don't

you drive down? I have to come up to Canada just to get back into my own country," he complained, "but we could meet in Point Roberts, have lunch and shoot the bull. I'll show you what I can."

"You're on, buddy. Let me know when." Quinn passed on his regards to Nate's wife and family before hanging up. As he sat alone in the semi-darkness of his office, he felt an exhilaration he hadn't experienced since being back on the job after Karyn and Tyler were snatched from him.

The powers that be might have forced him out of the RCMP, but his mission was far from over.

It wasn't until Quinn got into his car and was driving out of the underground parking lot that he realized he'd forgotten to check who had called while he was on the phone to Nate. His Honda was so much of an antique that his version of hands-free calling was to put his phone in his lap and switch it to speaker mode. As he turned onto Georgia Street he punched in his voice mail number. There was one message. The minute he heard Jordan's voice, he knew something was horribly wrong.

"*J.J.,*" she'd cried. "*Oh my god, someone just...*" Then the message cut off abruptly. It was all Quinn could do not to jam on his brakes. Instead, he veered wildly across two lanes of rush hour traffic before coming to a screeching halt by the side of the road. In an instant, he'd called Jordan back, but when it only rang once before going to voice mail, he dialed the West Van police dispatcher on a secure line. After receiving assurance they would immediately send a car to Jordan's place, he pushed his way back into a steady stream of honking cars heading north. He wasn't entirely sure where Jordan had called from but when she left the office earlier he remembered her saying she was going for a run on the seawall in front of her house.

Goddammit, he thought as he weaved in and out of traffic, why couldn't he have had his police lights and siren? Heart racing, he swerved into the bus lane, just missing the back end of the car in front of him. As the volume of honking horns increased, so did his anxiety. After the Sun had published that damned article on Jordan, how many times had he thought about asking for a security detail outside her house, only to quash it, knowing he couldn't call in any more favors? Now, begging didn't seem so beneath him. He dialed his old friend, West Vancouver Police Constable David Ho.

Chapter Nineteen

Twenty-five torturously slow minutes later, Quinn pulled up to the street side of Jordan's house on Argyle. His hunch that she'd called from there was immediately confirmed. Multiple black and whites lined both sides of the street outside her house, their flashing lights punctuating the darkening sky. At the end of a dirt lane that led across the railroad tracks and onto the seawall walk, an ambulance was parked, its doors open wide.

"Hey, you can't go down there," he heard someone yell as he raced toward it.

Laser-focused on his goal, at the same time praying he wasn't too late, Quinn sprinted past the ambulance, nearly colliding with two paramedics removing a stretcher from the rear. His chest tightened.

"Is there a woman down there?" he asked one of the paramedics, who nodded and pointed him toward the water.

Quinn all but slid down the last rise of the well-worn trail and onto the paved seawall walk. A few people huddled around someone on the ground.

Charging forward, he parted the small crowd with both hands and immediately saw the object of everyone's attention. It was Jordan, half-sitting, half-lying on the ground. Quinn's eyes jumped to the torn knees of her jogging tights, as well as her bloody palms. Then, he saw the look of sheer terror in her eyes.

"J.J.," she cried as soon as she saw him, "I...I was just coming down for a run and..."

"Move away. Everybody. Give her some space," Quinn shouted as he pushed the onlookers back. "Did anyone see what happened?"

A wiry, athletic-looking man in running gear stepped forward. He seemed about to say something when Quinn saw Dave Ho running toward them. "Wait," Quinn instructed the man, "I need you to tell this to the police. Constable Ho, this is..."

"Jared. I'm Jared Cunningham." The man looked about ready to burst. "I was just coming back from my evening run and I saw someone jump out at this lady." He looked at Jordan, still sitting on the ground. The paramedics had arrived and were kneeling beside her as she struggled to sit up on the asphalt. "He ran full into her and knocked her off her feet," Cunningham continued."

"Who did?" Ho and Quinn asked simultaneously. Ho cocked an eyebrow and Quinn backed off.

"I don't know. Someone jumped out from the shadow under that burned out light over there and attacked her."

"I'm fine," Quinn heard Jordan assure the paramedics. She reached out a bloodied hand. "Hey Quinn, can you just help me up?" She was clearly rattled, but there was no mistaking the iron resolve in her voice.

"Are you taking her to Lions Gate?" Quinn asked the medic who was trying to remove a blood pressure cuff from Jordan's other arm.

"I am *not* going to the hospital," Jordan glared at him. "I'm fine, but I'm getting a bit tired of sitting on my butt on this wet pavement."

Quinn looked questioningly at the paramedics. "Her blood pressure is a bit high," one of them said. "Not surprising, but she does seem to be okay except for some lacerations to her hands and knees. We'd like to take her in but it's basically up to her. We can't force her to go to the hospital."

"They're right, Quinn, and neither can you," Jordan challenged.

He looked at Dave, who shrugged. Gently they helped her to her feet. Ho got contact details from Cunningham and a couple of other bystanders, the small crowd dispersed, and Quinn, Ho and Jordan carefully made their way back to her house. Though a bit slow and wobbly, Jordan made it under her own steam. The constable suggested she might like to clean up the cuts to her knees and palms before he asked any more questions. She politely refused as she lowered herself gingerly into an overstuffed armchair.

The last time Quinn had seen Jordan look that tired was back on Annabelle Island. Now, as she stoically answered Ho's questions she seemed to suddenly wane before their eyes. Her face was deathly pale, and she appeared to be struggling for words.

"Hey, Dave," Quinn interjected. "Do you think

we could wrap things up here for now? I think Jordan is about done for tonight."

Jordan threw him a grateful look and tried to stifle a yawn. "Honestly, Constable," she shook her head, "I can't think of anything more. As I said, I literally was just about to walk by that light standard to start my run, when someone grabbed my wrist. I saw a glint of something shiny in their other hand. It all happened so fast. I just remember squatting down, leaning forward and bending my elbow toward his forearm until he dropped my wrist. The next thing I remember, he hit me full force from behind and I was on the ground, the wind knocked out of me."

The constable was furiously writing in his pad, trying to keep up with her.

"That's when I called you, Quinn. I was just starting to leave you a message when I realized I'd better call 9-1-1."

Heeding Quinn's cue, Ho closed his notebook and prepared to leave. "Thank you for your time, Jordan. Please, no need to get up, I can see myself out." He extended a hand to Quinn, who clasped his friend's shoulder and walked him toward the front door.

"Watch her," Ho said quietly. "I'm not sure she didn't hit her head when she went down." Then he leaned in closer so only Quinn could hear. "And, until we can get a full statement from the witness, don't assume this was a random attack."

Even though Quinn had been thinking exactly that, it knocked him off-kilter to hear it put into words.

When Quinn returned to the living room, Jordan had moved to the love seat and covered herself with a chunky hand-knitted blanket. "You make that?" he asked.

She looked surprised. "How did you know? Ah, Rachel told you I knit, right?"

"Yeah, what's so wrong with that?"

"Rachel being a blabbermouth, or me knitting?" She smiled despite her obvious exhaustion.

"How about I make you a strong cup of tea? Got any brandy I could lace it with?"

She shook her head.

A few minutes later, Quinn emerged from the kitchen. "Be careful, it's hot." He handed her a black mug that said *Put on your Big Girl Panties and deal with it*. It was the first one he'd grabbed out of the kitchen cupboard.

He sat across from her, watching her blow on the steam that wafted up into her face. He figured this was as good a time as any, and cleared his throat. "So where did you learn the Gracie Jiu-Jitsu technique?"

Her eyes registered a fleeting look of surprise. "What do you mean?"

"You know exactly what I mean." Quinn smiled benignly. He sat back in his chair, determined to wait her out.

"Busted," she finally said. "I, uh...started a self-defense course for women."

Quinn nodded but didn't say anything.

"I didn't want to tell you." Some color had come back into her cheeks.

"Why not?"

"I didn't want you to think I was afraid." Then her eyes filled with tears. "And weak."

Quinn got up from his chair and perched on the ottoman beside her. She drew up her knees to give him some room.

"Jesus, Jordan, the last thing I would ever think is that you're weak. Are you kidding me? In twenty-five years of police work I have never seen a victim—I'm sorry, a survivor—as strong as you. Ever." Without thinking, he reached out and lifted her chin. What he saw in her eyes nearly broke his heart in two. They held each other's gaze for a second. Then, as if they both realized the intimacy of the moment, Jordan looked away and Quinn dropped his hand and awkwardly stood up.

"You need to get some sleep," he said as he collected his jacket off the back of the chair. "Lock the door behind me and promise me you'll set the security alarm before you go to bed."

He heard her put her tea on the coffee table as he walked to the front door. "Hey, Quinn? Thanks. For calling me a survivor, I mean. I didn't realize how much I needed to hear that right now."

With his hand on the door handle, he turned. "I wouldn't want to be the one to say it at the risk of being called a misogynist," he winked. "But the mug says it all, kiddo."

"I do have one question, though." Quinn looked around the house. "Why do you insist on leaving all the lights on in your place after dark? For one thing, your electricity bill must be over the top. More importantly, you're an easy target for creeps like the guy on the seawall tonight."

Jordan looked at him with sad eyes. "I know, I'm working on that. Really, I am. It's just what I need to do right now to scare away the dark."

Quinn's reply was to nod and let himself out the door. Then, he swore a silent oath to get the fucker that did this to her if it was the last thing he ever did. Not even an expertly aimed bullet between the eyes of his family's murderer would bring Karyn and Tyler back. But now that he was no longer with the Force, doing the same to Jordan's kidnapper would give him the sadistic pleasure he craved by acting as both judge and executioner.

Chapter Twenty

What the hell had just happened? I had seen her in the light of her living room window putting on a hat. Like she had done every other night before her run. Standing under a burned-out street lamp, I saw her emerge from the side of her house and walk down the trail toward the seawall. This time, I wasn't going to make the mistake of waiting too long, as I had back on the island. But unlike then, I had decided not to kill her. Instead, I would slash that exquisite face to shreds. It would cause her infinitely more suffering than a quick death.

From my hiding place, I had watched her get closer, closer...relishing the thought that in mere seconds it would all be over, my mission finally accomplished. I took a long, deep breath and willed my heartbeat to slow down. I tightened my grip around the ice-cold handle of the knife. Then, at the split second she was beside me I clicked open the switchblade and leapt from the shadows.

I knew instantly that something was wrong.

She was taller than I expected, more solid. In one quick maneuver, she leaned forward and without a struggle, somehow dislodged my hand from her wrist. I stabbed the air with my knife. I must have pushed her because a scream told me I'd connected. But then I stood frozen in stunned disbelief. There she lay, on the ground, just a few feet away. I wanted to do something—linger and finish it—but I didn't dare. Instead, I turned and ran.

Chapter Twenty-One

For once, Jordan was glad Quinn insisted on accompanying her to the West Vancouver Police Department, where she was to be questioned further following the previous night's incident. After Constable Ho got them all coffee, and insisted Jordan call him Dave, the three of them settled into a space the size of a laundry closet. The air in the room was heavy and stale, enveloping them like a shroud. The walls badly needed a new coat of paint, although it was impossible to ascertain what the original color might have been. Anything other than a drab gray would surely have enhanced the interrogation room. But then, making people feel at home here probably wasn't the objective.

"So," Dave said. "We were able to get some useful information from our witness."

"What did he tell you that you didn't already know?" Quinn asked.

Dave consulted his notes. "He said he didn't get a good look at the assailant's face because the light on that section of the seawall was burned out. But he was firm that he or she was of slight build."

He or she? Jordan's stomach roiled. She put her cup down on the table so abruptly that Quinn had to grab it to keep it from going over the edge. *Slight build.* The skanky, skinny creature that visited her daily in the bunker.

"Jordan. Hey, kiddo, are you all right?" Quinn's voice pulled her back to the present. He shook her forearm gently, as if to wake her. He turned to Ho. "Is there any likelihood the witness might have seen this person before the attack? Maybe when he started out on his run."

Ho sat back in his chair and for a moment seemed to be choosing his words. "That's where it gets a little fuzzy."

"How so?" Quinn looked puzzled.

The policeman looked first to Jordan, then to Quinn. "The way he tells it, he had almost finished his run and was on the way back when he saw someone cross over the tracks and disappear into the darkness under a burned-out light. Then, a woman we now know to be Jordan, was just about to pass whoever was standing there. He said he saw the figure raise their arm and thought he saw the glint of something metal. Then he heard a scream and she was knocked to the ground."

Jordan nodded. "That's exactly what I told you last night, Constable Ho...Dave. But, whoever attacked me fled the scene. Obviously, I was just in the wrong place at the wrong time, as they say." She looked across the table at Quinn. "If there's nothing else I think we should be getting back to the office." She caught the two men exchanging a glance. "What?" She hesitated, part way out of her chair. "Is there something else you're not telling me?"

Ho never took his eyes off her. Quinn cleared his throat. "Jordan, Dave here believes this wasn't a random attack."

Jordan looked from one man to the other. Even as she was forming her question, she had an eerie feeling she already knew the answer. But she had to ask it anyway. "There was a handful of other people running or walking the seawall last night, I just happened to be the closest at the time."

The two cops looked at each other, and Jordan felt the color drain from her face. "You think whoever it was deliberately set out to attack *me*?" She reached for the edge of the chair and sat heavily.

The expressions on the two faces looking back at her said it all. She was not collateral damage; she was the target of a person of slight build who was still on the loose. And who most certainly now knew where she lived.

"There's just one more thing," Ho's voice penetrated her thoughts.

What the bloody-hell else could there be? Jordan was about to ask, but the words lodged in her throat.

"After we brought you up from the seawall last night," Ho said, "we did a thorough search of the area."

Jordan glanced over at Quinn. He seemed to know what was coming.

"And?"

"We found a cell phone on the rocks below where the incident took place," Ho said.

The RCMP had returned her work phone to her and she had her personal one with her, so she knew it wasn't hers.

"It was a burner phone. That is…"

"I know what a burner phone is," she snapped.

"There were photos of you, your house, and…" He produced the phone and held it so she could see the screen. "And these people," he said.

"You knew about this and you didn't tell me," Jordan lambasted Quinn as they walked around back of the police station to his car. "How could you have let Ho blindside me like that?"

Quinn took so long to answer, she was about to leap down his throat again. "Because I didn't think you'd believe me," he finally said.

"The police find a cell phone at the scene of the attack with photos of me and my parents on it and you didn't think I'd *believe* you. Are you kidding me?" Her voice broke as she screamed at him. "When were you going to tell me?"

"When were you going to tell me about your parents?" he shot back.

She stopped in her tracks, bent over, and held her stomach. She felt like she'd been sucker punched and for a moment, thought she might be sick.

"Jordan, when are you going to get it through your head that we're on the same side?" His tone turned soft and conciliatory in the hush of the dreary afternoon. The only sound between them was the steady drip, drip, drip of water as it slid down the police station's dilapidated downspout into a puddle below. Each droplet reminded her of the slow, quiet tears she had endlessly cried in the darkness of her underground prison. Knowing she could no longer shoulder the burden of that memory alone, she straightened up and hooked her arm through Quinn's. "Wanna buy a girl a cup of coffee and listen to her sad tale of woe?"

"I thought you'd never ask." Quinn gave her a crooked smile, then opened the passenger door. "Get in, I know just the place."

Chapter Twenty-Two

"Just the place," as Quinn referred to it, turned out to literally be A Hole in the Wall. It served as both the establishment's name, as well as the front entrance of what could only be called a dive-bar, just off Vancouver's notorious Granville Mall.

Jordan was reluctant to take off her raincoat or sit on the crusty-looking wooden chair Quinn gallantly pulled out for her. "How do you find these grotty places?"

"Ah, that's for me to know." He gently nudged the chair behind her knees, forcing her to sit.

"Hey, J.J.," a man emerged from behind the bar and strode toward their table. "Where you been, man? Haven't seen you for what, at least six months?" He clapped Quinn on the back and looked enquiringly between Jordan and him.

"Max, meet Jordan Stone." Quinn winked at Jordan and said, "Jordan, meet Max. He's the owner of this fine establishment."

She reached out to shake Max's hand.

"Nice to meet you, Jordan." He turned to Quinn. "So, what are you doing now? I heard you retired from the Force. We've missed you around here."

"Long story. Why don't I save it for a beer at another time? We just popped in for coffee." Quinn looked at Jordan. "Hey Max, can you make one of those fancy coffees for her? You know, like they sell at Starbucks."

"You mean a latte or cappuccino? Of course we can. What do you take this place for, some dive-bar?" Max joked.

Jordan felt herself relax and she looked longingly at a well-worn fireplace, its blackened hearth barren of any flame.

"Why don't I get that fire turned on for you?" Max said, following Jordan's gaze. "I take you for a double- or maybe even a triple-shot latte kind of lady. Work for you?"

In spite of herself, Jordan was starting to like the lived-in feel of the place. She shrugged off her coat. "That would be amazing, Max, thank you."

Not only did Max make the best triple-shot latte Jordan had ever had, but after apologizing that they were too late for breakfast and too early for lunch, he brought them out a plate of cheese scones, assorted cold-cuts and veggies. "The baking is day-old, I'm afraid, but I heated them up for you, so dig in."

"Thanks, Max," Quinn said, slathering half a scone with a healthy dollop of butter, and refilling his black coffee from the pot.

"Sure thing. Just gimme a yell if you need anything."

"So, where do you want me to start?" Jordan asked when their host was out of earshot.

"How about at the beginning? I usually find that's as good a place as any."

Jordan pinched the last crumbs of scone from her plate and realized just how ravenous she'd been. The gas fire was now blazing, and she could feel the heat from across the room. They were the only two people in the place, and she was becoming more comfortable by the minute. She took a deep breath and plunged in. "You know Castellano?"

"Well, not personally but obviously I know who you're talking about. He's been the bone of contention at most of our office meetings. Correct me if I'm wrong, but I get the gut feeling there is something personal for you about getting this guy. Outside of writing your investigative piece, I mean." There was no sign of Quinn's usual bombastic tone.

"Yes, well, I'd say your instincts on that front are pretty good."

"So, besides being in the illegal importation of drugs, what is it about him that causes you to lose all your inhibitions about putting yourself in danger?"

"Excuse me? What's *that* supposed to mean?"

Quinn leveled her with what Rachel referred to as his "X-ray eyes."

"*What*?" Jordan heard herself whine.

Quinn sighed, took out his wallet and pushed back his chair. "Hey, if you don't want to talk, that's fine. We should probably free up our table for Max's lunchtime crowd."

"Really? I can't quite see a lineup at the door," Jordan said. "Don't tell me. He takes reservations, right?" Quinn continued staring her down. "All right, I'm sorry," she said.

He threw a twenty on the table and remained standing.

"Oh, for god's sake, Quinn, sit down. Please?"

"Truth?" he asked.

Jordan nodded and then looked away as she felt the sting of tears.

"Hey, kiddo," Quinn sat down and reached across the table, lightly clasping her forearm. "Something is eating you alive and the way I see it you've got nothing to lose by taking this burden off yourself."

She whisked away a tear as it trickled down her cheek and took a deep breath. "Salvatore Castellano is, as far as the Italian authorities know, the last remaining foot soldier of the late Vittorio Constantine."

Quinn's expression changed from compassion to incredulity. "The mob boss who was ousted by the 'Ndrangheta clan?" He shook his head as if to clear water from his ears. "What the hell does he have to do with you? Was he one of the wiseguys you were writing about? The Italian gangsters living in plain view of Canadian authorities while going back and forth to Italy?"

"He was," Jordan said slowly. "Until he, or someone who worked for him, tried to run me off the road in Italy."

Quinn sat back in his chair. "Because you were investigating him for a story here in Canada? Am I missing something?"

Under the table, Jordan twisted what was left of her paper napkin into shreds. Her palms were sweaty, and she wished she could ask Max to turn off the fire.

"No, you're not missing anything. At the time, I couldn't believe it either." She thought of Giancarlo as she concluded what was surely the understatement of her life.

Quinn opened his mouth to say something, then, closed it. The two of them sat facing each other, apparently neither one knowing what to say. Finally, it was Quinn who broke the silence. "I think I've severely underestimated you."

"What do you mean?"

"Well, don't take this the wrong way but I kind of had you pegged as a holier-than-thou crime reporter who criticized the police, while sitting in your ivory tower postulating as to how we could have done a better job."

Jordan took in a long breath and let it out slowly. "Wow, that's kind of hard not to take the wrong way. With that low an opinion, why did you want my help writing reports for your PI business?"

Quinn took a loud slurp of his coffee. "That's easy. Everybody knows that in this city, the most irreverent PIs or reporters make the best investigators. They're always playing the devil's advocate. It's the ones who are really just wannabe cops that are useless as tits on a bull."

His colorful vernacular made her chuckle, releasing the tension somewhat.

"You fall into the first category, by the way."

"Thanks," Jordan said dryly. "Being a cop is certainly never something I've aspired to. No offense."

"None taken." Quinn looked at his watch. "So, moving along can you give me the CliffsNotes version of how you got involved with Castellano? More importantly, how did photos of your parents come to be on some scumbag's cell phone? For some reason, I didn't think your parents were still alive."

To Jordan's surprise, as the hands on the battered Playboy clock on the wall of Max's place approached noon, the front door opened and closed constantly as patrons arrived for lunch. When at last she had told Quinn as much as she felt she could, she glanced around to see virtually every table in the place was occupied, the noise level increasing by the decibel.

She agreed with Quinn that they needed to vacate their meeting spot, and while he unsuccessfully tried to talk Max into accepting some money for their meal, she pulled on her coat and waited for him near the door. She was self-consciously aware that several pairs of eyes were on her; the men's appreciatively. The cool once-over she got from the women wearing work boots and safety vests, not so much.

Chapter Twenty-Three

The next day, Jordan and Rachel were in the conference room when they heard Sassafras howling. Bolting out the door and skidding to a stop in front of the reception desk, they saw the feline hissing at Callie, who was pinned against the door.

"Oh my god, I thought it would be okay if I just walked in. I should have knocked first," she said.

"Sassy, come here, right this minute!" Rachel commanded. But when the cat didn't back off, she reached out and scooped her up. "Sorry, I'll just put her away. I'll be right back."

Callie remained rooted to the spot. "I'm sorry you got such an unfriendly welcome," Jordan said. "Please, come in, I don't know what got into poor Sassy."

"I…uh, I can come back if this is a bad time."

"No, no, this is fine. I'm ready for a break. Rachel and I were having coffee, can I get you one?"

"Mmm, no thanks, I have to start my shift downstairs pretty soon, but I wondered if I could pick your brain for a few minutes."

Jordan saw Rachel coming out of the conference

room, shutting the door behind her. Her eyes narrowed as she glanced quickly at Jordan. "Nice to see you, Callie," she said, "but I need to get back to work."

"Of course, no problem." Callie looked at her watch. "Oh my gosh, look at the time. I didn't realize my shift starts in five minutes. Jordan, maybe we could make it another time?"

"Sure." Jordan was still watching Rachel over Callie's shoulder. She reached for one of her business cards off the reception desk. "Maybe give me a call next time and we can make sure you don't get attacked by our guard cat," she said, trying to sound light. "She must be having an off-day."

"What?" Jordan asked Rachel when Callie had gone.

"What do you mean, *what*? Have you ever seen Sassy act that way before?"

"Only when she first met Quinn," Jordan laughed.

"Exactly! That's my point. She only does that with people she doesn't trust."

"Oh, Rache, maybe Callie isn't a cat person. They know, you know. I mean when people don't like them."

"Yeah, maybe. Anyway, I'm going to finish my coffee and see if she's calmed down." With that, Rachel headed into the conference cum coffee room.

Although their sense of style was at polar opposite ends of the fashion spectrum, Jordan trusted her lifelong friend to give her honest, impartial advice when it came to what suited her. This evening's shopping was no exception and she was delighted with the purchases Rachel helped carry as they sat down for an early dinner. They'd chosen an amazing vegetarian restaurant that although neither of them was vegetarian, they regularly went there to satisfy their respective cravings. They were there so often, the server dispensed with the menus, asking if they'd like the usual. Jordan checked her phone for messages. When she looked up, Rachel was frowning. "Sorry, kiddo, but I'm expecting some important messages."

"No, it's not that." She looked at Jordan with a puzzled expression.

"What, then?"

"So, after Callie left our office, I went down to get something to take out for lunch."

"And?"

"*And*, Callie wasn't working."

"Maybe you just didn't see her. Are you still dwelling on Sassy's reaction when she came into our office this morning? Sweetie, let it go. She was probably just feeling her oats now that the vet said she doesn't have to wear that damned collar anymore."

"Jordan, I asked the manager if Callie was around and he said she wasn't scheduled to work today. And get this, he said she was working the night shift."

"So?" Jordan helped herself to the curried cauliflower and baba ghanoush. "Maybe she got her shift confused. I'm starving, if you don't dig in, I swear I'll demolish this." But when Rachel virtually ignored the food, Jordan put down her fork. "This thing between Sassy and her really has you bugged. What's really going on, Rache? Come on, out with."

"I didn't tell you this, but last week when you asked if Callie knew Ash, she said she didn't, but I could swear I saw her getting into his car when I was at the club using the pool one night a couple of weeks ago."

"That is weird," Jordan conceded. "But what reason would she have to lie?"

"Exactly, that's what I asked myself. So, I did a little digging around."

Oh-oh, Jordan had heard that exact tone before with Rachel. When she was researching a story for her, she'd been like a dog with bone. God help anyone who was on the receiving end of one of her wily hunches. She was afraid to ask.

Chapter Twenty-Four

Quinn flashed his Nexus card at the lone border control officer who could prevent him from entering the US from Canada. Not that he'd want to; there was nowhere further into the States that you could go from the tiny spit of land. Someone once crudely described enigmatic Point Roberts as being like the foreskin of America; it probably should have been removed long ago, but keeping it provided some benefits.

"The purpose of your visit, Mr. Quinn?" The officer returned his Nexus card.

It grated on Quinn's nerves that he was no longer addressed as "Inspector," which basically had given him free rein in the past. The guard, whom he didn't recognize, barely looked old enough to be out of school.

"Just coming over to have lunch with an old friend," he said with a tight smile. Perma-grin, Rachel called it.

"Have a nice day, sir," the kid said.

Yeah, you too, you little twerp.

Quinn drove down the sleepy town's main drag, past the highest number of gas stations per capita he'd ever encountered, all competing for his attention. The next largest industry after fuel belonged to the five shipping and receiving outlets in town. Business always seemed to be booming no matter the time of year. He wondered how the approximately 1,100 full-time residents kept themselves occupied during the endless bleak days of winter. Somewhere behind the curtain of foggy drizzle, he knew there was a killer view of Mt. Baker, but she wasn't going to make herself known today. On warmer days, he'd often sat on one of the pebbly beaches of The Point, as the locals referred to the peninsula, watching eagles circle over the ocean and back to their nests. Perhaps it was the anticipation of seeing whales swim by their waterfront homes that kept the mostly retired residents content. They were the same inhabitants who took to their opulent yachts to flee from several thousand tourists who swarmed the five-mile peninsula during the hot summer weather. Most seasonal visitors were Canadians who maintained summer homes and flew the flags of both countries.

Just before reaching the beach, Quinn turned into the gravel parking lot. Situated where the famous tavern The Breakers once stood, the Whale's Tale had eventually been built in its place. It was a spot where he and Nate had met numerous times over the years. Sometimes, they were on official business, other times they met just to shoot the breeze. Seeing only two other cars in the lot, Quinn assumed he would have no trouble finding Nate, or a table. When he stepped through the door, there he was, shaking the rain from his windbreaker.

"Hey, it's good to see you." His friend greeted him with a hearty handshake. "How long has it been?"

Handsome, rugged-looking and black, Nate had always worked undercover and taken pride in his physique. Now Quinn noticed his jacket strained a little at the seams. "Long enough for you to pack on some extra tonnage, I see. What's Lily been feeding you?"

Nathaniel Winston Jackson had been a member of the elite Secret Service—or USSS as it was otherwise known—when at age twenty-six, he suffered a serious gunshot injury while protecting a senior White House official. If it had been anyone other than Nate, Quinn was positive it would have proved fatal; the man's stamina was legendary. While Nate was on indefinite leave, the Drug Enforcement Administration jumped at the opportunity and snapped him up. After almost a year of intense physical therapy and passing all the requisite physical and mental tests, he was recruited into the DEA. Outside of Quinn, only a handful of people knew of Nate's notable career before his devastating injury sidelined his USSS position. As a DEA agent and undercover operative, Nate's apparent easygoing manner masked a steel resolve that Quinn had witnessed firsthand. The list of arrests Nate Jackson was directly responsible for read like the who's who of the intelligence community. As a member of the RCMP, during the first cross-border case Quinn worked with Nate, he knew this man would always have his back.

Nate patted his belly as they headed toward a table by a window overlooking the water. "Hey, give me a break. I can still chase down a perp when I have to. But why should I? Let the young un's do it now, I've paid my dues." He gave Quinn an envious glance as he placed his jacket over the back of the chair. "You haven't changed a bit, man. Still as mangy as ever. How long before you have to go out for a smoke?"

"I quit," Quinn said, pulling out one of the two chairs parallel to the window. It was by unspoken agreement that neither cop would sit with his back to the door.

"No shit! Why?"

"Long story. Tell you about it later."

After wolfing down hamburgers and fries, they waited until the waitress refilled their coffees. Quinn would have ordered a beer, but now that he had no get-out-of-jail-free card he thought better of going back through the border crossing with alcohol on his breath.

"So, are you handling one of the Fleeing Fifties down here?" he asked Nate.

"I wouldn't know about that, and even if I did, I wouldn't tell you," his friend chuckled.

Both men knew they were talking about what many of the locals were aware of—that their quiet little town was reputed to be home to as many as fifty people in the US Marshals Services Witness Protection Program. Others, who were not officially in the program, found Point Roberts a good place to get away or hide from ex-wives and former associates. In effect, the border provided a quasi-restraining order. Certain Americans who could freely move around their own country but couldn't obtain a passport, couldn't easily access Point Roberts; the only way in by land was through Canada and then back into the US. It was the comings and goings of small boats and planes that often hog-tied the authorities who were trying to keep the bad guys out. Quinn knew the hideouts in the WPP were the subjects of one of the stories Jordan was working on when she was abducted. Or at least that's what he used to think until their chat at Max's.

Nate took another sip of his coffee. "Seriously, J.J., it's great to see you. You look good. Been doing okay?"

Wishing he had a cigarette to go with his coffee, Quinn replied, "Yeah, as well as can be expected, I guess."

"Do you miss the Force?"

Quinn shrugged. "Yes and no. I don't miss the brass breathing down my neck, that's for sure."

"I hear you, man." Nate's face turned serious. "You know I never take it for granted what you did for me, right? Like you said on the phone, I *do* owe you. That's why I thought we should talk in person."

Quinn held his old friend's gaze. "I know that, and you don't owe me anything. There was no way in hell that bastard should have stayed out on the street. I just had less to lose than you, that's all." The truth was that at the time, unbeknownst to him, Quinn was already on his way out of the Force. After Karyn and Tyler's murders, his conscience hadn't bothered him one bit when he was involved in a questionable shooting of an infamous gang member in one of Vancouver's east-side back allys. After Quinn had learned Nate's family was being threatened Stateside, he figured he did the city a favor by taking one more piece of trash off the street. But instead of receiving accolades, his actions essentially put the final nail in his coffin.

Twice, he had been brought up on disciplinary charges for overreacting to what he was sure was about to unfold between members of a known street gang and his partner. The brass gave Quinn the option of quitting them before they quit him.

Nate nodded and pulled a manila envelope from inside his jacket on the chair. "Is this the guy you're looking for? The Italian?" He swiveled a photograph toward Quinn. "It's a still-shot from the surveillance video I was telling you about. But as far as we know, his name isn't Castellano."

"Yeah, that's him." Quinn tapped the photo. "What name do you have him under?"

"Anthony Cassell, a.k.a. Tony Castle, and a slew of other aliases. He's the one I was telling you about—the guy we had to spring loose in '08. We knew he'd been going back and forth between Italy, the States, and Canada. It was a joint FBI-RCMP case. You were on stress leave, after...well, you know." He looked down at the table.

"It's okay, Nate, you can say it. After Karyn and Tyler were killed."

Nate shifted in his chair. "Yeah, after that. Anyway, about a year ago he just went underground. Couldn't find him anywhere. Until that is, he showed up on surveillance footage taken during a sting operation involving one of his associates. We caught his buddy with 125 kilos of marijuana stuffed into the headliner of his boat. Been watching him for two years and finally got him as he was about to do a trade for $1.4 million in cash. Didn't exactly make his day if you know what I mean."

Quinn whistled. "Yeah, I heard about it. Wish I could have been there."

"I wish you were too, buddy. Thing is, when your guys searched his house back in Canada they found a shit load of cash, multiple firearms, including two assault rifles. But get this, a couple days after we tossed our drug smuggler's place we get an anonymous phone call telling us where to locate a Glock handgun. Sure enough, we found it buried under an old outbuilding on his property and were able to raise the filed-off serial number."

"And?"

"It was the same gun that was used a few years back in an attempted execution of the late Vittorio Constantine, a disgraced 'Ndrangheta kingpin. The gun conveniently went missing from the local Italian constabulary and they never found out who had tried to take the old man out."

Quinn's head snapped back. "The guy you took down last week was connected to Vittorio Constantine?"

"It would appear so," Nate nodded. "You can imagine my surprise when you reached out asking me questions on behalf of Jordan Stone. She's the investigative reporter who was doing the story about 'Ndrangheta members living in Canada, right? The one who was abducted."

Quinn's mind was running on caffeine-fueled overdrive. Long before Jordan came clean with him at Max's, he realized he'd met her before her rescue from the bunker. In fact, they had first met, or butted heads would be more accurate, when he was investigating known members of Italy's most notorious organized crime family. As they'd talked about at Max's, these criminals were living right under the noses of Canadian authorities and Jordan had written a piece in which she severely criticized his RCMP unit for not doing more about the mob's blatant presence. Jordan's kidnapping was the last case Quinn worked before being taken off the Serious Crimes Unit. Prevented from finishing his investigation into the 'Ndrangheta was the final assault on his self-worth that had already been decimated. From there, he had nowhere to go but down. And he had been doing a masterful job of that until Jordan finally agreed to share an office and support him in his new business venture.

Quinn wrestled the memories to the back of his mind and put his hand over his cup to refuse the waitress's offer of a refill. "Why would someone call you about the gun?" he asked Nate when she was out of earshot. "What does that have to do with you taking down the dealer?"

Nate shrugged his shoulders. "Dunno, but we recently got another anonymous tip from the same person who called about the Glock."

"How do you know it was the same guy? What was the tip?"

"Not a guy. It was a woman. She disguised her voice, but our sound boys picked it up with their voice recognition software."

"A woman? Couldn't you trace the calls—either one of them?"

"Nope. Could have been made from different cell phones or she just switched out the GSM card. This time she told us where we could find some equipment that supposedly was used in a recent crime. Up in your neck-of-the-woods. Chilliwack. Your old buddies in the Special Crimes Unit were working it."

"So, you don't even know what geographic area the woman called from?" Quinn asked.

Nate rolled his eyes. "Of course, we do," he smirked. "The cell tower that both those calls bounced off was in West Vancouver."

"And you're sure it was the same woman who made the first call?" Quinn asked calmly while frantically doing the math in his head. The phone tip Nate was telling him about would have come in as he and Jordan were moving into their new offices.

"Positive," Nate replied.

Chapter Twenty-Five

True to his word, two days later, Nate forwarded Quinn the results of the mystery woman's anonymous tip. Reading Nate's email in disbelief, he nearly jumped out of his skin when Jordan rapped twice before opening his office door.

"What are you doing?" she asked.

"Nothing much, why?"

"Want to come shopping with me? Rachel's birthday is coming up."

"Not really." He shuffled files around his desk as if looking for something, hoping she would get the hint and leave.

"Come on Quinn, don't be such an old Grinch. I thought we could go in on something for her. We should be paying her a lot more for what she does around here. I'll buy lunch."

He was about to try another tactic to get rid of her when something occurred to him. "All right," he gave in. "But I get to choose the restaurant."

For a brief moment, she seemed to hesitate, possibly wondering if it would be another place like

Max's Hole in the Wall. However, she lifted his jacket off the coat stand and tossed it to him. "Deal."

"Hey, now that I've gone shopping with you," Quinn said between bites of his dripping beef dip, "maybe you can help *me* with something." He wiped his mouth with an over-sized paper napkin.

"How can you eat stuff like that?" Jordan asked, picking at her salad. "Don't you ever worry about how clogged your arteries must be?"

Quinn shoved the last of his French fries in his mouth and washed them down with a gulp of coffee. "No, can't say I spend much time thinking about that." He balled up his napkin and stifling a belch, pushed his plate away. "Anyhow, as I was saying, I could use your help for a buddy of mine. We used to work together in the Serious Crimes Unit."

"Sure, what do you need?" She nodded for the waiter to take her plate away.

"Well, Rachel mentioned that one of the things she researched for you was how criminals often secure their internet connections. You know, with virtual private networks aka VPNs?"

"Rachel *told* you that?"

"Hey, it was when she was telling me how much she admired your investigative skills. She was bragging about you, that's all." Jordan eyed him suspiciously. He plunged ahead to fill the silence. "So, my buddy needs to take a little time off work for personal reasons. *Very* personal reasons, if you get what I mean. But he's got to be available for the brass to call him on his cell. And if he had to get hold of someone, he doesn't want his call to be traced."

"So?"

"So, I was wondering if that VPN thing would work for him. On his phone, like it would on a computer."

Jordan's eyes hardened, and she motioned to the server for their bill. "What do you take me for, Quinn? You're a cop, you would know about these things. Cut the bull, what's really going on?" She threw some cash on the table and got up to leave.

"Geez, Jordan, you're so goddamn touchy." He grabbed his coat and followed her out of the restaurant.

She turned to face him. "I have no idea whether you can use the same technology for phones. And furthermore, you should tell your cheating buddy that maybe he should just do the right thing and leave his wife before he starts fooling around with another woman."

She marched into the middle of the sidewalk, causing busy shoppers to careen around her, and hailed a passing cab. "I'm late for an appointment. And by the way, you owe me fifty dollars for Rachel's gift!" She jumped in the back seat and slammed the cab door behind her.

After having gained Jordan's trust at Max's, Quinn was pissed at himself for upsetting her, and with such a stupid ruse. Karyn always told him he would never understand women. Back in his office, he printed out the confidential investigative report Nate had sent. After following up on the second anonymous tip, the RCMP had raided an old farm property they long suspected was a marijuana grow op. As Quinn read on, what stood out in the report was that after investigators hauled out a myriad of equipment, there was special note of a six-foot length of heavy gauge rope with what appeared to be two small blood stains on it. When the crime analysts ran the samples of blood for DNA through the National Data Bank, the first one came up frustratingly empty. No match.

The second was a perfect match. To Jordan Stone.

Chapter Twenty-Six

Ash Courtland paced the floor of his study in his home in the British Properties. He had purchased it in the early eighties when money and champagne had flowed like water. Given the downturn in his law practice in recent years, today he wouldn't have been able to buy a home in the increasingly wealthy neighborhood. In fact, he probably couldn't afford it even now. *Especially* now. Across the wide expanse of the pristine golf green, he gazed out the window, then removed his glasses and rubbed his tired eyes. At least the tranquil view was one thing he could count on as his world crumbled around him. Alone and wracked with guilt and grief for time gone by, it seemed that virtually everything in his life had been turned upside down.

He was about to turn back to his desk when he spied a lone coyote meandering across the dewy grass into the warmth of the early morning sun. The animal paused, cocking its head as if listening to something in the distance. With no natural predators, other than the occasional cougar or bear, the coyote no doubt knew it had no cause for fear. Just like certain types of humans, Ash thought, this deceptively beautiful animal could disembowel its prey in a heartbeat.

Mercifully, the Christmas holidays, along with all the festivities he dreaded, were over. The previous night after making excuses for leaving a client's cocktail party early, Ash automatically veered off to Callie's place. It was as if a peculiar magnetic force commandeered his vehicle. He felt guilty, as he'd been encouraged to bring a date to the party, but he'd said there was no one special in his life. Once at Callie's, he feigned an appetite for a meal she insisted on making the two of them, gave her a gift which she exclaimed was too extravagant, and then they had sex. She called it lovemaking and always donned the latest piece of jewelry he'd given her, but he knew it was just sex.

His thoughts reeled back to the first time they'd met. She was the new hostess at the Deer Ridge Country Club where he was a member. She was twenty-seven and hot. Not beautiful in a classic way, but exotic. She was a tall blonde, though as he quickly discovered, not a natural one. Her long, tanned legs seemed to go all the way up to her armpits. At least that's what his club cronies said. Along with other indecent remarks that made him blush with shame. Last summer, after closing the club down after one of many evenings of drunken debauchery, Ash drove Callie home and she seduced him into an act that neither of them remembered clearly the next day. Thus, started the clichéd May-December affair.

Now summer had turned to winter and her good looks had taken on a hard edge. Gradually, she became more intense and demanding, not of material things, but of his time. As much as continuing the relationship made him uneasy, Ash was still making late-night pit stops at her house.

And he was still ashamed of himself.

His hands shook as he stood in his study, absently polishing his glasses. He couldn't seem to block out the memories that came flooding back from the last time he left Callie's house. As he was about to get into his car, a well-dressed man had approached him on the sidewalk.

"Ashton Courtland?" the stranger asked.

"Yes."

The man handed him a plain white envelope, which he accepted without thinking. "You have a nice day, now," the man said, and was gone as suddenly as he appeared. Ash hoped it wasn't another summons. Resisting the urge to open it immediately, and wanting to get away from Callie's, he popped the package into his briefcase and drove off.

Once home, without taking off his coat, he poured himself a scotch, slit open the envelope and reached inside. Instead of the expected summons, or at the very least, a threatening letter from yet another creditor, all he saw was a DVD. He turned the envelope upside down and it rolled drunkenly across his desk blotter. After pushing the metallic disk into the slot of his laptop, he freshened his drink while he waited for it to load. When he turned back to his computer monitor, his blood ran cold.

On the screen, up close and in excruciating detail, he and Callie were captured in the most compromising position he could have imagined.

Shocked and unable to move, the blood rushed to his face and his legs weakened. He dropped into his chair and continued watching in disbelief. He was just about to push the eject button in an attempt to put an end to his agony, when a line of text floated across the screen. *Stop! You must watch to the end to see how you can make this go away.* Tempted though he was to fast forward, he watched for what seemed like an eternity until the vile retrospective of his most personal moment was over.

Ash Courtland didn't know how long he had been sitting in his leather chair in the darkness of his study that night. Or how many scotches he consumed. But he finally dragged himself off to bed, where he tossed and turned. At 5a.m. he could stand it no longer and got up to make coffee, then drove to his office. Like a robot, he went through the motions of shuffling papers and files, telling his secretary when she arrived at nine, to hold all calls. Until that is, she tapped on his office door to inform him there was someone on the telephone who insisted she interrupt him.

As was promised at the end of the DVD, the phone call was their first official contact. The muffled voice on the phone told him he had exactly forty-eight hours to come up with half a million dollars or the video would go viral.

Chapter Twenty-Seven

Jordan was supposed to be working on a client report for Quinn but instead, she spent most of the morning agonizing if she should confide in Ash what Simon had told her on the phone. As her parents' closest confidante and lawyer, Ash Courtland was both a counselor and father figure to her. After her parents went into the Witness Protection Program, Ash oversaw the funds from the trust fund Jordan's father, Gavin Stone had set up. If managed properly, even after her extensive house renovation, her investments would virtually guarantee her security regardless of what happened in her career. Comforting as that was, she knew she'd give it all up in a heartbeat.

Just as it was likely that Quinn was driven by the horrific death of his wife and son, Jordan's own ambition came from the fact that she would do anything to get her parents out of witness protection. The only possible way to do that was for the authorities to locate Salvatore Castellano, have her parents testify against him, and put the notorious thug away for life. Giancarlo Vicente had warned her that even then, there was always the possibility that one of

Castellano's associates would come after them. In his role as Special Prosecutor, Giancarlo could pull a certain amount of strings, but Jordan sensed his reluctance to give her false hope. "Very few witnesses leave the program and stay alive, cara," he'd said the last time she saw him. "I promise we will do everything we can to bring him to justice, but please, don't get your hopes too high."

Jordan could still feel the sting of Giancarlo's warning. It was as if he had cut out a piece of her heart. Or was it his sudden disappearance that had done that? After her abduction and rescue, she kept waiting to hear from him, but Giancarlo neither called, nor returned her messages. Shortly after, she'd read about his abrupt resignation from the prosecutor's office in Calabria.

Although Simon Grenville was not a prosecutor, it was obvious he was brought back from London to pick up where Giancarlo had left off. As Interpol's special agent in charge of liaising with Italy and Canada to bring former members of the 'Ndrangheta to justice, now it was Simon urging Jordan to leave the task of finding Castellano to his team. Quinn, who seemed to harbor some petty jealousy toward the British agent whom he had never actually met, agreed. However, following his little tête-à-tête with Jordan at Max's, he had agreed to use his stateside contacts to help locate the gangster, all the while echoing Simon's warning for Jordan to stay out of it.

Now, it was already the second week in January and Jordan hadn't heard anything useful from Quinn concerning Castellano's whereabouts. "Dammit, Quinn, where do you get off telling me to stay out of this when neither your buddies in the Integrated Crime Unit, or the supposed high-ups you have in Seattle, have come up with anything?"

But even she backed down when Quinn fixed her with an expression that could wilt spinach. "Don't play amateur cop, Jordan. I promise you, you will rue the day you cross me."

Fully aware she was about to engage in what her therapist termed "high-risk behavior," Jordan pushed both men's warnings aside and booked herself a flight to Seattle.

Chapter Twenty-Eight

I dashed through the rain toward the blue-lit entrance of the Twisted Bamboo, the lounge on the ground floor of Seattle's luxury, hip Hotel Distinque. Shaking off the last remnants of rain, I found a banquette table tucked into a corner where I could observe from a discreet distance. The heat from the gas fireplace chased away the chills, and I sank deeper into the upholstered couch and opened the drinks menu. It was early, and except for a couple of people sitting at the bar, the popular after-work hotspot had yet to fill up.

"What can I get for you?" The waiter placed a bowl of nuts on the polished burl table, interrupting my thoughts.

Hesitating for just a moment, I closed the menu. "I'll have a Dirty Martini."

"Certainly. Will there be anything else?"

"No, just the martini."

As he retreated to get my drink, I checked my watch, then compared it with the time on my phone, just to be sure. She should be here by now; her flight had been on time coming into Sea-Tac Airport.

Pocketing a cool fifty, the taxi valet had told me her destination and I'd jumped in the next cab in line. For another fifty, the driver made sure I got to the hotel in record speed. So what was taking her so long? Could she have decided to go somewhere else?

I had worked myself up into quite a frenzy, when out the window, I saw a taxi pull up to the curb. As my target emerged from the backseat, a sudden sense of calm settled over me. A few tantalizing seconds later, I watched as she entered the lounge, walked to a table on the far side of the room, and gave her order to the waiter. He seemed to know her by name and within minutes he reappeared with a glass of white wine. When he'd gone, she reached into a stylish leather briefcase, pulled out a thick sheaf of papers, and sipped from her glass as she read its contents.

My line of sight was perfect. I tingled with delicious excitement knowing Jordan Stone was blissfully unaware of me sitting across the room, watching her every move as I had so many times before.

The bar had filled almost to capacity and the quiet of two hours ago yielded to the animated buzz of multiple conversations which floated in and out of my consciousness. At times, the noise sounded overwhelmingly loud, and at others, everything was distant and echoed as if I were underwater. I wondered how much longer I'd have to wait. I couldn't leave without walking past her table.

I looked up when my waiter arrived at my table with a fresh martini. "A guest at the bar sent this over," he replied to my unasked question.

Sharply dressed and bathed in the warm glow of the lounge's lighting, my fellow barfly looked exquisitely attractive. A raised eyebrow and a warm smile silently asked permission to join me.

What the hell? Even once Jordan went up to her room, I would have a little time to kill. Besides, this could be an unexpected bonus.

"So, what brings you to Seattle?" my new friend asked after settling in beside me and ordering a Jack Daniels on the rocks.

"Oh, just down for the weekend for a little break, and possibly some business." I smiled.

A hand brushed my thigh, perhaps accidentally. "Oh yeah? What kind of business would that be?"

"I'm a travel writer, doing a little research on Seattle. How about you? What do you do?"

Something about a yacht brokerage business. Talked too much, but intense. Equally intense when we ended up in the elevator an hour later, both half-undressed on the way up to my room.

Chapter Twenty-Nine

Jordan rolled over and looked at the bedside clock. Ten o'clock! The blackout curtains of her hotel suite let in not even the thinnest sliver of light. She only had two short days to track down Castellano, and still didn't have a plan. She would call room service for breakfast, have a quick shower while she waited, and hopefully some stroke of genius would hit her, and she'd know where to start.

She lifted her head from the pillow and reached for the light, only to be overcome by a wave of nausea. Waiting a few moments until it passed, she gingerly tried again. She rubbed the back of her neck and groaned. She hadn't eaten anything in the bar the night before, but she'd only had two glasses of wine. Perhaps it was time to heed Dr. Danforth's advice and not combine alcohol with medication. The guys at the newspaper would laugh if they could see her now. Not so long ago, she could keep up with them drink for drink and still bound into the office the next morning. It pissed them all off as they passed around a bottle of Advil. Their editor always knew when they were hung over and took great delight in barking out orders. Then he'd wink at Jordan as he closed his door.

She placed her order with room service, and still feeling dizzy, headed into the bathroom. The hotel was renowned for its suites that had floor-to-ceiling windows between the bedroom and the luxurious bathroom, where the water fell from an opening in the ceiling into a deep, freestanding bathtub. As she walked through to the shower, she regretted not having the time to take an exquisitely long soak.

Something felt off. Other than her aching head. But Jordan couldn't put her finger on it. Her plan had been to stay an additional night, but for some reason her instinct, which she decided to trust this time, was telling her to check out early. After a quick breakfast, she repacked her suitcase, took one last look around, and went to open the door of her suite. *That's funny, I always put the safety lock on.* Quinn would go up one side of her and down the other if he knew how careless she'd been.

She stepped out of the hotel elevator and into the lobby. Nervously, she glanced toward the bar.

"I trust you enjoyed your stay with us, Miss Stone." The woman at the front desk smiled warmly. "I see you had another night booked. Was everything satisfactory?"

"Yes, absolutely. Everything was fine," she lied. "It's just that I have an unforeseen situation at home. Would you mind calling me a cab?"

Sitting in the back of the taxi, Jordan's head felt like it would explode, and her stomach gurgled in loud protest. Maybe breakfast hadn't been such a good idea after all. Her brain struggled to formulate a plan as she clicked through her limited options with sluggishly slow speed. She asked the driver to take her to a car rental place, but she still had no earthly idea where to start looking for Castellano. She couldn't reach out to Quinn's police friends in Seattle, even if she knew who they were. *What the hell were you thinking coming down here on your own?*

She felt the cell phone buzz in her purse. Her heart sunk when she saw Quinn's number come up. "Hello?"

"Hey, it's me."

Her mind switched to fast-forward as she thought of what she would tell him.

"You there?" he asked.

"Yes, I'm here. What do you want? I told you I'm away for a mental health weekend."

"I know. I'm surprised you answered. I was about to leave you a message."

"Well, you've got me now, but I'm in a hurry. What's up?"

"I'll be quick, but I think you're going to want to hear this. One of my contacts in Seattle just sent me a photo. I'm forwarding it to you now." Jordan heard the tone indicating the arrival of a new message but kept her ear to the phone.

"It's a surveillance photo of a guy on some fancy boat off Point Roberts. It was taken from land, so the image is a little grainy, but they've been watching him for a while. They just busted one of his cohorts for running drugs between the US and Canada, and they suspect the guy in the photo has been doing the same. He's a smooth operator. Dresses real stylish and all. Tells the locals he's out baiting and bringing in prawn traps, but they know that's bullshit."

Jordan was so focused on what she was going to say next that she hadn't realized the cab had pulled up to the car rental agency. "Hang on a second. What do I owe you?" she asked the driver.

"Where are you?" Quinn asked.

Juggling her phone and purse, she got out of the taxi while the driver retrieved her overnight bag.

"Thanks, keep the change. No, not you, Quinn. Hold on. I need to put my phone down for a minute." Jordan shoved the cell in her pocket, reorganized herself, and pulled it out again. "Okay, I'm good. Anyway, that's very interesting, but why are you sending *me* the photo?"

"Because we're reasonably sure that Salvatore Castellano is mister fancy-boat-guy and I want to know if you recognize him. This could be the break we need."

Suddenly, Quinn had her full attention. "Jesus, Quinn, I've only seen him that one time in Tropea that I told you about, and it was really brief." *Not brief enough.* She recalled regaining consciousness on the cold concrete floor of a remote outbuilding. Other than being paralyzed with abject terror, all she remembered were Castellano's cold, steel gray eyes leering at her, no doubt hoping he'd have some time alone with his prize before handing her over to Constantine.

Jordan stood on the curb where the taxi had dropped her. A shiver ran down her spine and she pulled her coat tighter around her. "Let me take the phone away from my ear and I'll have a look, hold on." She clicked on Quinn's text message and zoomed in on the attached image.

All at once, everything around her started spinning and she couldn't breathe. The shock hit her with the force of a two-by-four smashing into her gut. Grainy as it was, there was no mistaking the man in the photograph. It was Constantine's henchman, Salvatore Castellano. Simon had been right: He was not only alive and well, but from what Quinn was telling her, he was less than 140 miles north of her, in Point Roberts. She stood rooted to the sidewalk in a state of suspended disbelief.

"Jordan, are you still there? Jordan!" She was vaguely aware of Quinn yelling something at his end of the phone, but mixed with the sounds of traffic whooshing by, his words were snatched into the air and carried away.

Vaporized. Just as surely as her hopes of finding Castellano were before he found her and tried to kill her. And this time succeeding.

Chapter Thirty

Ash Courtland was thankful that at last Callie had ceased calling. In an effort to avoid her, he'd even stopped frequenting the club. Only once after the videotaping and DVD incident did he have contact with her. His stomach churned as he recalled the night that against his better judgment, he'd agreed to meet her at an out of the way restaurant for a late-night drink. She was wearing more makeup than usual, and she looked tired. Used up.

Callie's jaw dropped when he recounted the events from a couple of days before. "You mean someone broke into my house and planted a video camera in my bedroom? Oh, my god, what if they come back?"

She was renting the house she was living in which although modest, Ash had often wondered how she could afford West Vancouver. But to give her credit, she'd never hinted or asked him for money.

"I hate to say this, my dear, but it might be a good idea if you moved." She shrugged and promised she would think about it. As the effect of the drinks took hold, he enlisted every ounce of willpower he possessed not to suggest they go back to her place. He ended their evening with a chaste kiss on her cheek, even as he sensed her wanting something more.

He drove by her house several times after that, and seeing her car in the driveway, knew she had not heeded his advice. As he sat in his Jaguar at the end of her street, uncertainty threatened his resolve not to see her again. He missed her in an odd kind of way but pushed away the feeling. It was better like this. Even before the blackmail, he'd been thinking of how to extricate himself from the relationship. She'd been asking too many questions of late, wanting to know more about his personal life. This was the excuse he needed, but knowing Callie, he had a disconcerting sense that things were far from over.

It had been extraordinarily difficult for Ash to raise the kind of money his extortionist demanded, particularly given the short time period. Now, as he was about to take the next step his blackmailer demanded, he took a deep breath and quelled his rising panic.

The hand-off wasn't anything like he'd seen in the movies. The anonymous caller who had called Ash's office instructed him to leave a sports bag containing the money on the backseat of his unlocked car. Then he was to enter the food court of the adjacent office complex and stay there for at least ten minutes. The muffled voice told him if he even attempted to return to his car earlier, or anyone else did, the money would be gone, and the video would go out over the internet. For half a million dollars Courtland had nothing but a stranger's verbal assurance that they would keep their end of the bargain to destroy the original video, a deal that left him distinctly unnerved.

It was a strange feeling to know someone was probably in his car right now. In a futile effort to relax while he waited out the ten minutes, he bought himself a coffee in the mall and lingered longer than necessary. He tried to look casual as he held his cup between trembling hands and watched shoppers and passersby. Furtively, he scanned the crowd. Was someone watching him watch them?

When he felt it was safe to return to his car, he rode the elevator up to the top level of the parking lot. Most of the cars that had been there when he'd parked were gone. As he looked into the backseat, he realized he was holding his breath, praying it was all just a prank and somehow the sports bag would still be there. But it wasn't.

Barely conscious of the drive home, he agonized about what he would do if the blackmailer broke their word and released the sordid video online. Blackmailer and promise-maker. What a ludicrous oxymoron. He pulled into his driveway, turned off the ignition, and somehow mustered the strength to trudge up to his front door.

All he could do now was wait. And hope against hope that this would be the end of it.

Chapter Thirty-One

Jordan had been able to get on standby from Seattle to Vancouver but as short as the flight was, she felt as though she had been traveling forever. After lying to Quinn that she didn't recognize the man in the photograph and making an excuse to get off the phone, she decided against the rental car and asked them to call her an airport limousine. She knew she might have to wait around forever before getting on a flight, but it seemed her only viable option. Once at the airport, she couldn't stomach anything else to eat and sat quietly in a bar consuming cup after cup of strong black coffee.

She was completely wrung out when she eventually dragged herself home late Saturday night. Whether it was fatigue, or the buzz from the caffeine wrestling with her brain, Jordan was having trouble thinking back. How soon after she'd arrived at the hotel in Seattle had she gone up to her room? She still felt the effects of what seemed like a massive hangover. Was it possible she had more than two glasses of wine? She couldn't remember. A fine investigator you are, Jordan Stone.

By Monday, Jordan felt considerably better. Rising early, she showered, and on her way into the office, stopped at her favorite French patisserie. She got a café au lait to go. The *to go* part always felt like sacrilege. In Paris, she would have stayed and savored the ambiance. However, this morning was not one of those times, so she quickly purchased an assortment of rainbow-colored macarons for Rachel and went on her way. One of them would be sure to match whatever crazy outfit she wore today. For Quinn, she bought a chocolate croissant, then thought twice and got two.

"Okay. Well, let's get on with it then." Quinn opened his first file. "I don't know if Jordan has brought you up to speed on this surveillance photo." He turned the startlingly large image toward her and Rachel. Jordan felt her gut tighten.

"No, she didn't." Rachel glanced sideways at her. "I'm sorry, with all this fuss with Sassafras I forgot to ask about your weekend, Jordan."

Unable to peel her eyes from the photo, Jordan felt her face burning. "No worries. Quinn, have you been able to find anything more about Castellano's whereabouts? Is he in Seattle or Point Roberts? Do you know?"

"As a matter of fact, I do," Quinn beamed. "It would appear that mister fancy pants here is a close associate of one Domenic Grimaldi, the drug smuggler my Seattle police buddy's team took down last week. Castellano has a boat registered out of Whidbey Island, Washington."

Grimaldi. Jordan struggled to remember where she had heard that name, other than the prominent royal family of Monaco.

All at once it hit her. Quinn's voice became a distant echo in the background. It was a man named Grimaldi she'd been on her way to interview just outside of Tropea when the brakes in her rental car failed and she nearly ran off the road. She hadn't made it to the meeting, but more significantly, she was never able to contact Grimaldi to explain her absence and reschedule. Or even to find out why he had reached out through one of Jordan's contacts in the first place. After her terrifying experience was over, Giancarlo had told her she probably owed her life to the incident that prevented her from meeting with Grimaldi. Allegedly, the last person to have met with him was found hanging in his own apartment after the neighbors complained of a putrid smell.

"Jordan, are you all right?" Rachel's light touch on her hand jolted her back to the conversation.

She turned to her friend, unable to speak.

"You're so pale. What's wrong?"

Even Quinn looked concerned, but at the same time he cocked his head and eyed her suspiciously. "You said you didn't recognize Castellano. Is there something you're not telling me about this guy?" His index finger stabbed at the photograph in front of them. "Dammit, Jordan, I thought we were going to be honest with each other. If you know something, you need to tell me. Now."

Suddenly chilled to the bone, she pulled her sweater snugly around her taut body. Over the ensuing half-hour, she told them both she'd gone to

Seattle hoping to find Castellano. She filled them in on everything, *except* the niggling feeling she couldn't seem to shake from the night in the hotel bar. The weird feeling of being hung over after just two glasses of wine. And the image of the unsecured dead bolt on her hotel door that was seared into her brain.

Quinn waited until Rachel had gone to the post office before laying into Jordan. "For Christ's sake, I ordered you not to get involved in finding this guy on your own," he seethed.

"You can't *order* me to do anything," Jordan shot back. "I wasn't seeing any results from the friends you supposedly have in high places. What was I supposed to do?"

"You were supposed to let me handle this," he retaliated. "What is it with you? First, you drive to Chilliwack to meet some anonymous tipster and get yourself kidnapped. Then you go down to Seattle without telling anybody, to look for a wiseguy who is wanted here for drug smuggling, and in Italy for torturing and murdering at least two people." He barely paused for a breath. "What the hell's the matter with you? Do you have a fucking death wish?"

They stood in the middle of the office and stared each other down, only breaking eye contact when Rachel came in unexpectedly.

"Um, am I interrupting anything?" Rachel asked warily, looking from one to the other. "I forgot my purse. Is everything okay?"

"No, everything is not okay," Quinn said.

"Everything's fine," Jordan said. "But I'm glad you're back. I need some fresh air. I'll come with you."

"Come back here, Jordan," Quinn shouted. "We are not finished. You can't keep walking away from everything you don't want to deal with!"

Her answer was to follow Rachel out the door, slamming it behind them.

After walking to the post office, Jordan begged off going for lunch, feigning the beginning of a stomachache.

"You're getting one of your gastric attacks because you're under too much stress," Rachel said.

"I'm under too much stress because of Quinn. This isn't going to work out, I should never have agreed to share an office with him. I knew this would happen."

"You knew what? That he'd rightfully be pissed at you for taking matters into your own hands after what just happened to you? Really?" Rachel's voice raised an octave. "And you think *he's* being unreasonable." She stopped walking and turned to look at Jordan. "If you want my opinion…"

"I don't," Jordan snapped. Instantly, Rachel's eyes filled with tears and Jordan felt as if she'd just plunged a knife into her friend's heart. "I'm sorry, Rache. I didn't mean that."

Rachel shook her head. "You've changed, Jordan. Sometimes I don't know who you are anymore. And I know you've stopped going to counseling."

"And how would you know that?" She stopped short of accusing Rachel of snooping through her office.

"With our schedules networked on our computer system, I always avoided booking you for meetings when you have your weekly appointments with your therapist. When I went in to put something on your calendar, I noticed the time slots you'd blocked out were open again. I wasn't being nosy. I just care about you, that's all."

"I know you do, Rache," Jordan replied quietly. She hooked her arm through her friend's. "I don't know what I'd do without you. I'm sorry I overreacted." She gently tugged at Rachel to resume walking. "You know, I'm feeling better. If we hurry, we could do lunch *and* make the matinee showing of that movie you want to see. Let's play hooky," she said.

"I don't think so." Rachel slowly and deliberately unlatched Jordan's arm from hers and headed down the sidewalk without a backward glance.

Chapter Thirty-Two

The therapist fixed me with one of those annoyingly blank stares like you'd see on those professional poker players' faces on TV. "Why do you think you got drunk that night in the bar?" Doc asked.

"Why does anybody get drunk? It wasn't intentional, it just happened."

"Were you looking to be picked up by a stranger? Did that feel exhilarating—exciting to you?"

"No, of course not. Maybe. I don't know. Like I said, it just happened."

"We've talked about this before. Things don't just happen. You made a choice, consciously or not, to allow it to happen."

I sat across the coffee table from the doctor, silently.

"Do you think you were experiencing a hypo manic phase in the days leading up to the incident? Remember we talked about other times when you have felt increased self-confidence, as if you're invincible?"

The question didn't deserve a response.

"You said it yourself, you hadn't had much sleep and prior to that night in the bar you were engaging in very goal-directed activities."

"I'm always 'goal-directed,' as you put it. That's what I do. How does that make me different from anybody else?"

The doctor placed the writing pad and pen on the table. *"What makes you different from other people is that among other things, you suffer from post-traumatic stress disorder. So, when you go through these phases, which you know are exacerbated by alcohol, you are much more likely to seek out excessive pleasurable activities and engage in high-risk behavior. Do you understand that?"*

"Yes." I knew it was no use trying to explain what, in my lowly opinion, was responsible for my actions. *"It's just that I'm under an enormous amount of pressure right now."*

"Which is why you need to be particularly vigilant with your medication and your overall health. When you're stressed, drug or alcohol use, or even insufficient sleep, can trigger blackouts. Your brain is less able to buffer itself against what's happening around you."

I gazed out the office window, not wanting to make eye contact. Doc leaned forward and fixed me with a serious expression. *"Look, this is completely treatable, but you must understand that every time you stop taking your medication or use excessive alcohol, the higher your mood gets. Think of it as turning the heat in the room up a notch with each instance. You put yourself at risk for problems with judgment or risky behavior. You've already experienced that, haven't you?"*

"Yes. I'm sorry I keep letting you down."

"You're not letting me down. And this isn't about me judging you. I'm concerned about your safety, and that of others."

I looked at the clock prominently displayed on the wall.

"Our time is up for today. But if you feel the need to talk again before our next session, call me. Will you promise to do that?"

Then, as usual, the good doctor wrote something on a yellow sticky note, ripped it from the pad and slapped it on the top of my file before putting it in the out-basket. It was probably just a note to her office assistant, but it grated on me just the same.

I knew what I would write on that sticky note if I were my therapist:

Non sei niente ma un figlio bastardo. You are nothing but a bastard child. And your mothers were whores. Both of them. That worthless woman should never have adopted you. Your real mother should have aborted you, but instead she gave you up to someone else to raise. She didn't want you either. Nobody wants you. You've been nothing but trouble!

Although I had promised to call if I needed to, as I left the office I knew I wouldn't be back for my next appointment. Doc was right; I am a goal-oriented person and I'd never felt clearer about exactly what I needed to do next.

Chapter Thirty-Three

The bicycle courier stopped, ostensibly to give Sassy a scratch and throw her a treat, after dropping off an expedited package at the office. As Jordan reached for a letter opener, she was more convinced than ever that he was using his sudden love of cats as an excuse to flirt with Rachel. Ah, the tingle of new love, she thought enviously. She yearned to take up that dance again with Giancarlo.

"Bye, Miss Stone," he waved, his mouth full of one of Rachel's hermit cookies.

"Bye, Kieran," Jordan called back, slitting open the envelope he had just delivered. He and Rachel would make a cute couple, she thought as she pulled out a thick sheaf of stiff paper. A single typewritten sheet was clipped to the front page. *Thanks for a great night! Something for you to remember me by.* It was signed, *The Seattle Stranger.*

Jordan's heart hammered against her chest as she removed the paper clip with trembling hands. *Oh my god, no!* Frantically, she flipped through six full-color, eight-and-a-half-by-eleven glossies, then she rifled through them again hoping that somehow, the images would magically have changed. None of the photos were close-ups, but they were definitely taken in her Seattle hotel suite; she could see the distinctive tub through the glass between the bedroom and bathroom.

"Hey, I'm going for lunch. Want me to bring you something back?" Rachel called as she walked toward Jordan's office. She was buttoning her coat as she stopped just outside the doorway and looked in. "Jordan, what's wrong? You look awful, are you getting another stomach attack?"

Jordan struggled to make her lips move. "No, I'm…I'm fine." She wondered if Rachel could hear her heart thumping. "Just feeling a little lightheaded. Probably too much coffee on an empty stomach."

"Then I'm taking this away from you." Rachel reached across the desk and removed Jordan's cup. "And I'm bringing you back a bowl of soup. Don't even think about telling me you're not hungry."

Jordan nodded. She needed to be alone. And to figure a way out of this nightmare.

Chapter Thirty-Four

Ash Courtland's voice sounded strained when he called to arrange lunch.

"I was just thinking about you," Jordan said, trying to sound light. "Is everything all right with you?" *It's not all right with me, god knows.*

"Of course, dear. Just something I thought we should talk about, that's all."

Although his timing was fortuitous, it was unusual for him to plan something so last-minute. Usually, he booked their get-togethers several weeks ahead. Now, as she sat at her desk still reeling from the courier delivery, Jordan pondered whether she should confide in him.

She was anxious to see Ash, but at the same time she was nervous that Quinn might have mentioned her trip to Seattle to him; she wasn't sure if they stayed in touch after her return from the island.

"The usual place?" Jordan asked, referring to Ash's favorite haunt, the Deer Ridge Country Club.

"Ah, no," he cleared his throat. "Why don't we meet at the Spotted Giraffe? It's quiet there and we won't be disturbed by everyone I know."

Jordan thought it was odd, but with the sting of the graphic photos indelibly etched on her mind, she agreed to meet him at noon.

The popular restaurant was a hive of lunchtime activity. Jordan would have wagered they'd never get a table. Upon recognizing Ash, the hostess flew into a bit of a tailspin, clearly at a loss as to where to seat them. Her embarrassment was made all the worse when the proprietor magically appeared at the front desk. He greeted Ash by name and solicitously requested that they follow him. The only empty table was situated in a cozy corner, but in close proximity to the kitchen. Jordan knew it to be the owner's table.

With a flourish, their host scooped up the reserved sign and turned to Ash. "Mr. Courtland, if you and Miss Stone would do me the great honor of dining at my personal table, we can accommodate you immediately."

Ash graciously accepted and pulled out Jordan's chair. She thought she detected a slight bow from the proprietor before he snapped his fingers at a passing waiter and whispered something to him. The server took their lunch orders without writing anything down and brought their beverages.

Adding precisely two splashes of milk and a scant half-teaspoon of sugar to his tea, Ash then took an inordinately long time stirring it. They usually slipped into easy conversation on their monthly lunches. This time, Jordan sensed him holding back, as if unsure how to start the conversation.

"You said you needed to talk to me about something," she ventured. "Is it about my investments?"

"No, everything is doing well there. In the last few months you've averaged just over a ten percent return. I'm very happy with the results your advisor is getting. I wouldn't suggest any changes."

Good, I'm going to need it.

Ash cleared his throat and in a business-like manner said, "You've investigated a lot of crime stories in your career, Jordan."

He was stating the obvious and she wondered where he was going with this. He stopped stirring his tea. Carefully and deliberately, he placed the spoon on the saucer. "In your work as an investigative reporter did you ever come across blackmail situations?"

Instantly, her antennae went up. Ash twisted his bloodstone and gold signet ring round and round his buffed and manicured little finger. "Well, yes, but could you be a little more specific?"

"I have a client," he continued, "who is in a...shall we say a delicate situation."

What is it with men who get themselves into *delicate* situations? Jordan thought back to the scenario Quinn had tried to run past her a few days ago. Maybe your client should keep his pants zipped, she wanted to advise Ash. Instead she said, "Well, I'm sure as his lawyer you would have advised him to go to the authorities."

"I'm afraid it's not quite that simple." The server brought Jordan's warm scallop and spinach salad, and Ash's quiche.

She sighed. "It never is, is it?"

"Sorry?" he asked, looking puzzled.

"No, I'm sorry." She reminded herself to be grateful he wasn't lecturing her for going to Seattle alone; apparently, Quinn hadn't squealed on her. "Obviously this is very concerning to you, Uncle Ash. How can I help?"

They both toyed with their food while he related the high-stakes gamble regarding a client who appeared to be on the losing end of a business transaction with whoever was out to blackmail him.

"While I tried to discourage him from paying them any money," Ash continued, "I understand why he went against my advice. He was terrified that if he didn't pay them within forty-eight hours they would do as they'd threatened. That a DVD they had would, as they put it, go viral."

Jordan dropped her fork with a clatter, startling the couple dining beside them. She felt the blood drain from her face.

"Are you all right?" Ash summoned a passing waiter. "Could you bring more water, please?" He turned his attention back to Jordan and reached across the table to take her hand. "You're shaking my dear, and don't try to tell me it's nothing."

In slow motion, her mind reeled back to the package delivered to her office less than an hour ago. Attached to the last of the six photos had been a second typewritten sheet. On it was a single sentence: *If you do not come up with the money in 48 hours these pictures will go viral.*

After assuring the restaurant's owner there was nothing wrong with their virtually untouched meals, a waiter removed their plates and Jordan told Ash about the package. He listened without interrupting, nodding sagely. Mortified, she told him about the photos and blackmail demand.

"I'm so embarrassed, Uncle Ash. You must be incredibly disappointed in me."

He took an agonizingly long time to acknowledge her humiliation. "Jordan, you could never disappoint me. You are like the daughter I always wished I'd had. I am, and always will be, extraordinarily proud of you." He reached across the table and this time took both her hands in his. "Now, there is something I need to confide in you. And I pray that in turn you won't judge me too harshly."

Jordan squeezed his hands and waited for him to conjure up a minor peccadillo in an attempt to make her feel better about her situation. "The client I just told you about?"

She nodded.

"There is no client, Jordan. I'm being blackmailed. Like you, I was sent graphic images. In my case, it was a DVD, and I was instructed to come up with the money within 48 hours."

Ash paid the bill and helped Jordan on with her coat. She felt as if some slimy swamp creature had sucked the blood from her body and replaced it with ice water. All she could think about was going home to a hot bath and figuring out what to do with the rest of her life. And how much money she would have to liquidate. Ash was as confused as she was, but he was adamant they not go to the police. "My reputation and everything I've worked for is at stake, Jordan. Please, let's just keep this between us. No police. Please," he begged.

When they exited the restaurant a thick, gray fog had descended over the city. Jordan pulled her collar up against the rain and searched to find something positive to say to comfort the man who had always been her pillar of strength, but nothing would come. "Uncle Ash, can I ask you something?"

"Of course." He slid his arm through hers as they waited for the valet to bring their cars.

"You said the DVD was grainy. Do you know for sure it was you?"

He removed his arm and turned to face her. Inwardly, Jordan cringed at the agony she saw etched on his face. "Yes, my dear, I'm afraid it was."

Neither of them spoke. Could he have been with a prostitute? Sadly, she realized she knew nothing about Ash's personal life.

"And you," he broke into her thoughts. "Were the photographs definitely of you?"

They stood desolately on the sidewalk as people hustled by, all rushing through the rain and going about their business blissfully unaware of these two souls' mutual pain.

"I don't know." Jordan felt the sting of tears in her eyes. "I know I was there, but I can't remember anything about what happened that night."

Chapter Thirty-Five

It was as if the glory of an early spring was making apologies for the nastiness of winter. Crocuses and snow drops lined the driveway of Jordan's beach-side home. They were just beginning to poke their heads through the soil like newly hatched chicks too weak to leave their shattered eggs. Like the tender perennials, Jordan longed to turn her face to the sun and bask in its heat. But she couldn't stop. Not now. She had signed off on the investments Ash would need to cash in for her. He had already given in to his blackmailer's demands and prayed that would be the end of it. He urged Jordan to do the same. Now, all she could do was wait anxiously for the call.

On the drive into work she made one quick stop when she popped into her favorite little florist in Dundarave Village, a trendy area of West Vancouver. Once a landing point in the early 1900s for people who rowed their boats from Vancouver's mainland to their North Shore cottages, the upscale galleries, shops and restaurants still retained their old world feeling of time stood still. But time didn't stand still. It lurched forward, seemingly at breathtaking speed.

At that moment, Jordan's life felt like a runaway train hurtling dangerously down a rickety track.

She pulled into the lane that ran behind the flower shop and pulled open the creaky back door.

"I hope you're not expecting to get in early without having brought me a latte," a voice called out. "I'm in the front, come on through."

Easier said than done, thought Jordan. Weaving her way through Zsuzsi Schultz's flower shop at seven in the morning was akin to tiptoeing through a minefield. Like most florists, Zsuzsi's day started at four a.m. so she could be at the flower wholesalers by four-thirty. She did this, three times a week in order to snap up the freshest flowers at the best prices. Among hers and Jordan's social circle, everyone knew which nights their dear friend could join them for girls' night out—almost never. Judging by the lack of makeup and voluminous head of white-blond curls barely restrained by an elastic band, this had been another early morning for her.

"How did you know it was me?" Jordan asked, handing over a triple-shot, skinny caramel macchiato.

"Who else would park in back at this ungodly hour?" Zsuzsi grabbed the coffee with one free hand, a huge bouquet of flowers in the other. "You're a doll," she said, giving her friend an air-kiss. "I was just thinking about you the other day. Meant to call you."

Gingerly, Jordan stepped over an enormous bucket of freesia as she inhaled their unmistakably sweet scent. She perched on the only free surface she could find and took a sip of her own coffee. "Oh yeah, why's that?"

"Wanted to find out the scoop on Mister McDreamy." Zsuzsi reached out and plucked a fluffy cloud of baby's breath from a shelf. "You *do* have a life after all. You've been holding out on me, girlfriend."

Jordan gazed around the shop, taking in Zsuzsi's stunningly unique arrangements. "What are you talking about?"

"Don't play coy with me." The florist headed to the shop's front door. "Hold on, I just have to put these outside. He's been in here three times now, asking about your favorite flowers. I'll be back in a sec and then you must tell me all about him. And don't leave out any of the juicy bits."

"Zsuz, this isn't funny," Jordan said when she returned. "What did he look like? Describe him to me."

Her friend looked at her askance and suddenly stopped her flurry of activity. "You really don't know who I'm talking about?"

"What did he look like?" Jordan repeated. "Did you get a name?"

Zsuzsi shook her head. "No name, but tall, dark...a bit Middle Eastern-looking. Or maybe Italian. Hunky."

Italian. Jordan's chest tightened. She nearly gasped out loud. "You didn't give him my address, did you?"

"Of course not. What do you take me for?" She looked at Jordan aghast. "But he knew where you lived. Said he just wanted to make sure that when he took you flowers, they would be exactly what you liked. Of course, I assumed you guys were an item."

Jordan threw the rest of her coffee into the trash and fished in her purse for her keys. "I've got to get into the office for a meeting with Quinn, but if that man comes in again would you call me?"

"Of course, darling, but...what's going on?" Jordan had already started out the back door to her car. "Damn it, Jordan, come back here. I can tell you a bit more of what he looked like, but it would be a lot easier to just look at my surveillance video."

Jordan froze part way out the door and turned. "You have surveillance in here? Why?"

"Remember when we were having that spate of break-ins here in the village and that jeweler was shot? The West Van Police made a presentation to our merchants' association, suggesting we all put video cameras in. I have one in the back, and another out front."

Jordan looked at her watch. "Shit, I'm late for my meeting, but could I come back and see the surveillance footage? Please, Zsuzsi."

"Of course, but I wish you'd tell me what's going on." Her friend fixed her with an earnest gaze.

"I will but I've got to run," Jordan called over her shoulder. "I'll be back before you close."

Chapter Thirty-Six

As soon as Jordan arrived at the office it dawned on her that she had completely forgotten the reason for stopping at Zsuzsi's flower shop in the first place. She had wanted to pick up a little spring bouquet as a peace offering for Rachel. Although professional, Rachel had been cool since Jordan snapped at her when they had argued on the sidewalk a few days ago. Even Quinn had noticed and asked Jordan about it.

"You've got six messages, five of them important, one urgent," Rachel said, thrusting a handful of yellow notes at Jordan when she walked in the door. "And Quinn wants you to meet him at..." she looked at the clock on the wall, "um, ten minutes from now, at the West Van police station."

"Huh? Are you kidding me? I just raced from West Van to meet with him here. Why didn't you call me?"

"I did," Rachel said without looking up from her computer. "You'd know that if you ever checked your messages."

Damn. She had left her phone in the car while

she'd been in the flower shop. The day was rapidly going from bad to worse. She took a deep breath. "Rachel, could we talk later when I get back?"

"Whatever." Rachel had suddenly become fascinated with a pile of filing.

Exasperated, Jordan shrugged and debated the quickest way to get back over to the North Shore. She called Quinn from her car to let him know she was on her way but would be late. "What's so important that we have to meet over there?" she asked him.

"Something you need to see, and they won't let me take it out of headquarters," he replied.

Jordan drove into the police parking lot that ran parallel to Bellevue across from Ambleside Beach. If you had to work in a police department, West Vancouver would be the one. Across the street the sun glinted off the tops of whitecaps, the sea a blazing carpet of shimmering diamonds. She wondered if she saw dolphins jumping about a half mile off shore, or if it was just the frothy tips of wind-whipped waves teasing her. She pushed the hair from her face as she ran up the back staircase and through an adjoining outside passage to the front of the police department.

After checking in at the reception desk, where she received a visitor's pass, Jordan paced the floor of the small reception area before Quinn appeared and beckoned for her to follow him.

"We've been waiting for you." He walked briskly, steering her down a long hallway. As they rounded the corner, Jordan heard a familiar voice. They entered what appeared to be a small conference room.

"Jordan," Quinn said dryly, "I believe you know both Constable Ho and Miss Schultz."

Dave Ho stood to greet her. Sitting to his left, nervously fidgeting with a paper cup, was Zsuzsi. Absently, Jordan shook the constable's hand. "Zsuz, what are you doing here? Are you all right?" she asked.

"Please don't be angry with me, Jordan. I was just so worried after you left that I called the police liaison with our merchants' association."

Trying to disguise her anger at being railroaded, Jordan sized up Constable Ho with new eyes. At approximately five feet eight or nine, he was—well, compact. His crisp, meticulously pressed button-down shirt was open at the collar and tucked neatly into a pair of taupe chinos. He looked more as if he belonged in an office than a police station; certainly not like a street cop. What the hell did he have to do with Zsuzsi and the merchants' association?

"The liaison officer recognized your name from the incident sheet and referred it to Constable Ho," explained Quinn.

"What incident?" Zsuzsi piped up. "Jordan, you didn't tell me. What happened?"

She glared at Zsuzsi, who shifted uncomfortably in her chair and picked more furiously at the rim of her paper cup. "I told you I'd be back, Zsuz, why couldn't you have just left it at that?" Jordan could feel her face burning as her thoughts fast-forwarded and tumbled through her brain. How was she going to explain this to one cop and one ex-cop, the latter of whose eyes were shooting daggers at her?

"No disrespect, Jordan," Ho said, "but in Miss

Shultz's defense, we encourage our business partners to keep their ears and eyes open, and to report anything, no matter how trivial it might seem."

Jordan was still standing right inside the door, glaring at the three of them as if she were a trapped animal.

"Would you like to sit down?" Ho asked. "I'm going to show you a video and see if you can identify the man Zsuzsi says has been to her shop asking about you." He pulled out a chair for her. It wasn't a request. "Can I get you anything before we begin?"

Part of Jordan wanted to ask for a coffee, in the hope of putting off the video as long as possible. But the other part wanted to know the man's identity. Would it be, as she strongly suspected, Salvatore Castellano?

It couldn't have been more than a few seconds before her worst fears were confirmed. As soon as Ho froze the frame of a man about to enter Zsuzsi's shop, Jordan's gut did a double somersault. She swallowed hard to push back the bile that rose in her throat.

Three pairs of eyes scorched her face. It was as if the room had taken an enormous sigh and then it hung there like a giant pillow waiting to suffocate her.

Jordan decided on the offensive tack. "You're right, Zsuz," she forced a smile. "He is kind of hunky, but I have no idea who he is."

Zsuzsi seemed to let out a sigh of relief. But on the peripheral, Jordan was aware of an exchanged glance between Ho and Quinn.

"Are you sure you wouldn't like to see more of the surveillance footage, Jordan?" Ho looked slightly incredulous.

"Not necessary. I told you, I have no idea who that man is." She catapulted herself from her chair. "So, if there's nothing else—"

Quinn returned Ho's stare but just shrugged.

"All right then. Keep in touch, Quinn." Ho's eyes narrowed. "And Miss Schultz, we appreciate you coming in. Please keep us informed if this man visits your shop again."

Jordan was already on her way out the door without acknowledging either the constable or Zsuzsi, in part because she was so livid she didn't trust herself to speak. She thought her conversation in the flower shop had been in confidence.

"You'll have to excuse Jordan," she heard Quinn apologize as she bolted for the door. "We need to get back to the office for a meeting with a client." She was sure they knew he was lying, but she heard Ho and Zsuzsi utter polite acknowledgments as Quinn ran to catch up with her.

The look on his face as they walked out to the parking lot confirmed to Jordan that he was seething. However, to her enormous relief, when she'd told Ho she couldn't identify the man on the video, Quinn didn't offer up his identity either. Now, she wondered why.

"How the hell could you let that go on without telling them it was Castellano on the video?" Quinn demanded.

"I could ask you the same damned thing." She pulled up the collar of her coat. The wind had picked up and the sun was partially hidden by a bank of fog that rolled toward them. Instead of being charmed by the possibility of seeing dolphins on the horizon, she was fixated on the bleak, black tarmac that stood between Quinn and her escape. Their standoff reminded her of the time on Annabelle Island when she had run from him. She was sick of being in an adversarial position. Sick of everyone threatening her freedom. Jordan ignored him and attempted to skirt around him to her car.

"Oh, no you don't, lady." He grabbed her forearm. "I'm done with this. You are going to tell me everything about this guy and you're going to tell me now."

"Get your hands off me," Jordan hissed, conscious of several uniformed officers passing by on their way into the building. When they were out of sight, she wrenched her arm free and looked Quinn straight in the eye. "I'm going to get in my car. I'm going straight back to the office. And I'm going to pack up my things and get the hell away from you."

"Oh no, you're not. We're going back to the office, all right. But you're going to tell me the rest of the story about this guy who keeps showing up in surveillance videos and photos. The man you said, twice now, that you didn't recognize. The one who now appears to be stalking you."

Jordan clicked the remote key to unlock her car door. Quinn stepped in front of her, blocking her way. "Get this straight, Jordan, this guy is a ruthless killer and until now was thought to be in Seattle or Point Roberts. Clearly, he's been right here in West Vancouver. And he's looking for you. Correction: he's not looking for you, he knows *exactly* where you live. He knows your friend, Zsuzsi, and he's asking about your habits and favorite flowers. Do I have to fucking spell this out for you?"

Distantly, Jordan heard a seagull's haunting cry as it circled in slow motion overhead. Then, all the sounds stopped. The air became close, like the eerie vacuum just before a tsunami. An inexplicable sense of rage erupted inside her, threatening to spew its way to the top. She wanted to run. Instead, weakly—ashamedly—she grabbed for Quinn's forearm just as her trembling legs buckled like crepe paper.

Chapter Thirty-Seven

Jordan finally understood why Quinn hadn't divulged the identity of the man on Zsuzsi's security tape at the meeting with Constable Ho. He had hoped to connect this case with that of his friend Nate Jackson's, his contact in Seattle. It turned out Jackson wasn't a run-of-the-mill police officer. Instead, he was high up in the DEA and Quinn confided to Jordan that he felt he owed it to share the Castellano collar with him. Whether she liked it or not, by neither of them divulging the gangster's identity to the police, she and Quinn had essentially become allies.

Quinn had wanted to request twenty-four-hour surveillance on Jordan's house but without coming clean with Ho, that was out of the question. He'd asked her to meet in their office late afternoon.

"I think you should leave town for a while, just until we can get this guy," he announced.

"He's right, Jordan." After Quinn had filled Rachel in on the past forty-eight hours' events, she had bounced back to her usual manner of being deeply concerned about her best friend.

Quinn nodded his appreciation for her support.

"This is not someone to trifle with. He's ruthless and he *will* resurface when he's ready. Like it or not, by knowing where you live and in contacting your friend, Zsuzsi, he's insinuated himself into your life."

And Uncle Ash's life, Jordan thought, but she wasn't going to bring him into this mess until she could figure out the connection. The memory of the night in Seattle made her flush. She shook her head and refused to meet Quinn's gaze.

He took her gently by the shoulders, turning her to face him. "Jordan, he's taking his sweet time before coming after you for whatever reason, but it can't be good. For all we know, he was behind your abduction. And although he doesn't fit the physical description that the witness gave, he was probably behind your attack on the seawall." He reached into the breast pocket of his jacket and handed her an envelope.

Jordan stared at it blankly.

"Just open it."

She took the envelope gingerly as if it might ignite in her hand. *Please don't let it be more photos.* In the last few days she'd been on the verge of confessing everything to Quinn, including the blackmail, but something always held her back. Now, she wondered if what she held in her hand was going to make the decision for her. With a sinking feeling in the pit of her stomach, she opened the flap. Instead of the expected photos, what she pulled out was a photocopy of an airline ticket, with her name on it. Destination: London, England. The departure date was for the following day. After years of booking Jordan's flights, Rachel would have supplied all her personal information, including a passport number.

Shocked, she stared at them both. Why the UK, and how could she just up and leave on such short notice? What if the other shoe dropped and her blackmailer surfaced? She *couldn't* leave now. She glanced over Quinn's shoulder and saw Rachel nodding her head earnestly. She had tears in her eyes.

"Jordan, take J.J.'s advice. It isn't safe for you here. Please do this. Do it for me," Rachel pleaded.

Jordan looked again at the ticket and then to Quinn. "Why London? And business-class. I thought we couldn't afford the Starbucks bills."

"Rachel said you've always wanted to fly Virgin Airlines again."

She had treated herself to a flight from New York to Toronto when the airline was new to Canada, and she had raved about it to all her friends.

"They're now flying out of Vancouver direct to London, where apparently," he looked at Rachel, "you have an old college friend. The firm will pay for it. That's a long way and you need a break."

"You're kidding, right?" But his expression told her he was deadly serious.

"Okay," she sighed. "But I'm only staying until they get this guy. I don't like running away."

Quinn raised his eyebrows.

"Usually, anyway." She chuckled in spite of herself. "And don't think I'm not going to work on my investigative piece while I'm over there."

Quinn opened his mouth to protest. Jordan noticed Rachel shake her head for him to be silent. "All right, but for god's sake, try not to attract attention to yourself."

Under any other circumstance, Jordan would have been ecstatic at the prospect of getting out of another drizzly Vancouver month. As the folksy saying went, spring could come in like a lamb, or a lion. This one was definitely in the lion category. But instead of looking forward to leaving, she wandered aimlessly back and forth while she packed, her arms and legs as heavy as lead. On the beach side of her house the view was almost obliterated by a huge dark cloud hanging over the sea. What was it, she wondered, that made everyone feel they had a right to move her about at will, like a pawn in a chess game? First, she was literally imprisoned. Now, she might as well be.

She had asked Rachel to promise she wouldn't let their mutual friend in London know she was coming, saying that she wanted to surprise her. But Rachel wouldn't hear of it.

"Don't be silly, Jordan. With Olivia's insanely busy schedule, you can't just drop in on her." Their friend had a high-end, ridiculously expensive gallery on New Bond Street where she represented some of London's most notable up-and-coming artists. Apparently, the days of artists not being rewarded monetarily until after they were dead was a foreign concept to Olivia and her protégés. They lived and played large.

After Rachel took it upon herself to phone Olivia ahead of Jordan's visit, she had no choice but to go to London. However, there was nothing to say she couldn't stay for a couple of days, feign an excuse, and then take off for greener pastures. If she was to be forced into a vacation, she might as well use her time more productively than hobnobbing with Olivia's endless highbrow friends and hangers-on.

Resentment mounting, she snatched clothes out of drawers, placed them in her suitcase, then changed her mind and threw them back in the dresser. London would most likely be the same as it was in Vancouver: damp and dreary. On the other hand, the temperatures at this time of year in Tropea, situated in the small municipality of Vibo Valentia, Italy, were usually in the low sixties. The nights could dip down as low as forty, then unexpectedly, the days would shoot up to seventy-something and you would be peeling off layers of clothing.

Now, as Jordan sat on the edge of her bed that was covered with clothes, she reminisced about her first, also spontaneous venture to the little Calabrian town. Her all too short stay left her smitten with the people and their seemingly stress-free, simple way of life. If one based their knowledge of Italian food on the many upscale Italian restaurants in Vancouver, they'd be disappointed. Like the Tropeans' way of life, the local cuisine focused on simple preparation, a lack of heavy sauces, and incorporating exquisitely fresh ingredients. No self-respecting Italian would use cream, butter, or even garlic in the preparation of classic spaghetti alla carbonara. Likewise, they would turn up their noses at adding bacon. Instead, they would use guanciale, a cured meat made from pork jowls. The word, "guanciale" literally meant "cheek" in Italian. That said, one wouldn't totally lose face if on the rare occasion you couldn't get guanciale, you substituted pancetta, which was made from the pig's belly.

In Vancouver, Jordan avoided ordering spaghetti carbonara because it was usually smothered in a rich white sauce. That all changed last year when the owner of the café around the corner from her apartment in Tropea, made it for her family and had invited Jordan to join them. For the remainder of her stay she seriously thought she would die if she didn't savor Sara's light, fresh specialty, several times a week. Giancarlo used to tease her that only a foreigner could become a pasta addict in Calabria.

Giancarlo. She reached into her closet for a sleeveless red linen dress and held it up to the light, then clasped it to her face and breathed in its scent. Feeling ridiculously girlish, she had stubbornly refused to have it dry-cleaned after returning from Tropea.

"Has anyone ever told you that you remind them of the Lady in Red when you wear that dress?" Giancarlo had asked that magical evening last September. "You look *molto bella*."

Jordan recalled that moment sitting across from him at a candlelit table, listening to his lightly accented English. She *felt* beautiful. And surprised at the unexpected tingle of excitement. They were at her favorite outside bar overlooking the magnificent Santa Maria dell'Isola, the grand monastery that stood on a promontory just off the mainland. Lonely and struggling with emotions she was grappling to understand, she had started going alone to Ristorante Al Cannone every evening at six o'clock to have a glass of white wine and watch the sun sink slowly into the sea. Sometimes, she could have sworn she heard the sizzle as the fat, red-hot globe made its final descent and kissed the Tyrrhenian Sea good night.

Several weeks after her arrival in Tropea, Giancarlo asked if he could accompany her to the sunset bar. It had been a particularly grueling day of hunting down tips that might lead her to her father, Gavin Stone. When she first met Giancarlo, she'd told him she was there to research an article about the region's gangsters who were living in Canada while thumbing their noses at the system. His interest was from an entirely different angle, and he'd insisted on following Jordan's tracks, a tactic that had her decidedly on edge. It was difficult enough to get the locals to talk about Mafia activity in the area. It was next to impossible when they thought she was conspiring with the region's Special Prosecutor.

The heat had been stifling that day, unusually hot for late September, even in southern Italy. She had wanted to stop by her apartment quickly to change but didn't want Giancarlo to see the inside. She hadn't made the bed since she'd arrived and undoubtedly had left the kitchen in its usual shambles. Reticent about sharing her private sunset ritual with him, Jordan was even more reluctant to show him her lack of domesticity.

"I have an important errand I need to run first. I'll meet you in Canon Square," she had told him. "Don't be late, I like to be there exactly at six."

"Yes, ma'am," Giancarlo had said with a salute, attempting a Canadian accent, but which sounded more like an American from the Deep South.

Whether it was having indulged in more than one of her usual pre-dinner glasses of wine, or it was the setting so exquisite that it defied description, Jordan recalled softening toward the man who up until then had done his best to foil her investigation. As they soaked up the remnants of heat from the disappearing sun she had felt her face flush and an unfamiliar flutter in her belly.

Now, alone in her beach house, Jordan allowed herself to savor just one more moment from that extraordinary evening. Clutching the red dress, she closed her eyes. In her mind, she could see rivers of fuchsia bougainvillea running riot down the sides of the chipped and weathered buildings across from where she sat in Canon Square. Briefly, she and Giancarlo had inhabited their own little slice of paradise, their initial awkwardness gradually melted by the heavenly smells that assaulted their senses.

Jordan took a deep breath and let it out through tight, pursed lips. As she listlessly resumed her packing, this time, she had a different kind of feeling—that of having a knife slowly twisted in her gut. She wished she could recapture the excitement of returning to Tropea instead of the fear and apprehension of what she was running from. Suddenly, her decision was clear. Rather than continue to beat herself up over what she might have done to cause Giancarlo to disappear from her life without a word, she would kill two birds with one stone: She'd go to Italy and find out what happened to him, for herself, as well as finish up the investigative piece she had been working on before she was abducted. If she couldn't get her old job back at the paper, she knew for certain she could file it as a freelancer.

If only she could contact her parents. Were they somewhere in Europe? They could still be in Italy and she wouldn't even know. Or they could be on a completely different continent. No one knew but their handlers.

She looked at the clock on the bedside table. Quinn would be there in five minutes to drive her to the airport. She threw the last of her things into the suitcase and swung it off the bed onto the floor. Then she walked through the house and for the first time since her rescue, turned off all the lights.

"I just want to see you safely on board that plane," Quinn said gruffly, as he threw Jordan's luggage in the trunk. "Let's get this show on the road." He opened the car door for her. "Then I can stop babysitting you and get to work on nailing this bastard. Doesn't seem like the police are having any luck."

During the forty-five-minute drive Quinn filled her in on the scant details of his latest conversation with his Seattle buddy, Nate. Former Inspector J.J. Quinn apparently did have friends in high places. Now if they could just deliver.

As Jordan climbed out of the car and said goodbye to Quinn at the terminal, she couldn't help but wonder if this was just another way of escaping her demons. What if her blackmailer tried to make contact and she was nowhere to be found? If he carried out his threat, the rest of her problems would pale in comparison.

Chapter Thirty-Eight

Keeping a discreet distance, I followed Quinn's Rav-4 to the Vancouver airport. Then I watched her get out of the car. He removed a suitcase from the trunk and set it on the sidewalk outside the international departure entrance. He gave her an awkward hug before getting back in the car. She turned and disappeared through the open sliding doors. I wanted to jump out and follow her, but cars were honking their horns and a security guy was frantically signaling for me to drive on.

I was barely conscious of the blood that congealed under my fingernails as I scratched at my upper arms. I had missed her twice, and just like on the island, she was escaping my grasp again. My therapist was right; one minute I feel invincible, only to be left deflated and wallowing in despair at my own ineptitude. But I'm strong.

This would take longer than I'd planned, but I would prevail. Just like I did when that pathetic excuse for a father had finally given in and pushed a Mou candy through the gap between the bottom of the closet door and the weathered hardwood floor. It was always gusto d'arancio. The mere smell of anything orange still makes me gag.

The first time, my pudgy child's fingers grabbed at the crystallized jelly candy as soon as he slid it under the door. Greedily, I bit into it and then held what was left in my hand to look at the other half of my treasure. There in the center of the sweet was half of a wiggling white maggot. I had eaten the other half. I threw it to the floor and gagged on what I'd swallowed. I heard him laugh from outside the closet, then curse in Italian as his heavy footsteps faded away. When he finally returned, I had pulled a coat from the rack above to keep warm and had fallen asleep in the dark.

Ever since then, I would put off something I relished as long as I possibly could. It brought back a sense of exquisite pain, as if I alone controlled my outcomes. Even now as an adult, I was capable of going an inordinately long time before having to use the bathroom or consume food or water. But this time I had waited too long. I had been within striking distance of her on the seawall. Hidden in the dark, I had imagined inhaling her sweat, mixed with the muskiness of her perfume as she jogged past me. Now, I just needed one more opportunity. A quick twist of the knife and it would all be over. His knife, the one he'd brandished at my mother and me as he railed and hovered over us in his drunken stupor.

Chapter Thirty-Nine

Jordan had just gone through Vancouver's airport security when she got a call from the general manager at the club. Since her abduction and rescue, the staff there knew Rachel was using the Stone family membership for the gym and swimming. For whatever reason, they had turned a blind eye and made her feel quite welcome. Or they did, until her "digging around" about Callie went a bit too far.

"You have to stop this obsession with Callie," Jordan told Rachel on the phone as she walked toward the first-class lounge. "The GM from the club just called and said you'd asked one of his guys to see some archived security videos. What the hell were you thinking?"

"I know, I'm sorry. I guess I overstepped my bounds a little. It won't happen again."

"A little? What were you looking for, anyway?" Then the penny dropped. "Are you still bugged that Callie didn't admit to knowing Ash? Maybe the old dog is having a fling with her and she didn't want us to know."

"Ew! She's about our age or maybe younger.

You're disgusting!" They both laughed, breaking the tension.

"Anyway, save your sleuthing skills for Quinn, and leave that poor woman alone."

"No worries, she's not at the restaurant anymore."

"Really? She probably couldn't handle the manager letching over her. Did you see the way he looked at her? Now, *that's* disgusting!"

"Yeah. He said she just never came into work again."

"Well, good. Maybe now you can focus on other stuff. Like Kieran. How are you guys doing? And don't leave any of the good stuff out." Jordan had been right about her hunch that the bicycle courier had a crush on Rachel.

The rest of the conversation turned light and breezy, and Rachel was back to her old self. As Jordan hung up she realized how much she already missed her. And yes, even Quinn.

After a glass of wine and a light lunch in the Club Lounge, Jordan made her way to the departure area in time for priority boarding. While in line, she scrutinized her fellow business-class passengers who were waiting their turn to board. With a sigh of relief, none appeared to resemble anyone she would suspect as being tied to either Castellano or Grimaldi. Then again, how would she know?

Thankfully, the flight to London via Toronto was non-eventful. On the second leg of her journey, Jordan took a sleeping pill as soon as the plane departed Pearson Airport, choosing to slumber through the perks of flying business class. Except for the chatty fellow across the aisle, whom she politely dismissed by putting a blackout eye mask on, no one seemed the least bit interested in her.

Arriving at London Heathrow, Jordan followed her fellow passengers through customs, then to baggage claim to await their belongings. Finally through security and into the arrivals area, she formulated her plan. She scrolled through her phone until she found Olivia's number.

"I'm sorry love, but something's come up and I'm not going to be able to stay in London after all." She recited her perfectly rehearsed speech into her friend's voicemail. "I was *so* looking forward to seeing you, but I'll give you a call when I eventually get settled." Then, nervously she added, "Olivia, please don't say anything to Rachel. I don't want her to worry. Everything's fine—but I have to be in Calabria for a story I'm writing. I'll fill you in when I call you in a few days." Her heart hammered as she rang off and made her way to the Alitalia ticket counter. She berated herself for lying to Olivia, but if Rachel and Quinn knew where she was headed, they would be livid.

Only a few passengers were carrying on to Lamezia Terme from Rome, and in the quiet of the boarding lounge, Jordan reflected on how best to handle her lie when it eventually surfaced. She tried to put herself in Olivia's frame of mind as she listened to the message she'd left. Olivia had always been closer to Rachel and it would only be a matter of time before she alerted her that Jordan wasn't in London.

The time of reckoning came sooner than Jordan had expected. Apparently, Olivia was so incensed at having canceled several events and her own travel plans in order to accommodate Jordan's visit, she had called Rachel immediately. While still on the tarmac at Lamezia airport, Jordan switched on her phone to find a litany of scathing texts from both Quinn and Rachel. Between the time she'd left London and arrived in Italy, the shit had hit the proverbial fan and somehow, no doubt thanks to Rachel's stellar investigative skills, Quinn managed to get a line on which flight she was on and alerted Interpol Agent, Simon Grenville to Jordan's arrival. *Are you out of your mind?* his text demanded. *Of all bloody places to go right now, Tropea is NOT one of them!* Yup, that would be Rachel; she knew every detail of Jordan's previous visit there. Quinn's message instructed her to look for Simon, who would drive her the sixty kilometers from the airport to Tropea. So much for a few days of anonymity.

In one respect, after three grueling flights, she was grateful she wouldn't have to take the train from the airport to Tropea; it stopped at every tiny town and country crossing and took double the time as driving direct. Simultaneously, she was nervous about seeing Simon again. She wondered what Quinn might have shared with him. Did the roguish Interpol agent know about her relationship with Giancarlo and should she risk questioning him about the former Special Prosecutor's sudden disappearance? As she no longer trusted the instincts that had previously served her so well, she decided she'd have to play that one by ear.

Twenty-four hours after leaving Vancouver, Jordan arrived at Lamezia airport. Instantly, she was assaulted by the buzz of barely organized chaos. Unlike Rome, none of the signs were in English and her Italian was rudimentary at best. Dazed, she tried to get her bearings inside the terminal. She decided to follow the herd, assuming they were heading for the baggage claim area. As was the custom in Italy, passengers hurried off their flights to collect their luggage only to wait endlessly for their arrival. Tourists in particular, seemed anxious to be on their way. Jordan, on the other hand, relished the time she had to put her thoughts in order. Should she duck into the restroom to freshen up? The sight of her bag hurtling down the baggage chute made the decision for her and she headed out to the passenger pick-up area.

"Jordan, this way," she heard Simon's unmistakable Oxford accent. He waved from a crowd of people who were waiting for friends and loved ones. "Over here," he called again. For a moment, her heart seemed to stand still. Since reading Quinn's texts, she'd been mentally preparing for this moment, playing it over and over in her mind. How would she react to seeing Simon after almost two years, as well as her affair with Giancarlo? Had she misjudged what could only be described as sexual tension when they were both in London? Jordan took a deep breath and waved back, but Simon had already left his spot in the crowd and was weaving his way to the front where he arrived just before she did.

"Jordan, this way. Over here." He stood amongst a group of welcomers holding up cards with travelers' names on them. "You look marvelous," he said, a bit too enthusiastically. He seemed about to hug her, but then withdrew, looking flustered as he reached for her bag. "How was your flight?"

"Flights, plural," Jordan replied, trying to ignore the flush she felt creeping up her neck. "Twenty-one hours' worth," she added. "And a three-hour layover in London. I'm exhausted."

"Well you don't look it." He hesitated as if considering what he would say next. "I, ah, understand you had a change of plans. That you were originally to stay in London."

"You talked to Quinn." She could almost hear his salty language as he paced the office like an angry lion. Poor Rachel. "How mad is he?"

Simon stopped dead in the middle of the concourse, causing people to career around them. His cornflower-blue eyes studied Jordan's face, somewhat unnerving her. His full head of gingery blond hair that had become streaked from the sun, matched the four-day beard he sported. He cocked one eyebrow, adding a few more megawatts to his rakish smile. "Well, let me put it to you this way: nine thousand kilometers is about the only thing separating you from being thrown into full lock-down mode."

"That bad," she winced, her stomach tightening.

"Mm-hmm, but let's not dwell on that just now." His face broke into a full grin. "I've managed to convince him you're safe with me for the time being. Come on, I have a car waiting."

Time diminished any remnants of awkwardness there might have been between her and Simon as they sat in the backseat talking all the way to the historic center of Tropea. His driver, a lovely man by the name of Roberto, wove his way expertly through a string of small towns to their destination. Jordan was stunned when they pulled up outside the converted palace that had been her home when she was there the previous year. She turned to Simon. "How did you manage...?" Roberto deposited her bags on the cobblestone walkway outside her building and politely bid her farewell before discreetly walking back to the car, leaving them alone.

"I knew you'd stayed in one of the flats here before," Simon said. "I'm afraid the only thing available is one of the small loft apartments, but hopefully it will do for the time being."

They had been so involved in their conversation coming from the airport that she had forgotten to ask Simon if he knew of a small hotel she might book into for a few nights until she could make other arrangements. "I don't know how to thank you. And you haven't lectured me on being *here* when I'm supposed to be in London."

He simply smiled. "Plenty of time for that. But right now, as marvelous as you look, you need some rest. Why don't you call me when you've caught up on some sleep, and let me know if you feel like a bit of dinner tonight? We can talk about things then."

"I *am* tired," she admitted, feeling the fatigue at last. "This is so kind of you, Simon. I'm sorry that Quinn had to get you involved. I know how busy you must be. You could have just sent your driver."

"I thought it would be nice for you to see a familiar face when you finally made it here," he said.

SCARE AWAY THE DARK

"Have I told you yet how marvelous you look?"

"Yes," she laughed self-consciously. "Hopefully I'll look much better when I've had a shower and some sleep."

"Impossible. By the way," he called out over his shoulder as he sauntered down the lane toward the car. "You look exquisite in red. Call me."

She remembered the red dress she'd worn on her first date with Giancarlo. Now back in his beloved Tropea, Jordan realized, for the first time, she was wearing a red lace top with white linen trousers.

Chapter Forty

Jordan awoke parched, in the upstairs loft of the tiny studio apartment. After Simon and Roberto deposited her at the door, she had let herself in with the key the owner had left. As was his custom, he'd also left a bottle of local red wine, fresh fruit, bottled water, and coffee. Enough to get her through until she could get out to the market. Not bothering to unpack, she took a quick shower and lay down, doubting she would be able to sleep. That had been four hours ago, and it was now dark outside. She could hear a couple quietly talking as they made their way down the cobblestone lane below her open window. Going to dinner at the restaurant at the end of the block, no doubt.

Dinner. She was supposed to call Simon. Was it too late? If she called him, would she appear overly anxious?

"It's not too late at all," he assured her when she called. "Besides, nothing decent opens here until eight, so take your time and unpack. I'll pick you up in an hour."

She fixed her hair, having slept on it right out of

the shower, and applied a bit of mascara and lip-
gloss. Then remembering how tanned Simon was, and
how pasty she felt, she brushed a shimmer of bronzer
across her face. Careful to avoid wearing anything
red, she chose a pair of fitted black jeans and a white
long-sleeved tee. As she had discovered on her last
visit, the various restaurants around Tropea were
generally casual, and at this time of year, could be a
bit cool.

The last time Jordan stayed in the converted
palace that was built in 1720 and renovated in 1921,
she had taken the massive two-bedroom ground floor
apartment. However, as reasonably priced as it was, it
had been ridiculously large for her needs. During that
uncharacteristically hot September, however, she had
been eternally grateful for the cool air provided by the
three-foot-thick stone walls. In truth, she only needed
a place to sleep, shower, and make coffee. But as she
unpacked and surveyed her surroundings she *did* find
this room a bit claustrophobic. Since her abduction,
she noticed she'd become increasingly uncomfortable
in small spaces.

As she contemplated what might be involved in
requesting a move to the larger apartment, Jordan
heard the unmistakable sound of Simon's vintage
Triumph TR3 outside. He had brought it from the
UK, and Jordan had wondered if he still had it here in
Italy. When she teased him in the past, commenting
that the car was oh-so-British and older than he was,
he'd indignantly pointed out that it was designed by
an Italian. Giovanni somebody or other. Not wanting
him to see the mess of her partially unpacked
suitcases, she ran downstairs from the loft, grabbed

her purse and keys off the kitchen table, and dashed out to meet him.

"I didn't think it was possible." He stood on the cobblestone street, arms thrown wide, beside the Hunter green roadster convertible.

Jordan looked behind her. "What?"

"That you could look any better than when I dropped you off. You must have had a good sleep. Are you hungry?"

Jordan was grateful for the dark, so he couldn't see her blush. "Thank you, and yes."

"Good," he said opening her car door. "I thought we'd try something a little different."

The evening was chilly, and Jordan was glad he'd kept the top up. "Perfect. I'm in your hands, Special Agent Grenville."

Leaving the historic town center of Tropea behind, Simon pushed the car into high gear and they raced along the SP22. The route looked vaguely familiar, but it wasn't until Jordan saw the first road sign that she realized they were heading for Ricadi and its main attraction, Capo Vaticano. By daylight, the 124-meter-high white granite cliffs provide an unequaled view of miles of sandy beaches and secluded coves with crystal-clear turquoise water. Once a sacred place, priests and fortune-tellers came to the cape to prophesy futures based on the flight of the indigenous birds. She'd been awe-struck by the exquisite beauty only a twenty-minute drive from Tropea. Even the locals didn't take it for granted, proudly taking visiting friends there at the first opportunity. Other than a few hotels, restaurants, and a little bit of shopping, Capo Vaticano existed purely for its natural beauty.

"Are we going to Capo?" she asked Simon, hopefully.

"We are," he replied. "But just for an *aperitivo*."

Jordan recalled thankfully, that an aperitivo in Italy usually included some kind of light fare. That and Simon's company would hopefully get her through until however, and wherever, dinner presented itself.

After settling into the rustic but comfortable bar, Jordan happily let Simon order two *Negronis*, a typical Italian cocktail comprised of gin, vermouth, and Campari. As was the custom, a dish of olives and another of potato chips came with the drinks. As if reading her mind, Simon asked the waiter to bring a platter of prosciutto, bresaola, and fresh mozzarella.

"Dig in," he encouraged, when the food arrived. "You must be starving."

"Does it show?" Jordan snatched several items off the large plate.

"Only by the crestfallen look on your face when you thought potato crisps and olives were the main course." He laughed, digging in as well.

They nibbled and chatted easily about what had been going on in their respective worlds. Warmed by the cocktail and some solid sustenance, Jordan relaxed, letting herself be pulled into the familiar electricity that still appeared to exist between them. Or were the butterflies in her stomach really about missing Giancarlo? She was pondering that question when the waiter brought their second drink. Breaking the spell, Simon folded his napkin and laid it deliberately on the table.

"I will make good on my promise of dinner, but first I want to talk about your abduction and this individual who appears to be stalking you." He held her gaze just long enough to be unnerving. Jordan could practically count each blond-tipped eyelash and the laugh lines that crinkled the corners of his eyes.

"How much did Quinn tell you?" In spite of basking in Simon's exquisite good looks, she felt her hackles rise. *Please, do we have to go there tonight?*

"I don't need to speak to Quinn. I have my finger on the pulse anytime I wish. You must know that." He shook his head. "Much as I'm very happy to see you, he's right—you should have stayed in London."

She contemplated Simon's last remark and nodded. "I've put this all behind me and am leaving it in Quinn's capable hands. I reluctantly agreed to leave Vancouver, but now that I'm here I thought I'd research some of the local attractions and try my hand at freelance travel writing. I need to get back to what I do best." The guilt of her lie made her cheeks burn.

Simon sat back in his chair and examined her soberly. The muscles in his jaw clenched, as he appeared to search her face for some hidden clues. "Jordan, give me more credit than that. You and I both know you're not here as a travel writer."

She looked away, fussing with the swizzle stick in her drink. He leaned forward in his chair, and for a moment, she thought he was going to take her hand. "Look, I don't want to ruin a perfectly delightful evening, and I promised you dinner, but swear to me you'll be careful. Don't take any foolish chances. All I ask is that you keep me apprised of where you're going while you're here."

As if sensing the protest she was about to launch, he held up his hands in mock surrender. "Not that you have to. You're a grown woman. But I can focus better on my own work when I'm not worried about your well-being."

Not wanting to ruin their evening, she agreed. Simon graciously changed the subject, and they chatted easily while polishing off the last of the antipasto platter. She was screwing up the courage to casually inquire what he knew of Giancarlo when he signaled the waiter for their bill.

"And now my dear, I am going to feed you properly before you keel over from starvation. I will not have that on my watch."

Chapter Forty-One

The wind whipped Jordan's hair around her face as she sat on the hard metal bench of the ferry that crossed from Reggio to Messina, Sicily.

"Ladies and gentlemen," came the captain's announcement in English. "Today we have a gift from the Tyrannean Sea. If you look to the starboard side, you will see a lively school of dolphins playing with us around the boat."

She had been to Messina once before when on assignment with the newspaper. As she often did when working on an exhaustive investigative piece, Jordan groused that the known gangsters she was researching for her story were living off Canadian taxpayers' dollars and claiming social assistance while driving exotic cars and living in luxurious mansions.

"What is wrong with these people?" she frequently railed against the Canadian authorities. "Can't they see these high-level thugs are simply thumbing their noses at us? We should deport them all back to Sicily where they came from."

She imagined her former editor wagging his

arthritic and gnarled index finger at her. "I don't need to hear all the wailing, girlie, just get me the damned story," Ernie would bark. "And close the door *quietly* when you leave."

Though she used to silently curse him each time she slammed his office door, she had to admit she missed the curmudgeonly, award-winning editor. And the stellar investigative pieces he somehow managed to coax out of her, despite her tirades. Silently, she thanked him for putting the fire in her belly that she would no doubt need all too soon.

The crackle of a loudspeaker interrupted her thoughts with an announcement for passengers to return to their cars before docking in Messina.

Sitting in the lineup waiting to get off the ferry afforded Jordan some perspective from which to consider her relationship with Simon. Correction: *if* there was a relationship with Simon. She was confused as to where their professional association ended and their personal one began.

She thought back to the evening she'd spent with him just two nights before. For a glorious few hours, she'd been able to put the stress of recent events behind her and focus on something nice: just two old friends reconnecting over drinks and dinner, the spark between them evidently still there. Was that why she still hadn't brought up Giancarlo's name?

Always the gentleman, Simon had dropped her outside her apartment and leaned over to give her a chaste kiss on the cheek. She'd turned her head to say something, and the kiss turned into something warm and delicious. That memory, and his scent of sandalwood, lingered in her hair long after she had climbed into bed.

As Jordan started the engine in preparation for disembarking, she felt a twinge of guilt that she hadn't told Simon the real reason she was leaving Tropea for a few days. She had said she was getting claustrophobic and was going to Sicily for a change of scenery until she could move to a bigger suite at the end of the week. If she had told him the truth, or asked for his help, he would have shut her down in a heartbeat. And time was of the essence. She already worried she might be too late.

Jordan followed the directions on the rental car's GPS. The forty-five-minute drive along the picturesque coastline to the resort town of Taormina gave her an opportunity to re-acclimatize herself to the area. If her hunch was right, and her father had come out of witness protection voluntarily—or, god forbid, otherwise—he could be anywhere between Taormina and Palermo.

Lost in thought, the next ten kilometers flew past and all too soon, Jordan realized she had reached her destination.

Taormina, though touristy, was an achingly beautiful town, perched on the side of a mountain overlooking the Gulf of Naxos and Mt. Etna. Today, the elusive tip of volcanic Etna was visible through the usually ever-present haze. Jordan circled a three-block area several times before finally finding a place to park just off the main drag, Corso Umberto. Displays from the high-end shops and boutiques, which demanded a king's ransom just to enter, beckoned fetchingly. But shopping would have to wait. As she had several hours to kill before she could check into her *pensione*, her plan was to grab a quick bite of lunch.

She locked the car and set out by foot in the direction of the main corso. The instant she walked through the historic Porto Messina gate, it all came back to her: The sights of freshly baked goods turned bakery windows into blazing canvasses of temptation. Smells of prosciutto, salami, and smoked cheeses, that wafted out of the many delicatessens and *alimentaris* lining the streets, rendered her willpower useless. Fanciful deep-fried zucchini flowers and pungent, nubby brown truffles appeared to jostle for space beside trays of more standard fare like fresh stuffed pasta, olive oils and wine.

Focused though she was on her mission, her nose and her grumbling tummy propelled her into one of the bustling shops. She scanned the corners for stacks of spiny, blushing prickly pears, a Sicilian delicacy she discovered on her previous visit. Initially, she'd been taken aback by the market hawkers' boisterous shouts of *"Bastardoni,"* big bastards, before learning they referred to the fattest, most succulent fruit produced from the second bloom of the common cactus plant. A waiter had shown her how to peel their porcupine-like skins without embedding their tiny quills in her hand—a painful experience that could last for days—exposing a fragrant pulp that could be white, yellow, or if you were lucky, a stunning shade of crimson. Now, as she took one last look around the shop she remembered they wouldn't be harvested until the fall.

The market was getting crowded and lunchtime was approaching. Reluctantly, Jordan left the culinary delights behind and continued on.

The town of Taormina spanned a mere five square miles, but proudly boasted more than two hundred restaurants. Jordan located the café just off the Piazza Vittorio Emanuele, almost at the northern end of the corso. She recalled being intrigued by the wording on the awning of the trattoria: "Wine House, Coffee, Piecemeal," and she had taken a photograph. From there she had enjoyed the breathtaking view of the church of Santa Caterina, after whom her biological mother Kathryn was named.

As before, the restaurant was brimming with Italians, which Jordan took to be a good sign. There was still a slight chill in the air, but ever hopeful for sunshine, she chose a table outside. Her hunger had become more insistent, so she perused the menu quickly, deciding on a Caprese salad with buffalo mozzarella to start. And of course, a glass of the local white wine. Grateful Dr. Danforth wasn't there to lecture her, she relished her newfound freedom.

After placing her order, and with an hour still to kill, Jordan sat back in her chair and soaked in the warmth of the early noonday sun. As she watched a few typical-looking tourists juxtaposed with trendy passersby, the waitress brought her wine and some bread. She took a sip of the cool liquid. Ah, this is how life should be.

Pondering that thought, she was aware the outside deck of the café was beginning to fill up and she heard several *permessos,* "excuse me," as new arrivals squeezed past her table. Nothing ever came quickly in Italy, but with a newly-acquired sense of patience, she blissfully people-watched, savoring her wine. Eventually, she sensed her server approaching and looked up to acknowledge her. Instead, a gasp caught in her throat. *It couldn't be!* Seated at a table nearest the entrance from the street, was the man she had seen twice now: once in the photo J.J. had texted her when she was in Seattle, and then again on Zsuzsi's surveillance video.

The milieu and sounds of the chic little café crashed to a halt. For a fleeting second, Jordan and the man made eye contact. He was handsome in a dark, swarthy way but there was something about the way he looked at her that made a chill creep down her spine. In that nanosecond, she knew he had recognized her. Furiously, her pulse raced, and droplets of perspiration broke out on her upper lip. Suddenly, what started as a leisurely lunch, turned into a moment of blind, heart-thumping panic.

"Signorina, va tutto bene? Are you all right?" The waitress leaned over her, looking concerned.

Jordan's initial urge was to look around for an escape. But it was impossible. Other than jumping over the iron railing onto the sidewalk and making a complete spectacle of herself, there was no way to exit the patio without walking directly in front of his table. Even if she could get past him, the scant crowd so early in the season wouldn't provide enough cover for her to retreat into anonymity.

"Avete bisogno di un po' d'acqua?" the waitress asked.

Water? Do I need water? No! What I need is an escape plan. Then, as rational thinking kicked in, it hit her: She didn't need an escape plan. If the man *was* Castellano, he was obviously following her. Staying put would be safer than running and having him give chase.

She had no sooner shooed the waitress away, when a young woman about her own age emerged from inside the restaurant, perhaps having been in the restroom. She wore a white linen sleeveless dress and the effect against her tan skin was stunning. Ignoring the maître d', she strode purposefully to the man's table and sat down. *He has a companion; a much younger one, by the looks of it.*

Now Jordan was second guessing herself. Had she just imagined she'd recognized him? Perhaps it was coincidence he looked eerily like Castellano. The woman had sat down across the table from him without a greeting, not the way you would if you were intimate. He leaned in and appeared to be admonishing her about something. She tossed back her shoulder-length auburn hair and hissed something back in Italian. Hmm, not a happy couple, Jordan thought. There was something vaguely familiar about the woman. Maybe she'd seen them on the ferry and her mind was playing tricks. Perhaps Dr. Danforth was right; meds and alcohol don't mix.

As Jordan struggled to remember where else she might have seen the couple, a sudden commotion vied for her attention. On the road, a policeman was shouting in Italian, trying to tell the driver of a red Audi they couldn't park in front of the café. A statuesque blonde in a snuggly fitted animal-print dress and high heels jumped out of the car onto the sidewalk, yelling and directing rude gestures toward him. The noise was getting louder, a rising cacophony of Italian voices. Jordan looked behind her to see how the cop was handling the verbal assault. Even in these days of cops and reality shows, at home you wouldn't see such brazen behavior toward a police officer. This one, however, simply threw up his hands in frustration and made some coarse-sounding remark of his own before shrugging and walking away.

When Jordan turned back to her lunch, the mystery couple was gone. Evidently, they had vacated the restaurant during the commotion. Without thinking, she snatched some money out of her purse, left it on the table, and bolted from the café. Standing in the middle of the street, she scanned up and down the block and across the square, but they were nowhere in sight.

Chapter Forty-Two

If a town could break your heart, Taormina would be the one. Like an indulgent lover, it laid all its glory at your feet, urging you to steal and horde every delectable morsel for yourself. Around each corner, resplendent in its exquisite beauty, a cobblestone alley might beckon you down its path. If one ventured all the way to the end, the magnificent Piazza San Domenico captivated visitors with its astounding 360-degree sea view. And if you were lucky, you might see a multi-million-dollar yacht floating majestically between the sea and horizon. Then, as it sailed quietly out of sight, would come the rude reminder that its luxury was unattainable but for an exclusive few. Was that what Jordan was afraid of with Simon? That he would seduce her with his charm, only to be taken from her, or leave as Giancarlo had.

Still reeling from the shock of recognizing the man at the café—or did she?—Jordan left the beauty of the piazza behind, her mind grasping for something just outside her consciousness that continued to elude her. No matter how hard she concentrated, she came up frustratingly empty. She tried distracting herself by purchasing gifts for Rachel and Quinn, but she still couldn't get Castellano and the woman out of her mind.

She checked her watch. Still almost an hour to go before she could head over to her pensione on Via L. Pirandello. Once checked in, she planned to catch up on a half-dozen emails from Quinn, who had calmed down somewhat, but still had an inexplicable need to know where she was, every moment of the day. In the meantime, she would work her old sources and formulate a plan. While the Mafia's reign of terror had greatly subsided, and was seldom spoken of, many of Taormina's shopkeepers had signed an anti-extortion charter. From experience, Jordan knew which proprietors were plugged into the criminal underbelly that still existed outside of the town center.

The air was cool and fresh as Jordan wound her way through the maze of back alleys which ran between the shops and galleries. She prayed Tania, the talkative owner of the local ceramics gallery was still there, and that Jordan could find her shop. In this part of town almost every cobblestone lane looked the same. She was about to give up and retrace her steps when she heard the melodic sing-song of a familiar voice. There was Tania, dragging her sign out onto the curb, and calling a friendly *buongiorno* to passersby.

The daughter of an Australian mother and an Italian father, Tania had come back to her native Taormina and opened her studio six years ago. While there on assignment, Jordan had met the colorful woman when no other shop owners in the chic area of Taormina would answer her questions about the Mafia presence. All but one, that is. In the alimentari where she had stopped to buy prosciutto and cheeses, an old man by the name of Guiseppe had hastily written down a name and address, pressing the crumpled note into Jordan's hand before all but pushing her out the front door of his shop. And that is how she and Tania first met.

"Tania?"

Hearing her name, the woman looked up. The instant their eyes met, a broad smile illuminated her face. "Jordan, oh my god, what are you doing here? It's so good to see you!"

The two old friends caught up in the back office of Tania's studio over espressos and biscotti. As customers came and went, Jordan marveled at her friend speaking in perfect Italian. Then once they left, she'd revert to her heavy Australian accent.

After the two women had delved into what had been happening in each other's lives, Jordan brought up the reason for her visit. "Tania, I really need your help."

"Anything, my darling, you know that."

"What do you know about Mafia members living in bunkers underground?"

Tania's cheeks drained of color and her eyes widened like copper pennies. "My god, Jordan, I thought you'd finished that investigation a year ago!"

Jordan nodded. "I did, but this is important." She tried to keep the emotion out of her voice, but it was too late. She felt her eyes sting with hot tears.

Tania reached for her hand. "Oh, my goodness, child, what is it?"

Jordan hesitated. If she expected this woman to help her she would have to tell her the truth. "It's my father. He's been in witness protection since I last saw you." Tania's eyes grew wider. "I have reason to believe he may have come out of the program and is being held somewhere near here."

Tania removed her hand from Jordan's as if she'd been burned by a hot poker. "You can't be serious," she said, her eyes darting back and forth toward the door.

"I am deadly serious." Jordan brushed away a tear. "Tania, please, is there anything you know that could help me? *Please.*"

With a promise extracted from her old friend that she would check around and call her back that evening, Jordan headed down the main street towards the Giardini della Villa Comunale, Taormina's resplendent public gardens. Until Tania got back to her, there was little else she could do today, and she thought the gardens would bring her some peace. Besides, she needed to walk off the three espressos she'd inhaled in the last hour.

She knew she was getting close to the gardens when she passed the Galermi Aqueduct but stopped a passerby to ask for directions anyway. The woman spoke no English, but she nodded encouragingly, pointing further downhill. Sure enough, just a minute or two later, Jordan found herself in front of the public gardens' majestic gates off Via Bagnoli Croce.

As if anticipating her arrival, a bronze sculpture of a winged man and woman sitting on a bench, greeted her just inside the entrance. Whether they were free spirits or perhaps angels who looked after their sacred space, she didn't know. Jordan reached out to glide a hand over their wings and silently thanked them for their warm welcome. From there, she took the path along the top of the gardens, ambling through a line of olive trees planted in memory of the soldiers who died in World War II. There were virtually no other visitors at such an early hour, and Jordan got caught up in the welcome distraction of wandering aimlessly.

She wove her way down to the lower part of the park with its stunning views of the sea and Mount Etna. Then slowly, she worked her way back up, taking in all the sights and reading the signs that explained the history behind each one. But her curiosity kept beckoning her into little nooks and crannies. Marveling at each quirky structure and other delights, she was shocked to realize she had completely lost track of the time. And so, she picked up her pace, following the winding trail she hoped would lead her out of the park.

Eventually, she came out into a small square of sorts. Still blissfully alone, she was startled to hear a phone ringing. She hadn't encountered a single person since entering the park. In the clearing she had stumbled upon, a small structure housed a public restroom, and beside it sat a semi-circular cement bench. Jordan looked around. No one else was there, but the ringing continued. Walking closer to the bench, she saw it. A cell phone in a black and white zebra-patterned case.

Her cell phone.

Her spine tingled as she felt the familiar panic and urge to flee. Instead, as if she were floating out of her body, she watched her own hand reach down to pick up the phone. She held it to her ear but said nothing.

"Jordan, aren't you going to say hello?" a man's voice asked. "You shouldn't be so careless with your mobile. Or your safety for that matter."

With her free hand, she dug furiously through her shoulder bag. When had she last used her phone?

"It was so nice to see you at lunch. Are you enjoying the rest of your day?"

He must have taken it off the restaurant table when she had her head turned, watching the disturbance on the street. Had he orchestrated that entire incident in order to distract her?

"You son-of-a-bitch, who is this?" she shouted into the phone, turning around and around in the square, her eyes frantically searching the surrounding trees and structures. She was trapped. Alone. Was he watching her?

"Such feistiness. You excite me, Jordan. Like you excited me in Seattle. We should…"

She punched the red end-call icon and blindly ran down a path, fully expecting to crash into him, head-on at every turn. Which direction had she had come from? Was she running deeper into the park or out toward the entrance? If she could just get to the street and yell for help. But right now, that seemed like a hopeless possibility. Her phone rang again. She wanted to throw it into the bushes and keep running, but she knew she had to keep her wits about her. Later, perhaps the police could trace the call. If there was a later.

Breathlessly, she answered the phone while continuing to run, only to find she was getting deeper into the woods. "What do you want from me, you bastard?"

"Jordan, what's the matter?" It was Simon. "Where are you?"

"Taormina. I'm in the public gardens!" Which path should she take next? "A man...I think it's Castellano...he's chasing me." She stopped dead in the middle of the path. Coming toward her was a woman with a screaming child in a stroller.

"Jordan. Are you still there? Speak to me, goddammit! Is there anyone else around?"

"Yes, I'm here," she replied, stepping aside to let the young mother pass. "A woman with a child just went by." Phone in hand, she bent over, trying to catch her breath.

"What? Go with her. Right this minute! Go with her until you're safely out of the park."

The young mother had stopped up ahead and was looking back at Jordan, as if sensing her anxiety. "But she's going in the direction I just came from," she argued to Simon.

"Just do it! I'll see if I can get a policeman there. I'm putting you on hold for a minute. Do *not* hang up, do you understand?"

"Signorina, do you need some assistance?" Jordan heard the woman call to her above the bawling of her child.

"Yes," she replied weakly. Presumably, Simon still had her on hold.

"Come. Come with me, I can help you." She took Jordan's elbow with one hand and pushed the stroller with the other. "I know my way," she smiled.

Grateful for the reassurance, but heeding Simon's instructions, Jordan kept her mobile to her ear. At the same time, she allowed herself to be guided up the path until they reached a fork which veered off in opposite directions. To the right, the gate by which she'd entered was up ahead. As Simon had promised, Jordan spied a Carabinieri officer waiting on the sidewalk outside the gate. She turned her attention back to the woman only to see her running down the left-hand path, screams coming from the child in the speeding stroller.

"Signorina Stone?" the policeman asked, with a thick Italian accent. He wore the regulation short-sleeved light blue shirt and dark navy trousers with a thick red stripe down the outside seams.

"Yes."

"Agent Grenville asked that I bring you to the *stazione di polizia*. I have a car waiting." He gestured toward the road. "This way, please."

Though relieved to see the policeman, she thought it odd that Simon had summoned Italy's military police rather than the local Polizia di Stato.

Bewildered, she pointed behind her. "But aren't you going to check the park first? The man who was following me…"

He nodded. "It is being taken care of, Signorina. Two of my colleagues are checking now for a man of his description. You need not worry," he smiled.

"But how do you know what he looks like?"

"Agent Grenville. He sent us a photograph."

Quinn. *Damn.* Grateful though she was to be safely out of the park and in the company of the police, Jordan suspected what this latest development meant for her freedom going forward. However, with a member of Italy's military police waiting patiently, she had no choice but to accept a ride to his headquarters.

As the police car pulled away from the curb, Jordan looked out the rear window to see two women arguing on the sidewalk outside the park's gate. One woman gestured frantically while attempting to pull a stroller away from the other. After a short skirmish, one relinquished control of the carriage and shoved it violently toward the other, then fled down the street. Shocked, Jordan raised her hands to the back window. The woman running away was the Good Samaritan who'd helped her out of the park.

After spending a fruitless hour answering questions at Taormina's police station, the Carabinieri had someone drive Jordan to her hotel, where she checked in. Several messages from Simon awaited her.

"But we don't know for sure he was even in the park," Jordan said to him, using the hotel phone in her room that night. "He might have just been trying to frighten me."

"Uh-huh. And a little birdie just flew into the park with your phone and plopped it down on a bench for you to find. And a woman was about to lead you the wrong way, rather than out of the park, and who appears to have used someone else's baby to enable her ruse. Jordan, for god's sake, listen to yourself."

She wasn't about to admit that she couldn't come up with a better explanation, so she changed the subject. "Speaking of phones, when do you think I can get mine back from the Carabinieri?"

"Fairly quickly, I would think," Simon replied. "I don't suppose you used a handkerchief when you handled it, did you? I'd be surprised if they get any usable prints."

"Well, excuse me for not having the presence of mind to pull a tissue from my purse before I picked my own phone off a bench in a public park."

"No need to be defensive. I was just asking." With only silence from Jordan's end, Simon continued. "I've made arrangements for someone to escort you back here tomorrow. A member of the police force has a meeting here at eleven, so you'll need to be ready to leave by seven a.m. sharp."

"That's out of the question. First, I have a rental car, and secondly, I've got interviews lined up in Trapani and Salemi. I let Quinn talk me into leaving Vancouver. I'll be damned if I'll let you dictate when I leave Sicily."

"Interviews for what?" Simon shot back. "Don't be so bloody stupid, Jordan. This guy has stalked you from Seattle to Vancouver, and now he's there in Taormina, perhaps with an accomplice. What the hell does that say to you? That he happens to like traveling to all the same places you do? If so, you're delusional and I won't allow you to keep up this nonsense."

"You won't *allow* me? What are you going to do, arrest me?" Her words came out more shrilly than she'd intended.

"Look, I'm not having this argument with you. Be checked out of your hotel and waiting in the lobby at seven sharp," he snapped. With icy deliberation he added, "Do not test me, Jordan."

And the line went dead.

Jordan was still mulling over what to do as she took the wide marble staircase down to the hotel lobby. Should she comply with Simon's orders or should she check out tonight before her police escort arrived in the morning? No longer hungry after getting off the phone, she decided to get some fresh air and take a *passeggiata* along the corso. At this time of the evening, the locals' tradition of leisurely walking around the community ensured she wouldn't be alone.

Handing her key to the concierge, Jordan detected a slight awkwardness. "You are going out, Signorina Stone?" he asked loudly, quite unlike the discreet way he usually addressed guests. As if by magic, a well-dressed man in a suit appeared at her side.

"May I suggest dining in our hotel this evening, signorina, rather than going out?" he said.

She looked questioningly at the concierge. "Allow me to introduce to you our head of security, Signorina Stone," he said.

"It is a pleasure to meet you, Miss Stone," the man said in perfect English. He extended his hand. "Mr. Grenville has asked that we make you comfortable until your departure tomorrow."

Jordan simply stared at him, ignoring his outstretched hand. "Are you telling me that I am not free to leave the hotel?"

"Mr. Grenville feels you would be more comfortable dining in this evening," he repeated. "Or if you would prefer, I would be pleased to have dinner delivered to your room."

It was then that she realized she was essentially under house arrest.

Chapter Forty-Three

It had been three days since Jordan's police escort back to Tropea. Three long days during which she had ignored repeated calls and messages from Simon. She still seethed when she thought about how yet again her world was closing in on her. Damn Quinn and Simon. She couldn't go back to Vancouver, and now she couldn't leave Tropea. Admittedly, this prison was warmer and more picturesque, but a prison nevertheless.

Upon her return, the move from her studio into the larger two-bedroom apartment in the same building provided somewhat of a distraction. Simon called the first day back, asking her out to dinner. She ignored him. Instead, once the shops re-opened after *riposo*—the Italians' version of siesta—she boldly walked the few blocks to the market. Knowing one of Simon's men was tailing her, Jordan delighted in popping into virtually every little shop, where she lingered for an inordinate amount of time. She particularly relished the hour she spent in a bikini shop, trying on every bathing suit she could find in her size. Two can play this game of cat and mouse. If you're going to waste an officer on me, Special Agent Grenville, I'll make it my mission to bore him to death.

"Goodnight," she called to her guard as she unlocked the gate leading from the street to her apartment. *Hope it's a long one*, she mumbled under her breath.

When the phone woke her at 8:30a.m., Jordan was shocked at how late she'd slept. The only good thing about being escorted from Taormina to Tropea was that the policeman had given her back her cell phone. As suspected, there were no discernible prints on it other than her own. Assuming it was Simon calling again, she grabbed her cell off the bedside table, ready to let it go to voicemail. But the caller I.D. told her it was Rachel.

"Rache?" Jordan was excited as she spoke into the phone. "What are you doing calling at this hour? It's past midnight where you are. Do you just miss me?" She swung her feet over the side of the bed and padded into the kitchen.

"Jordan, I'm sorry to call you like this, but…"

"Don't be sorry, I'm delighted. I'll make myself a pot of coffee while we talk. But to what do I owe this pleasure? Are you suffering insomnia again, Sweet Pea?" She was glad they were back on their old footing.

"I need to tell you something."

Jordan's heart constricted as she scooped coffee into a glass carafe and waited for the kettle to boil. Her quirky friend's usual carefree tone sounded strained and ominous. She inhaled. Waiting.

"It's your uncle."

Her breath caught in her throat. "Ash? Is he alright?" Jordan knew he'd been exceptionally tense following their lunch meeting before she left Vancouver. She worried at the time that his high blood pressure was back and had told him so.

"Don't worry, my girl," he'd assured her. "Once we get through this nasty situation, I promise to go see Doc Mackenzie for a complete overhaul." It was his attempt at adding a little humor to an otherwise dismal conversation about their respective blackmail.

"Jordan," Rachel started. Then her voice broke. "Ash is dead. His housekeeper found him in his study."

Jordan's fingers opened, and the coffee carafe fell from her hand and crashed to the marble floor. "How?" She grabbed the kitchen counter for support.

"They don't know yet. There was a lot of blood. I'm so sorry, I know how much you loved him and…."

Oh, dear lord, no.

"I need to come home, Rachel. I have to be there," Jordan cried into the phone. Someone was pounding on her gate. *Go away! All of you. Just go away and leave me alone.*

Leave me alone to die. Do whatever you want to me. I may never see my parents again, now Ash is dead, and Giancarlo has disappeared. Everyone I love either vanishes or dies.

Quinn had contacted Simon, who, when Jordan didn't open the gate, had his officers try to break it down: an impossible feat, as it had stood for four centuries. Not one to be denied, Simon and his men scrambled across the scaffolding between Jordan's building and the one adjacent, which had been undergoing renovations since her arrival.

When they found her, she was sitting on the cold marble floor, covered in coffee grounds, her face dripping with tears. Her phone lay beside her; Rachel frantically called her name from the other end of the line. Simon picked it up.

"Why the bloody hell didn't you wait until I could tell her in person?" He was squatting beside Jordan, shouting into the phone. He listened for a few seconds then snapped, "All right. I'll have to call you back. Get Quinn to call me again, ASAP."

Jordan felt his strong hands under her arms. "Come on love, you're bleeding. We need to get you up from all this broken glass. Hold onto me."

She didn't remember breaking a glass. "He's dead, Simon." She rose unsteadily, like a newborn colt, as he led her to a kitchen chair. "I want to die too."

"No, you don't, Jordan," he said gently, tilting her chin upwards, forcing her to look at him. "Quinn will get whoever did this. I promise you."

She twisted her head from his grasp, unable to bear the pity she saw in his eyes.

"Look at me, Jordan. We *will* get these bastards. You must believe me." He turned to one of his men, "Get me the first aid kit out of the car and call an ambulance."

Jordan could hear Simon speaking with someone in Italian on the other side of the emergency room curtain. A doctor, no doubt. A tube of some sort was taped to her index finger and several gauze bandages were tied around her right wrist and hand. Someone clutched the curtain and pulled it back.

"The doctor says you're going to be fine," Simon said, smiling. "They were superficial lacerations." He pulled a chair up to her bed. "How are you feeling?"

She was too exhausted to make her lips move. Instead, she turned her head away as she felt her face getting hot with fresh tears. She hated him seeing her so weak and vulnerable.

"Jordan, I know you want to go back to Vancouver, but please hear me out."

When she didn't respond, he came around the other side of her bed. "It's not safe for you there. Whoever did this to your uncle is almost definitely involved with what happened to you." He picked up her non-bandaged left hand and held it gently in his. Jordan longed for the intimacy missing in her life, but she couldn't make herself respond. Suddenly, she could hardly keep her eyes open.

"Not safe here, either," she whispered.

"Possibly that's true," Simon agreed. "But at least we can protect you here. *I* can protect you here."

Uncle Ash used to hold her hand like that in the days and weeks after she was reunited with her parents, only to have them torn from her again. His hands were warm and reassuring. She always felt safe, she thought, as she drifted into what she was sure was a sedative-induced sleep.

Safe. My parents gone, perhaps forever. And now Ash. I will never ever feel safe again.

Chapter Forty-Four

For J.J. Quinn, Jordan's absence was both a blessing and a curse. On the one hand, while she was in Italy and under Simon Grenville's watch, he wasn't constantly worried about her safety. That gave him both the time and momentum to insinuate himself into the investigation to find her kidnapper. From what Jordan was able to tell his former colleagues in the Serious Crimes Unit, one thing was certain: whoever held her captive during those two weeks, it was not Castellano himself. Undoubtedly, he was behind it though. He probably hired the guy who did it, but he was not the emaciated, disgusting excuse for a human being that Jordan had described to the police.

What puzzled Quinn and made him wish that he could pick Jordan's brain, was that her kidnapper hadn't come up on any of the sex offender databases. Judging by the quantity of pornography, souvenirs, and obvious objects of fetishes the police had found in an abandoned building on the property, he couldn't believe this piece of shit was still flying under the radar. It had been months and the investigators still didn't have a solid lead. Except, that is, for the anonymous tip that led them to find a section of rope with Jordan's blood on it.

Since his meeting with Nate Winston, Quinn couldn't stop thinking about the two tips phoned in by an unidentified woman, both of which went through a cell phone tower in West Vancouver. He thought about the first call which came in around the time he and Jordan were moving into their new offices. He felt guilty he'd actually considered the possibility the tip had come from her. But that made no sense. Then the second tip came in. Certainly, Jordan had no reason to make a call that would lead investigators to evidence containing her own DNA.

Someone was playing games with them, but who? More importantly, why?

Chapter Forty-Five

Jordan was released from the hospital the next day, with the promise she would stay in her apartment and rest. The same plain-clothes officer, who had been not so subtly tailing her, was now officially posted in the alleyway outside her gate. Judging from the back and forth banter she could hear through her open terrace doors, he was well acquainted with the locals.

Rachel had been wonderful, calling daily to check on her. Jordan couldn't bring herself to speak to Quinn, as she felt angry and betrayed that he had talked to Simon behind her back. Rachel assured her she would update him and that she didn't need to worry about returning home right away. The coroner hadn't released Ash's body yet, as they were still analyzing the results of the autopsy. Whenever Jordan asked Rachel for details, she avoided answering, instead asking solicitously if Jordan was eating properly and getting enough sleep. Out of frustration, Jordan searched online for articles about Ash's death in the Vancouver and North Shore papers, but there was virtually nothing except that it had been ruled a homicide and was still under investigation.

"Wait until this is all over, sweetie, and everyone is in a better place," Rachel advised. "Then come home and have a true celebration of his life. That's what Ash would have wanted."

In the meantime, Jordan paced her apartment and cried. She picked up an British novel a previous guest had left in the apartment but found herself reading the same page repeatedly. She tried writing, but couldn't focus, and gave up. At home, she would have cleaned out closets and rearranged drawers, but here, in someone else's space, there was nothing that needed doing. She no longer was as claustrophobic as she had been in the loft studio, but she still felt imprisoned. By day three, she was going out of her mind.

As if psychic, Simon called to say he would be round before noon to pick her up for lunch. "You must be going bonkers," he said on the phone. "I'm taking the rest of the day off and I have a surprise for you. Are you up for it?"

Jordan glanced at the clock. It was only ten a.m. How would she pass the two hours until noon? "Yes. I'll be ready."

"Good. Oh, by the way, wear comfortable shoes and something modest."

That told her they were staying in town. From experience, she was aware that most locals wouldn't think twice about Europeans being topless on the beach. However, they favored a little less flesh when in the town center.

Despite her general malaise, Jordan had to admit, Simon's promise of a surprise and lunch got her attention. The mound of clothes lying discarded on her bed was growing. It didn't seem to matter what she tried on, she had lost so much weight since her arrival in Tropea that everything looked ghastly on her. If she were to wear sensible shoes, as Simon suggested, a dress or skirt was out. Her appearance distinctly reminded her of an under-nourished librarian in orthopedic shoes. That left jeans, which although they were no longer tight, Jordan wasn't sure they'd fit the bill either. She fished through the armoire for a pair of beige linen pants. As they had a drawstring, she could cinch them to snugly fit her waist. She teamed them with a long-sleeved black silk tee and slipped into a pair of Birkenstocks.

After brushing her hair into a ponytail, she applied some mascara and lip gloss. Taking a closer look into the mirror, her hand stopped in midair. Staring back at her was her mother. She had her widow's peak, something she cursed as a child because the front cowlick meant she could never wear bangs. No matter what she did, they always sprung up somewhere inconvenient. Now, Jordan wore her shoulder-length auburn hair off her forehead. Although she was only thirty-two, she already had telltale lines around her emerald green eyes, also identical to her mother's. She missed her so much. And yet, they'd only just me be afraid of having lines around your eyes, Jordan," Kathryn had said in the brief time they had together the year before. "It means you laugh with your entire being. I don't trust someone who only smiles with their lips."

Hmm, I should be super trustworthy, Jordan thought as she lightly ran her finger over the lines she was sure weren't there a few days before. The bandages were off her hand and wrist but like her face, the telltale scars were still there.

She heard the unmistakable honk of Simon's Triumph outside and took one last look in the mirror. *This is as good as it's going to get today.* She ran outside to meet him.

Simon drove down the road that curved steeply from the historical area of Tropea, where only residents and government officials were licensed to drive. It was the same way Jordan usually walked from her apartment to the beach, thus avoiding the one hundred stairs down and back via the alternate route on the other side of town. They made their way slowly along the lower road, Lungo Mare, past the Port of Tropea, eventually pulling into the parking lot at the foot of the imposing former Benedictine monastery, Santa Maria dell'Isola. As far as Jordan knew, there was nowhere along this stretch of road to have lunch, save the few cafés and *granita* stands that would pop up when tourist season began in June.

Simon came around to open her car door. "Do you know where I'm taking you for lunch?" His eyes twinkled as he offered his hand.

"No," Jordan shook her head and looked around. "Not unless Papa's Granita has opened early this year." But Papa's was still securely boarded up for the off-season, a family of seagulls the only diners on the beachside deck.

"Well, let's see what we might have in the boot," Simon winked.

Curious, she followed him around to the back of the car and watched as he pulled out a blue and gray backpack.

"We're going backpacking?" Jordan asked, trying to hide her disappointment. She looked down at her feet. Birkenstocks sure wouldn't work for a hike.

"In a manner of speaking. Here, hold this for a minute, would you?" He handed Jordan the heavy backpack and ducked his head back into the trunk. "Voila," he announced triumphantly, pulling a bottle of wine from a small cooler. Taking the backpack from her, he inserted the bottle into an insulated sleeve on its side and closed the trunk. He turned to look up at the towering monastery above. "Shall we go?"

"Go where?" she asked, puzzled.

"Up there." He pointed to the winding stone staircase that rose beyond a strip of orange construction tape that cordoned the monastery off during its extensive renovations.

From what Jordan had been able to glean, it was believed the monastery dated back to the fourth century AD, but because of the frequency of earthquakes in the region, it was rebuilt numerous times. It had only been in its present form since the eighteenth century. Built on limestone, over time the elements had eroded the foundation of the present-day church, rendering it constantly in danger of literally sliding into the sea. After nine long years, true to Calabrian construction schedules, renovations would be going on for the balance of the year. Jordan had been colossally disappointed that once again, she wouldn't be able to get in to see it.

Simon walked several steps ahead of her through the gravel parking lot. "Well, are you coming?" he held out his hand. There were huge *divieto di ingresso,* "no entry" signs everywhere. "It's closed," she said, stating the obvious.

"Not if you know the right people." He grinned like the Cheshire cat. The corners of his twinkling blue eyes crinkled with laugh lines. Her mother's refrain ran through her head as she ran to catch up with him.

Chapter Forty-Six

It was a good five-minute climb up the stairs to the church, and they were both out of breath when they finally reached the top.

"Turn around," Simon instructed, taking the backpack from his shoulder and placing it on the tiled terrace in front of the church.

Jordan was still trying to catch her breath from the steep ascent, only to feel it knocked from her again. What she saw, defied belief. Except from the road on her walks, she had only viewed the former monastery from Canon Square, her favorite sunset bar, high above the isola. Beautiful by day, it was truly spectacular when lit up at night. Standing in front of the church's three-arched façade, she looked back at Tropea, standing in all its glory—a fortress four hundred meters above the clear turquoise water of the Tyrannean Sea.

"Like it?" Simon asked. For a moment, Jordan had forgotten he was there.

"Like it? My god, it's spectacular." Her voice broke. "I...I've never seen anything like this. Thank you, Simon." Then she turned and looked into his eyes. "I mean it. I don't know what you had to do to get us up here, but I am so grateful. How did you know?"

"That you wanted to see it?"

Jordan nodded, uncertain she could trust her voice.

"Quinn told me."

"Quinn?"

"Yes. He dug up an article you had written when you were here last year, in which you stated you would literally give anything to get inside the monastery."

He drew closer, putting his hand lightly on her arm. Jordan felt a jolt of electricity.

"Did you really mean that?" he whispered.

She hoped he didn't mistake her silence for disinterest. Filling the gap, he brightly changed the subject.

"Are you ready to go inside?"

"Inside? But I thought during renovations—"

"It depends on who you know," they both chimed in unison.

"Now I know why they call you *Special* Agent Grenville." Jordan looped her arm through his as they went inside.

Once her eyes became accustomed to the semi-darkness, Jordan was surprised how small the interior of the former monastery was. From everything she'd read, most of the renovations seemed to have focused on the exterior, leaving the inside pretty much as it was. A woman inside the sanctuary greeted Simon effusively in Italian, and although Jordan didn't understand the conversation, it was clear they were expected. Their hostess opened her arms wide indicating they had free rein to walk where they pleased.

"May I take photos?" Jordan asked Simon, pulling out her cell phone.

"Possiamo fare delle fotografie, signora?" he asked the woman.

"Si, si. Per favore!"

Simon gave Jordan plenty of time to poke around and take pictures, saying he'd meet her outside in the gardens. Finally satisfied she had taken her fill of photographs, in case she couldn't get back in again, she entered the tiny gift shop where the equally tiny woman was sorting through a basket of scarves and placing crucifixes in a glass display case. With the monastery closed to the public, Jordan wondered if the woman was there just for them. She spotted the sign pointing out to the gardens and wondered what plant species could possibly sustain life high atop the windswept outcropping of rock that jutted over the sea.

Jordan ducked through the low-threshold of the doorway and found herself stepping onto a dry and weather-beaten path lined with foliage that resembled salal. At the very end of the promontory was an enormous iron cross, below which was a commemoration plaque, dated December 24th, 1999. It was inscribed in Latin and she looked around for Simon to see if he could translate it for her. At the furthermost edge, which seemed to hang precariously above the sea, he leaned with arms outstretched, against a rough-hewn wooden railing. Seemingly lost in thought, the wind ruffled his blond-streaked hair. Jordan wanted to let him know she was behind him but for some reason didn't want to break the spell. He turned his head in profile as he looked out over the water that sparkled and danced in the sun. It was a perfect moment. If only she could freeze it in time.

Jordan thought she saw him sigh deeply as his broad shoulders rose and settled back down. Then, as if sensing she was there, he turned. Over his shoulder she took in the breathtaking view of the nearly deserted white sand beach that stretched all the way to the breakwater that protected the historic Port of Tropea.

"Getting hungry, yet?" He smiled lazily, squinting into the sun.

"Starving," Jordan answered, surprising herself.

"Well then," he said. "Let me lead you to our picnic spot so we can do something about that."

"Really? We're having lunch up here?" Before he could answer, she added, "Right, it's all about knowing the right people."

What Jordan had thought was a backpack, revealed itself to be a fully-outfitted picnic basket. After leading her to a cobblestoned alcove that protected them from the wind, Simon motioned for her to sit while he proceeded to unpack plates, napkins, and cutlery. He even had plastic long-stemmed wine glasses into which he poured generous servings of one of the region's local white wines.

"For the lady," he said, handing her a glass.

She watched as he unwrapped various cheeses, prosciutto, black salt-cured olives, bread, and fruit.

He ripped off a hunk of the bread and cut a slice of some type of red-colored sausage. It was soft, a bit like a coarse pate, and he spread it over the bread with a butter knife. On top, he plunked a generous piece of pecorino cheese.

"Just to tide you over so you don't chew off my arm from hunger," he said, handing it to her. "I hope you like spicy."

Jordan took a bite. The bread was warm from the sun. The rich, fiery spread seared her tongue.

"Too hot?" Simon asked, waiting for her reaction.

"No, it's incredible. What is it?"

"Don't tell me you didn't try 'nduja when you were in Tropea last time. And here I thought you were a foodie."

The name sounded familiar. "I think I did but it was in a jar, like jam."

"For wussies." He shook his head and bit into his own. "And tourists. This, my dear, is the real thing. From pigs raised locally, and then manufactured by hand in a *charcuteria* factory in San Vincenzo. I'm a hopeless addict," he confessed. He polished off his first piece and licked his fingers.

Time melted away as they basked in the sun, sampled a smorgasbord of the local cuisine, and drank the entire bottle of wine.

"What are you smiling at?" Simon asked as he packed away the remnants of their picnic.

"You. I was just thinking how lovely this is. Chatting like two normal people, enjoying each other's company." Silently, Jordan was thinking how nice it was that Simon hadn't brought up any of the unpleasantness of the past few days. And how much she didn't want this day to end.

"Like a date?" he asked, looking up from his packing.

She could feel the color creep up her neck and into her face. *A date.* They held each other's eyes for a second or two. "Simon, I know we need to talk about this. I mean, what happened to me at home and then in Sicily."

He nodded. "And we will. Just not today." He took her hand. "Today is your day. It's good to see you relaxed and eating again." He tucked the last of the refuse and utensils into the picnic bag. "And you've done a masterful job of that, by the way. You've practically eaten us out of house and home."

"Me?" Jordan laughed. "You didn't do too shabbily yourself." She reached down to fold up the blanket they'd been sitting on at the same time Simon did, and their heads bumped. They pulled back and found themselves looking into each other's eyes. She could feel his warm breath on her face and smell his subtle cologne.

Softly, he kissed her.

"Are you ready to make our way back down?" he asked, gently pulling away.

"Yes," Jordan replied, savoring the moment. "At least it will be easier going down."

"And for that, madam, I thank you. That backpack was damned heavy." He pulled her to her feet and they made their way back to the gift shop and thanked their gracious hostess. She beamed at them and spontaneously came out from behind the gift case to give Jordan a hug. The little woman probably thought she and Simon were young lovers, perhaps even there to plan their wedding.

After exiting the church, they stopped on the landing at the first set of stairs and looked down. "This would be a hell of a place to cliff-dive, don't you think?" Simon asked.

Jordan put her hands on the railing and peered down at the deep aquamarine sea several hundred feet below. On a warmer day, she could see how it might be tempting. Two small pleasure boats rocked gently on deceptively slow-rolling waves. But where the water met the rocks below, the quiet sea became an angry abyss of frothy white foam. She and Simon pushed off again, down a short gravel path before the next set of stairs.

"What's this for?" she asked Simon, stopping in front of a sun-bleached wooden door recessed into the limestone rock face. Above it was a small rectangular opening, almost like a breezeway. On the climb up Jordan was so focused on getting to the top that she hadn't noticed it. She reached out to see if the door would open, but it didn't budge.

"Ah, that is a lesson in history itself," Simon replied.

"Really? Why?"

"Even though the monastery goes back to the fourth century, those are not original doors."

"Those?" she asked, seeing only the one they stood before.

"There's another one down here." Simon led her down a few steps to the left. "So, the legend goes," he whispered conspiratorially, "that after the monastery became a church, the priest of the day enjoyed a little extra-curricular activity, if you know what I mean."

"Like…?"

He nodded, flashing Jordan a wry grin. "Exactly. This door, and that one," he pointed back to where they had been standing previously, "was his little secret so he wouldn't be observed coming and going through the main doors."

"But why two doors and so close together?"

"Apparently, the padre had a rather voracious appetite. Legend has it that as his next visitor arrived, one of his minions would be showing the previous one out."

Jordan put her hand over her mouth to stifle a giggle. "Oh my. Where did you learn all this? Is it in the history books?"

"Hardly," Simon rolled his eyes. "But I have been inside those tunnels and it's fortunate our priest liked them young and sylph-like. You can't stand up fully and you wouldn't want to be carrying any extra weight. Fortunately for us, the gangster we were trying to capture found that out the hard way. He got himself quite stuck."

"Oh my," Jordan said again. "What happened?"

As they walked the rest of the way down to the parking lot below, Simon regaled her with his story. Even though no one in Tropea, or the surrounding areas for that matter, would acknowledge it, Jordan knew from her research that there was still a significant Mafia presence in the region. Long suspecting they were on to a key player, one of Simon's special investigation units had followed their target into the church on a busy Sunday and observed him going into the confessional. Only thing was, he never came out. After this happened two Sundays in a row, Simon, who went back with one of his agents, burst into the confessional in time to see the gangster exiting a hidden door behind the red-curtained booth. While the junior agent rousted the priest who supposedly was hearing the man's confession, Simon bolted down the tunnel after their man.

"Was the priest in on it too?" Jordan asked.

"No, but he needed considerable calming down," Simon chuckled, "As did the congregation. The fellow I was chasing got completely stuck. More of the limestone walls had caved in since our man had last used the tunnel. They're always having tremors here, as you know. Anyway, he was trying to crawl the last few feet on his belly in order to get to the exit. When I found him, all I saw were his lower legs and feet and he was squealing like a pig stuck in a poke."

They were both laughing so hard Jordan had tears streaming down her cheeks. "How did you get him out?"

Simon produced the keys to the car and walked around to open her door. "We had to go in from the other side, drill away some of the limestone and hope to hell we didn't kill him in the process."

"And did it work?"

"Yep." Simon started the car. "He lived long enough to testify against his boss, the real kingpin, who we were able to put away. However, as luck would have it, some Italian bureaucratic idiot put them both in the same wing of the prison and they killed each other. Poetic justice, some would say."

Jordan felt thoroughly relaxed as they wound their way back up the hill toward the town center. The sun was sitting low in the azure sky. She could smell the wine on Simon's breath and feel the heat from him beside her in the small car. Instead of stopping and turning in toward her apartment, he kept driving.

"Where are we going?" Jordan asked, looking over her shoulder at the missed turnoff.

"To our favorite sunset bar," he said. "But we have to be there by six." Briefly, he took his eyes off the road and winked. "I don't like to be late."

After returning home from the afternoon at the monastery, followed by a simple, but authentic dinner at Canon Square, Jordan slept soundly. It wasn't until she saw the little blue sleeping pill on the bathroom counter the next morning that she realized she had forgotten to take it. Since her abduction, the pills had been her defense against the dreaded nightmares. But last night they didn't appear. She popped the tablet back in the prescription bottle.

The previous evening, Simon had referred to *our* sunset bar. Was she reading more into that than she should? Could she ever really share what used to be hers and Giancarlo's special spot? Finding that too painful to ponder, she pushed the memories from her head and opened her laptop. It was more than time to get back to why she'd come to Tropea: to find out what had happened to her father.

Although she still reeled from Ash's death, Jordan was more determined than ever to track down the vile man from Seattle, who apparently was at least as close as Sicily. Unfortunately, along with Ash's demise went any possibility of knowing if the same individual was behind his blackmail as well as her own. Still worse was the fact that she hadn't told anyone about it. Not Quinn, and certainly not Simon. Why hadn't she? Was it because she felt stupid for putting herself in such a compromising position after her abduction? She should have known better. Or was it the shame she felt for not being able to remember what happened that night upstairs in her hotel suite? Guilty as she felt for not coming clean with Quinn, at least now she could put her time to good use and hone her investigative skills.

Having said that, she seriously doubted Quinn would approve of what she was about to do next.

Chapter Forty-Seven

J.J. Quinn crawled out of his disheveled bed with his usual resignation. He'd accepted that each night the nightmare would come. He only hoped he would be able to go back to sleep afterward. Usually, he would manage to snatch a few hours of uninterrupted rest before morning, but by afternoon he felt as if he could just close his eyes and sleep for a century.

This morning, as he walked through the foggy drizzle of East Vancouver, he scrutinized his environment for what could go wrong. What *would* go wrong. He scanned his surroundings for potential dangers, his mind on high alert as he determined if the guy coming toward him was removing a gun from his pocket. Quinn reached for where his service revolver used to sit, firm and reassuring, on his right hip. The approaching man pulled out his cell phone as he passed, taking little, if any notice of the ex-cop.

After his forced retirement, the shrink assigned to him warned the department higher-ups that Inspector Quinn suffered from post-traumatic stress disorder and was at high risk of experiencing another episode that could trigger the original trauma. Sure enough, the doc's prophecy came true. But even after leaving the Force, the depression, anger, and guilt continued to stalk him. The psychiatrist advised him to continue therapy as a private citizen; it would be paid for, but Quinn knew it would be fruitless. The only thing that would snuff out the rage that festered inside him would be to hunt down and kill his wife and son's executioners. He woke up with that thought each morning and went to bed with it every night.

Today though, his lust for vengeance would have to wait. Simon Grenville had pressed Quinn to follow up from his end on a possible connection between Ash Courtland's killer and Jordan's abduction. Neither cop was the model of patience and feeling the RCMP wasn't making any inroads in Jordan's case, Quinn was all too happy to oblige. As such, he was on his way to meet with the forensic accountant working the Courtland homicide, who as luck would have it, was another former RCMP member and old friend. All his accountant buddy was willing to tell him over the phone was that there were *inconsistencies* in Courtland's financial accounts.

Henry Blasco handed Quinn a mug of surprisingly good coffee and took a sip of his own. "You sure this wasn't a suicide?"

"Absolutely. Courtland would have had to be a cross between Houdini and Jack the Ripper to have caused his own injuries." Quinn sat down across the table from the former investigator with the RCMP Commercial Crime Program. "Why do you ask?"

"Well, judging from Courtland's bank records he was going down the tube. Rapidly." Henry pulled a sheaf of computer printouts from an over-stuffed accordion file and laid them out in front of them. "He was drowning in debt. His house was mortgaged to the hilt, and all his cards and lines of credit were maxed out. He was at least two mill in the hole." He handed Quinn a sheet of paper. "But, as you can see, he recently got an influx of five hundred thousand dollars, only for it to go out again a day later."

Quinn himself owed about ten thousand on credit cards; he couldn't imagine being six-figures in debt. "Geez, where the hell did he get that kind of money all of a sudden?"

"That, good buddy, is why they now pay me the big bucks." Henry leaned back in his chair and put his hands behind his head. "By the way, how's your new P.I. business doing since you left the Force? You know, you should have done it a long time ago, like I did. You'd be sitting on easy street by now."

Quinn glared at Henry across the table, "Are you going to share your thoughts regarding the five hundred grand, or did you just summon me here to gloat?"

"Nah, I'll save the gloating for when we get together for that beer you owe me." Then, with the aplomb of a magician, he pulled another sheet of paper from his file. "Did you know Courtland had Power of Attorney for your partner, Jordan Stone? And that he handled her trust fund?"

Quinn sat back with a start. "Jordan is a trust fund baby?" No wonder she seemed so superior at times. "Where'd the family dough come from?"

"Inter vivos," the accountant replied.

"Sounds like a fertility program," Quinn grumbled.

"That would be *in vitro*, you schmuck." Henry shook his head. "It appears Jordan's father, Gavin Stone, put a sizable portion of his assets—maybe all his assets—in what's called an inter vivos, or living trust."

"Living trust? So, Jordan's father isn't dead?"

Henry looked up. "Should he be?"

Quinn thought back to Jordan's confession at Max's. He had wanted to believe her parents were still alive and well in witness protection. Although he didn't tell Jordan, the chances they'd been found out, or decided of their own accord to leave the program, would most definitely not result in a good outcome. "So, what does this have to do with Courtland's murder?"

"It wouldn't appear that Ash Courtland is named as POA for any of his other clients," Henry said pointedly.

"So?"

"So, I think if we could get a warrant to search Jordan Stone's bank records, they might show a corresponding amount coming out of her trust account."

"Embezzlement? Courtland was helping himself to Jordan's money." He stared at Henry. "To pay off his debts." He tapped the copies of Courtland's bank statements. "But that would barely have made a dent in his financial woes."

"You're right about that," Henry agreed. "Don't you think it odd there was no ransom in the Stone woman's kidnapping?"

"Not really. That's not unusual for a sex-crime," Quinn said. "What are you getting at?"

"You didn't work a lot of white-collar crime, did you? As in high-profile businessmen with dirty little secrets to hide."

"No, I didn't," Quinn said, barely concealing his irritation. "What does that have to do with..." Then the penny dropped. "Blackmail?"

"That's what I'm thinking," Henry nodded. "Do you know if the investigators have gone through Courtland's computer? They sure as hell should have by now."

Quinn pulled his cell from his jacket pocket and hit speed dial. "Hey, it's me," he said into the phone. "Do you know if IHIT has finished going through the computers in the Courtland case?" He nodded to Henry to top up his coffee while the clerk at the other end clicked through her records. "Computer, as in singular?" he asked when she came back on the line. "Didn't he have a laptop? Really? Just a desktop at his office. That's a bit archaic." He nodded, thanked her, and hung up.

"Seems Courtland only had one computer. A desktop at his office and nothing unusual was found on it," he told Henry.

"No laptop or tablet?" Henry asked. "Doesn't mean there wasn't one. Just means it wasn't there after his murder."

Quinn scratched his head. "You mentioned businessmen with dirty secrets. What would Courtland have to hide? An affair? He wasn't married or even in a committed relationship that I know of. What could someone have on him?"

"When I worked with the Force, we investigated a number of cases where women contacted high-profile men—often single—online, or through social media. Lonely and hard up for a little romance, if you know what I mean, the men were convinced to engage in sex acts on camera. The women were scamming them for money. Blackmail. One of our victims was a Supreme Court judge."

Quinn let out a low whistle. "Jesus, what would possess someone at that level to engage in such behavior with someone they'd never even met?"

"Loneliness coupled with a lack of sex, my friend, can be a powerful aphrodisiac."

"Whatever happened to just meeting a woman in a bar?" Quinn groused as he got up to leave.

"Where are you going?"

"To follow up a hunch." He slapped his old friend on the shoulder. "Thanks for the coffee and intel. I'll call you later.

Chapter Forty-Eight

Jordan's hands trembled as she waited for the page to load on her laptop. Though she had resisted inquiring into Giancarlo Vicente's whereabouts after he left the Special Prosecutor's office, the time had come to face her fears and get some closure. She finally had plucked up the courage to ask Simon if he knew Giancarlo, to which he replied that he knew *of* him in his prosecutorial role for Tropea and the surrounding region. "I heard he got fed up with the bureaucracy and moved back to Rome," Simon said, seemingly with little interest. Did that mean Giancarlo had moved back with his former girlfriend and her young son? That certainly would explain why she hadn't heard from him.

The first link she followed was a short article about Giancarlo's resignation, dated November 20, 2015. Something about the date seemed familiar. She clicked on one of the related links at the bottom of the page and was startled when his face popped up larger than life on the screen. It was an old announcement from when he opened his law firm in Rome prior to rejoining the prosecutor's office. There were those eyes: the ones she had slid into like a vat of warm dark chocolate. And the small chicken pox scar above his right eye that she used to trace with her finger as they lay in bed after making love. But instead of a radiant grin of perfectly white teeth above a sensuous bottom lip, there was a strained smile. She studied his expression as if staring at it long enough would unlock the secret of why he'd disappeared without a word. Her chest tightened. *Why, Giancarlo? Couldn't you have had the courage to tell me you wanted to be with someone else?*

She couldn't bear to look at his face any longer and went into the kitchen to make coffee. There was something so familiar about the date of his resignation. She thought back. Where was she then? Her cup hit the counter with a crack as she grasped the significance. November twentieth was the day she was released from the hospital after her abduction. The same day she had gone over to Annabelle Island.

Unlike Giancarlo, private investigator Michele Abruzzese was easy to find. Since using his services the last time Jordan was in Tropea, little had changed in Michele's life. He still doted on his wife and daughter, who was a baby when Jordan last saw her. But now they had added adorable twin boys to their growing family. As before, Michele began their meeting proudly showing her family photographs on his phone.

She ushered him into the large living room of her apartment. "How can I help this time, Miss Stone?" he asked. Still early spring, it was warm enough that she had left the French doors open, and they could hear children kicking a soccer ball on the cobblestone street outside.

She made them each an espresso and put out a plate of anise cookies, which he accepted gratefully. "Michele, I thought we were friends. Please call me Jordan."

"Very well, as you wish." He smiled warmly, hovering above his chair until she was seated.

She saw little point in beating around the bush. "Tell me what you know about Giancarlo Vicente." Even to her own ears, she sounded desperate.

Michele took a moment to drain his espresso, and slowly returned the cup to its saucer. "Ah, our good friend, Giancarlo," he said quietly, not looking up.

"Did you know he was leaving the Special Prosecutor's Office?" For a *second* time, she thought.

"No, his resignation was apparently quite sudden." Michele's eyes still avoided hers.

"Do you know what prompted him to leave?"

"Well," he appeared to measure his words carefully, "we both know Giancarlo did not take well to the politics from his superiors, as well as other prosecutors in the region."

Jordan pursed her lips and nodded slowly. In the past, it had been almost impossible to get Michele to stop talking, their meetings often running so late that his wife would call. Now, it was like wrestling a bone from a bulldog. "Michele, what aren't you telling me?"

At last, he looked up to meet her gaze.

"Please," she begged. "I have to know."

He hesitated, then wiped his forehead with a crisply pressed handkerchief he had fished out of his pocket. "It was after your abduction that he was threatened."

"Threatened, how? What did my abduction have to do with Giancarlo?"

"We think it was one of Castellano's men. They said if Giancarlo didn't drop the investigation into the case involving your parents testifying against him, they would kill you."

Jordan froze. Her parents couldn't come out of protection until the authorities could capture the late Mafia boss, Vittorio Constantine's remaining soldier, Salvatore Castellano and bring him to trial. While in Vancouver, Giancarlo promised her he would do everything in his power to find him. He stopped short of promising her parents' release from the program. Nevertheless, Jordan clung fiercely to the ray of hope that faded a little more with each day that passed.

"Oh my god, Michele," her hands covered her mouth. "Do they have Giancarlo? Did they kill him?" Overcome with dizziness, she had to remind herself to breathe.

Clearly alarmed, Michele leapt from his chair and came around to sit beside her on the love seat. "Perhaps you should lie down, you look very pale. Please, I do not want for you to worry." He spoke quickly now, his accent thicker, his words tumbling over each other. "I have no reason to believe Giancarlo is dead, but…"

Jordan reached out to grasp Michele's wrist. "Please, tell me everything you know." She had been devastated when Giancarlo hadn't called when she was in the hospital. She would have known if something was wrong. But would she? She really hadn't known him that long. Although he was warm and demonstrative with her, she had seen the other side of him. On those rare occasions, she vividly recalled thinking she wouldn't have wanted to cross him.

Lost in thought, Jordan hadn't noticed Michele had left her side to fetch a glass of water. "You must drink this," he pronounced, handing it to her. "And eat something," he added, offering the plate of cookies.

"I can't." Jordan waved away the plate but accepted the water. "I'm an investigative reporter, I should have known something had happened to make Giancarlo just disappear like that." She berated herself for thinking he'd simply abandoned her.

Michele nodded solemnly and went back to his chair across from her. "Once Giancarlo was threatened, he went public with it. He told his bosses, then went to the media. He declared in the newspapers and television he would not be intimidated by such, how do you say, scum."

Jordan stared at Michele, her eyes wide. "What would possess him to do that? He of all people knew what could happen if you thumbed your nose at those thugs." Constantine had raped and tortured Giancarlo's own mother. What was he thinking?

Michele shrugged, throwing his hands in the air. "I cannot say what was in his mind but shortly after it hit the newspapers, you were abducted. Giancarlo was devastated. He blamed himself."

"But I was following up on an anonymous lead for a story I was writing when I was kidnapped." That wasn't exactly true, but she didn't see a need to tell

Michele that. "What could that possibly have had to do with Giancarlo and the Castellano case here?" And my parents, she thought as her chest tightened.

Michele shook his head again. "All I know is what he told me, Jordan. That it was directly after he challenged Castellano in public that you were kidnapped. He held himself responsible for the awful things they did to you." He looked at his hands in his lap. "He couldn't face you knowing it was his fault."

How did anyone know what that disgusting creature had done to her? She hadn't shared it with a soul, not even Quinn. The only person who knew much of what she'd endured, was Sergeant Stella King, following the intimate details that came from Jordan's physical examination and subsequent interview. Jordan had even considered canceling the hypnosis session at the last minute, afraid she might divulge the hideous secrets that only she and her perpetrator knew. Secrets that were the stuff of her nightmares, ones she was determined to take to her grave.

They talked a few minutes more, but it was clear Michele wanted to get away before she asked more questions about Giancarlo.

"I have said too much already." His furrowed expression said it all. "Giancarlo would want us to let him handle things his way. It is not for us to interfere."

It struck Jordan as odd that as a private detective, Michele was so reticent when it came to Giancarlo. But she genuinely cared for the man and didn't want to put him in the awkward position of having to choose between her need to know more, and his loyalty to Giancarlo. It became clearer than ever she would have to find a way to break through this all too familiar paternalistic smokescreen. Speaking of which, she discreetly glanced at her watch as she showed Michele to the door. J.J. would be calling in fifteen minutes. It would be the first time they had spoken since Ash's murder.

Chapter Forty-Nine

"I can't say I agree with you about not coming back to Vancouver," Jordan told Quinn when he called late in the afternoon. "But I'm beginning to realize how few choices I have."

"What the hell is *that* supposed to mean?"

"It's always men who seem to be making decisions for me."

Quinn sighed. "Jordan, nobody is trying to make decisions for you. We're all just trying to keep you safe."

"Yeah, yeah, it's for my own good," she replied testily. "Let's get back to Ash's murder. What have you found out?"

Quinn sighed. "Were you aware of any financial issues Ashton Courtland might have had?"

No one could accuse Quinn of not getting to the point. "What do you mean?"

"Well, the forensic accountants have found some suspicious transactions in his bank records."

"They're going through his private financial affairs?" Jordan gasped.

"Don't be so naïve. It's a homicide investigation,

of course they're going through his financials. And everything else about his life for that matter, with a fine-toothed comb. I would think you'd be grateful for anything that would help track down his killer."

"I am, of course. It's just that…never mind, can you just tell me what you know?"

"Can you just answer the question?" he sparred.

"About Ash's finances? No, I'm not aware of any problems he was having. What are you getting at?"

"Well, for one thing, he had some pretty significant debt. There's no other way to say this. He was basically going down the tube."

"Ash? There's no way." She laughed despite being irritated by Quinn's line of questioning.

"You can't argue with the numbers, Jordan. I've seen them myself." He cleared his throat. "Now comes the awkward part. I have to ask you something. Is there any chance that Courtland was being blackmailed?"

Her pulse quickened. She desperately tried to harness her thoughts as her brain switched to fast forward.

"Jordan, are you still there?"

"Yes, I'm here." *Just breathe.*

"Well?" He sounded impatient again.

"I can't imagine what anyone would blackmail him for. He's one of the most honest people I know." *Knew,* she mentally corrected herself.

"Do you know about any relationships? Did he like women?"

"Oh, for god's sake, he wasn't gay if that's what you're intimating. But no, I don't think he had anyone significant in his life. I'm sure he dated, but he's never introduced me to anyone."

"Okay, don't get testy. I don't care one way or the other, but I have to ask. What about clients? Anyone who might have had a vendetta against him?"

"What are you saying? Ash was like a father to me. He handled my trust...uh...my financial affairs. Otherwise, he was a corporate lawyer. Pretty boring stuff, he used to say. Have they considered a home invasion? Perhaps he refused to open his safe and the intruders killed him." The thought of Ash's last moments made Jordan physically ill. *There was so much blood,* she remembered Rachel saying.

Jordan wrapped her arms around herself and thought of the last hug Ash had given her as they stood outside the restaurant that day. She felt guilty she hadn't told Quinn they were both being blackmailed, but Ash was dead, and she couldn't bear to tell Quinn what appeared to have happened in Seattle. "So where do we go from here?" she asked.

He cleared his throat before coming out with it. "Jordan, I need to ask if you'd voluntarily agree to allow access to your bank records. I wouldn't ask unless it was important to solving Courtland's murder."

Her face burned with anger. Or was it shame? How could she have thought there'd be a way out of this convoluted mess?

Oddly, this time there was no hint of impatience on the other end of the line. It was as if Quinn was holding his breath, hoping to get the answer he wanted.

"What on earth could opening my bank records have to do with Ash's murder?" She tried not to sound indignant. "Where are you going with this? I'm obviously not a suspect. As you know, I was right here in Italy when it happened."

"Then you shouldn't mind cooperating. I have to tell you, Jordan, if you don't give permission to look at your bank statements, the police are prepared to get a warrant."

"*What?*" All Jordan could think of was how did she get here from there? Would this nightmare never end? If she was responsible in any way for Ash's death, she couldn't live with herself.

She took a deep breath. "J.J., do you have a while? What I have to tell you is going to take that, and longer."

After she got off the phone, Jordan slowly walked around the apartment, turning off all the lights. She moved sluggishly, as if wading through quicksand. It was relatively early, but after she told Quinn the whole sordid story about her and Ash being blackmailed, an overwhelming feeling of remorse and fatigue permeated every cell in her body. Hopefully, sleep would give her a temporary reprieve from the wracking guilt she felt over Ash's murder.

Was it possible that had she spoken up sooner, he might still be alive?

Chapter Fifty

This time, Jordan put up no protests about keeping Simon abreast of her comings and goings in Tropea. Once the forensic accountants in Vancouver had perused her bank records and subsequently interviewed her by phone, she held nothing back. They told her there appeared to be a direct correlation between whoever had blackmailed her and Ash, and they suspected both extortion attempts were somehow related to her abduction. No matter how many times she played the scenarios in her head, she couldn't conceive of how one could be related to the other. What single thread could have connected her and Ash?

What was most devastating, however, was the irrefutable proof that Ash had taken money from her trust account in order to meet his own blackmail demand. That in itself was incomprehensible, not to mention a heavy hit financially. It meant that she was effectively out half a million dollars. If it hadn't been for her fleeing the country and presumably the demands of her own blackmailer, it could have been more like a million. Though she wasn't destitute, not working for money was no longer an option.

The heat of the uncharacteristically warm spring morning forced Jordan to seek out a shaded table at the outside café. She had wandered around the corner from her apartment to have breakfast and take advantage of the free internet connection. After inhaling her usual *marmellata cornetti,* the first order of the day was to track down the individuals whose names Tania had given her. Going back to Sicily under Simon and Quinn's radar was, for the time being, out of the question. And so, she pondered her next move.

Idly, Jordan watched as the local citizenry went about their early morning marketing. It hadn't escaped her how fortunate she was to be back in the charming little town of Tropea, where daily life seemed to revolve around having coffee with friends and stopping in the street to talk to each other. Looking around the sleepy Piazza Ercole, Tropea's central square, she envisioned her father sitting in this very café back in 1985. By all reports, the town hadn't changed much, and she felt as if she were seeing it through his eyes. She could understand what he had found so endearing; it was the perfect place to fall in love with her mother, Kathryn. The couple had lived in Tropea for several years, until Vittorio Constantine's lust for revenge forced them to flee for their safety. And *that* had opened the Pandora's Box of her life.

Jordan had a fleeting thought of Cynthia Stone, the woman she had always thought of as her mother.

Shuddering, she recalled her last encounter with the bitter, hysterical woman who had screamed her innocence while being led away from a Vancouver interrogation room, and back into the general prison population. She had been convicted of being an accessory to the murder of a Vancouver private investigator who possessed the information that proved she was not Jordan's biological mother. As well, she had carried out two attacks on Gavin's then lover, Kathryn. At the time, Jordan would have been hard-pressed to decide which of her two mothers she held most in contempt. But as time went on, she had the opportunity to reunite with her father and to meet her real mother for the first time. It was immediately following that meeting, held under extreme security, that her parents entered the Witness Protection Program.

Jordan wrestled the bittersweet memories to the back of the cavern that lay buried deep within her psyche. The place where she stuffed everything she couldn't deal with. For now, she had to concentrate on one thing, and one thing only: finding the individual known to have constructed at least one elaborately appointed underground bunker. Tania had told her what she could, but it was very little to go on.

The sun crept close to the shady side of the café's patio. She was perusing her notes when an email from Quinn popped up on her computer screen. *Your kidnapping and Courtland's murder connected.* In a split second, her world lurched to a stop. If only she could get off, she thought. She took a ragged breath and sped through the email, trying to take it all in.

Quinn's message centered on a set of tire marks found at both crime scenes: the site of her abduction in the Fraser Valley, and Ash's driveway. From her own extensive investigative experience, Jordan was aware that every tire had what are called *sipes* that are designed to grab the road and prevent hydroplaning. Over time, each car's tires will form a different pattern of sipes. The tracks found in the bog around where she was buried underground, and the ones found outside Ash's home, were identical. A stone lodged in the tire tread was in exactly the same position as the photographs taken at both crime scenes. Quinn concluded that there wasn't a shadow of a doubt Jordan's abduction and Ash's murder were inextricably linked. The only question was how.

Jordan was still pondering her connection to Ash's death, something she had guiltily been going over repeatedly when her phone dinged with a text message. She opened it and saw a series of headshots from Quinn. *Recognize any of these? And don't lie to me!*

She scrolled through each photo. They were all men; some were obviously mug shots, others looked like close-ups, perhaps taken by surveillance. She thanked God she didn't recognize any of them. *Until the second to the last one.* A chill ran down her spine as she stared into the vacant eyes of someone she would never, *could* never, forget.

Her hands shook as she tried to type a reply to Quinn into her phone. *Recognize this guy?* Three little bubbles to the left of her sent message told her he was awaiting her immediate reply.

Jordan's fingers froze above her cell phone screen.

Do you recognize him?

She was trying to catch her breath without drawing the attention of anyone at the café when her phone rang. It was Quinn. Of course it was; when she didn't reply immediately, he'd hit the call button.

"What the hell?" his voice blasted in her ear before she could say hello. "I'm here working my ass off trying to find your kidnapper, as well as who might have murdered your uncle, and all you can do is lie to me. Really?"

"I wasn't going to lie. I just...I just wasn't sure that's all—"

"Wasn't sure what? Do you recognize him, yes or no?" She opened her mouth to speak but nothing came out. Her hands shook so badly she reached out and gripped the table.

"Yes or no, Jordan. It's pretty simple."

"It's the man who held me prisoner." Her voice betrayed her and broke. "Where did you get his picture?" Closing her eyes, she silently prayed Quinn would say they'd apprehended him. Then she could go home to Vancouver and part of this would be over. She would even be willing to let Simon find Castellano, and hopefully, her father. This was no longer her fight.

Quinn remained silent for what felt like a full minute. "Jordan, are you all right? Are you sure it's him?"

She felt dizzy as all the disgusting smells and vile sounds flooded her brain. It was as if she were back in the underground prison, feeling the guilt and shame oozing from every pore of her skin. She struggled to focus her blurry vision, and she thought she was going to be sick.

No, do not feel sorry for me. "Yes, I'm sure it's him and no, I'm not all right." Her mouth was so dry she could barely move her tongue. "But I don't understand what he could have to do with Ash's murder."

Quinn's voice lost its hard edge and he spoke more slowly. "Remember my Seattle buddy, Nate, who's been working that case in Point Roberts? And the guy who came up on their surveillance footage that you said you didn't recognize?"

"Give me a break, Quinn, I told you and Rachel everything after that."

There was not a sliver of doubt in her mind. It was the scumbag who'd kept her in the bunker. She shook her head in response to the waiter who offered her a second cappuccino. Another sip and she knew her stomach would revolt. "But why would he have gone after Ash?" she asked Quinn.

"This guy showed up on a security video taken in the food court of a Vancouver mall, not far from Courtland's office," he replied. "And before you say no, I already have Simon putting a security detail on your apartment. If he's connected to Castellano, I guarantee you will not get a second chance, Jordan."

She had no recollection of how she came to be sitting inside the café owner's private quarters while his flustered wife pressed a cold cloth to her face. The last thing Jordan remembered was her phone dropping to the ground and then she felt a strange tingling throughout her entire body before her legs went numb. Mrs. Franchetti tried her best to communicate in broken English, but then reverted to Italian. "*Devi riposare, mia cara,*" she urged.

That was several hours ago and now she was thankful to indeed be resting, but in her own apartment. With two policemen outside. After Simon had collected her from the Franchettis' he called Quinn to let him know she was safely home. The two men said their goodbyes and Simon handed the phone to her before discreetly letting himself out of the apartment.

After Quinn solicitously inquired how Jordan was feeling, he explained how he had followed up a hunch that Ash might have met his blackmailer at a nearby mall. Tapping one of his contacts in the security business, he had located the mall's security footage that showed a nervous Ash Courtland sitting in the food court, looking distinctly out of place. Next, Quinn had the security company run through the surveillance of the rooftop parking area, focusing on the exact time Ash was sitting inside the mall fidgeting with a cup of coffee.

Through some sophisticated imaging, they matched the man seen removing a sports bag from Ash's unlocked car to the guy Nate's people had observed going in and out of Point Roberts by boat. To put a finer point on it, Quinn explained, the police narrowed their search based on the date Courtland had taken money from Jordan's account.

So, now she knew her suspicions were correct; it *was* Castellano who'd been behind her abduction. But why would he have any interest in harming Ash, either by blackmailing or killing him?

Still frustratingly without answers, but secure in the knowledge that two of Simon's sentries were standing guard outside her solid iron gate, she gave up the struggle to put the pieces together and fell into a deep and dreamless sleep.

Chapter Fifty-One

My therapist was startled when she looked up from her desk and saw me standing at her open office door. I had actually been watching her for a full minute before she knew I was there.

Her cheeks had lost their color. "I...I wasn't expecting you," she stammered, as she rose unsteadily from her chair. She gripped the edge of her desk with white fingers. "I'm afraid I don't have time for a session now, but I'm sure if you call the office tomorrow, my assistant can book you in during regular hours."

Her eyes followed me as I stepped into her office, closed the door, and turned the lock. I wondered if she was scanning her brain, trying to remember what distinguished me from all the other loonies she saw every day.

"Sit down," I said.

"All right." She fumbled for the chair behind her and sat heavily. "What, uh...what brings you here today?"

For some reason, I couldn't think of anything else to say. "I want to talk more about my family," I blurted.

Doc's head went up and down like one of those bobble dolls on the dashboard of a car. I would have thought she'd have had more experience staying calm.

"All right, let's start with your mother. Were you close to her growing up?"

A little voice pushed its way into my head. You are living proof why mothers eat their young. "Yes, she was amazing," I said. "Always wanted the best for me. She used to call me dolce, sweet one."

"And your father, what was he like? Was he away a lot?"

You must have been dropped on your head as a baby to be this goddamned stupid. "No, why would you ask that?" Even to my own ears I sounded defensive, but I had to keep my story straight. We had discussed my father before, but I couldn't remember what I had told her. Soon, it wouldn't much matter.

The psychologist's finely-drawn eyebrows knit together as she reached for a writing pad. "You said he was in real estate development, wasn't it? In Europe. Wouldn't that have required him to travel quite a bit?"

She was trying to trip me up on purpose, the bitch. "I don't see whether my father traveled or not has to do with my issues today. Why do you keep trying to change the subject?"

"Do I?"

"Yes, you do."

"All right, what would you like to talk about?"

Now she was trying to act all casual, but I could see the thin blue vein in her left temple that pulsated ever so slightly when she was frustrated. I wondered if shrinks went to shrinks when they had problems.

"I actually don't want to talk about anything. It's only because my doctor referred me that I decided to come see you again."

"That isn't true, is it?" She stared at me smugly. "It wasn't your doctor who referred you. It was the chief psychiatrist at the remand center who ordered you to come here. It was one of the conditions of your probation rather than sending you to jail."

"Do you think I belong in jail?"

"Do you?"

"Of course not. It was a complete misunderstanding, what happened with that b... that woman."

"There was a restraining order in place. She reported that you'd been stalking her for weeks." The doctor took off her glasses and rubbed her eyes. "You tried to push her through a plate glass window." She sighed. "Look, I can't help you get better until you start being honest with yourself. You can lie to me all you want, but you know the truth."

"Really? What truth is that?"

Now the vein was throbbing in the double digits. She put her glasses back on.

"That is," she repeated slowly, "that you have what is called intermittent explosive disorder. You've had several psychotic breaks and tried to harm people. You are in denial about what happened in your childhood. That in itself is not uncommon, but it is something you have to acknowledge if we're to have any success at treatment."

"In denial about what, exactly? What do you

think happened to me in childhood?"

"Look, we both know you have a history of being abused."

She was looking more confident.

"I have the notes from the hospital psychiatrist's file. When you were little your adoptive father would lock you in a closet for hours, sometimes days at a time. He mistreated your adoptive mother as well. Is that why she left him?"

I clenched my teeth, just as I had all those years ago when I sat in total darkness on a cold closet floor and willed the tears not to come. The time I wet my pants because I couldn't hold it any longer.

My mouth was suddenly dry, and I reached for a bottle of water the doc always had sitting on the table.

She persisted. "Do you blame your mother for not taking you with her? It would be perfectly natural if you did."

This wasn't how I had planned it. The color had come back into her cheeks. She was pushing back.

"Look, the bottom line is that if you stay on your medication and start to take psychotherapy seriously, I'm confident we can make some real progress. But I want you to think about what I've said before your next appointment. Will you do that?"

Shaking, but determined to exit the room calmly, I nodded and walked stiffly out of her office. Without looking back, I knew the good doctor would be doing what she always did after our sessions. She would peel off a yellow sticky note, scrawl something on it, and place it in her out basket. Then she would forget about me for another week. But not this time. I held my head high as I said goodbye and walked through the empty reception area.

I opened the door to the outer hallway and while remaining inside, I made sure I closed it just loud enough for her to assume I'd left.

Chapter Fifty-Two

Except for sunset, the early hours of dawn were Jordan's favorite time of day in Tropea. Her first visit to the Calabrian town had been later in the season, when the temperatures could easily soar into the eighties and nineties. Because of the heat, she'd developed the habit of running early in the day before it became oppressive.

As a concession to her going stir-crazy from essentially being under house arrest, Simon had agreed to let her go out for a run, provided an unmarked police car trailed her. Is this how the president feels, she wondered as she ran past the marina toward the majestic limestone cliffs of the monastery. She stopped to catch her breath and savor the crisp morning air. Her escort slowed accordingly.

She watched mesmerized as glistening blue waves gently licked the pristine white sand beach that ran the length of the seaside road. The town was quiet in March, but the many pizzerias and seafood restaurants, boat rentals, and shops would soon be open and swarming with tourists.

Jordan wished she could stay until then.

Although she welcomed the quiet and peacefulness before the summer holiday season began, her soul longed to hear music emanating from the restaurants and feel the electricity that turned the sleepy town into a pulsating community. Her life of late had been *too* quiet. It had felt dead, like her soul, until she had returned to this magical place. All that was missing was Giancarlo.

She was gearing up to finish her run, remembering to conserve a last burst of energy for the steep hill that led up to the town center, when she became aware of another car slowing down beside her. Without turning to look, she knew it was Simon. She would have recognized the distinctive growl of his Triumph TR3 blindfolded. Obviously, her "secret service" detail had told him where to find her.

"Hey." She stepped off the curb and folded her lean frame into the open passenger side window. "This is awfully early for you. Have you come to take me to breakfast?" The moment their eyes met she knew something was wrong.

He attempted a half-hearted smile, but it was tight and forced. "I'll just pull over." Warily, she watched as he neatly slid the car alongside the curb and got out.

"I've actually brought breakfast to you." He reached in and plucked a bakery bag off the passenger seat. "Thought we might go for a walk."

Something inside her—a feeling she couldn't identify—made her stand perfectly still on the curb. "Simon, what's wrong?" *Please don't let it be my parents.*

He took her elbow. "There's something I need to

tell you before you hear it from someone else. Let's sit here." She had been completely unaware that he'd led her across the sand, toward a picnic table outside Papa's granita stand. Looking across the road, she saw the police car pulling away.

Simon sat beside her and took her hands in his. "Jordan, there's no easy way to tell you this. Your therapist in Vancouver was viciously attacked and left for dead in her office last night."

Jordan's heart felt like the runaway pendulum of a clock as it swayed and bounced wildly from side to side. "Dr. Danforth? What happened? Is she dead?"

Simon shook his head. "She was stabbed in the chest, neck, and abdomen. Her patient appointments were finished for the day and she was catching up on some paperwork. Her assistant had gone for the day, but as luck would have it the cleaners were getting out of the elevator when they were nearly knocked down by a woman flying out the door and down the stairs. They discovered the doctor on the floor of her office and called 9-1-1."

Jordan covered her mouth with her hands. Several times while in Tropea, she had nearly taken Dr. Danforth up on her offer to counsel her over the phone. Now she wished she had called her. "Is she going to be all right?"

Simon nodded. "They've upgraded her from critical to serious condition. Hopefully, there won't be further complications or infection. She was very weak, but when she regained consciousness after surgery, she was adamant someone at the hospital call your office." He shook his head slowly. "She is one extremely lucky lady. Had it not been for the cleaning people, she would have bled out."

"Thank god for that. But who would want to hurt her? And why would she have had someone call Rachel or Quinn?"

"I don't know. I haven't been able to reach Quinn. It was Rachel who called to tell me. Were you and Dr. Danforth friends outside of your professional relationship?"

"No, not at all. As you said, I was merely a patient." She cared about the therapist, but outside of their doctor-patient relationship there was no reason she would contact Jordan personally. "Has anyone been able to identify the woman they saw fleeing the building?"

Simon shook his head. A cold shiver ran down her spine.

He took off his jacket and wrapped it around her shoulders. "I don't imagine you're too hungry, love. Let's get you home so you can have a hot shower."

Her body felt like a dead weight as she reached for his hand. As if mirroring her mood, the gentle cool breeze of the morning suddenly turned blustery, and storm clouds huddled ominously over the sea. Just as the darkening sky gave way to torrential rain, she wondered when her life had begun to resemble a wild, out of control tempest that brought death or destruction to everyone around her.

Chapter Fifty-Three

It had been three days since Simon had broken the news about the attempted murder of Dr. Danforth and Jordan was wrung out from all the grief. Because he needed every officer on a security detail for a visiting politician, Simon reluctantly agreed to temporarily pull the unmarked car that had been following her every move. Without telling him, she rented a car for the day. Her first destination would be Capo Vaticano. He had taken her there several times for dinner, but this time, besides feeling the need to get out of Tropea and spend some time alone, she wanted to witness the cape's majesty in the daylight. Situated on the last strip of land before the Straits of Messina, the small center sat like a throne above the breathtakingly clear turquoise waters of the Tyrrhenian Sea. Equally feared and respected by sailors for centuries, the waters deep below the grayish white granite cliffs hid relics of shipwrecks. And as the legend went, secrets.

Tourists often assumed the name given this beautiful gem of Calabria was related to the Vatican. Instead, it meant "place of prophecy." Now as Jordan stood on one of the hidden beaches usually only known to the locals, she surveyed tufts of heather and clusters of prickly-pear cacti that dotted the sand among the palm trees. Lithely swaying in the breeze, the giant palms appeared to bow in welcome. Had her father brought his beautiful young lover, Kathryn, here over the years they were forced to live in secret? Or, perhaps he had come here to wrestle with his feelings about leaving Jordan and her mother for Kathryn, the true love of his life. Was it after one of their visits to this sacred place that Jordan was conceived, blissfully unaware she would grow up as the love child of a forbidden and dangerous union?

Her brain hurt from trying to figure out how she'd come to be in this place, possibly walking in her parents' footsteps thirty-two years later. And now her heart was torn. Should she stop pining for Giancarlo, who, as Michele had said, didn't wish to be found? If so, what would that mean for her budding relationship with Simon? She suspected he'd been holding back, sensing she didn't have room in her heart for him as long as she was saving that space for someone else.

The gulls' haunting screams startled her from her reflections. She'd come to the far end of the beach and the rock steps that led up through the underbrush to the vista above. Carefully, she picked her way up the snaking path until, breathless, she arrived at the top. There were just a few other cars in the parking lot, and some hikers taking photographs of the unparalleled view. In front of a small family-run *osteria*, sausages hung from a wide olive tree to cure in the sun. No doubt some of them would make their way into the region's famed 'nduja she and Simon had enjoyed at their picnic atop the cliffs of the monastery.

She walked past a woman sitting on the rock wall that surrounded the promontory. A fluffy blond puppy played happily at her feet. "Hello." Jordan smiled as she passed by her on the way back to the car.

"Hello. It's a beautiful day, no?" Though the woman spoke perfect English, her voice, soft and melodic, possessed just a hint of an Italian accent.

"Yes, it is." Jordan looked into the woman's chocolate eyes, momentarily taken aback by the deep sense of serenity they exuded. Dark chestnut curls framed her olive-skinned face which lit up when she smiled. The puppy reached out to sniff Jordan and she bent down to rub its soft muzzle. It was then that she noticed a deck of tarot cards sitting in a neat stack on the wall beside the woman. The light went on. She was a gypsy here to hustle tourists for tarot card readings. Jordan turned to leave. "Your puppy is sweet. Have a nice day."

"And you, signorina. I hope you have healed your heart while you were here."

Jordan turned to look at her. "Excuse me?"

"Please, I do not wish to offend you, and I do not want your money." The young woman's eyes held such warmth and kindness Jordan found it hard to look away. "But I believe I can help you with a decision you are struggling with. The answer is not as difficult as you may think."

She seemed so genuine Jordan hated to appear rude. "I...I'm sorry, but I don't believe in fortune-telling."

The woman's smile widened. "That's alright, belief is not necessary. I am not a fortune-teller. The cards you choose are simply a reflection of the energy you currently possess around a situation or circumstance. They do not predict your future. You are in control of your life and nothing I say or show to you can change that." She seemed to take Jordan's silence for permission. "Would you like to see what your cards show?"

As if to persuade her, the puppy jumped up and nuzzled its face into Jordan's hand. What the heck, it's not as if she had anywhere she needed to be. It might be fun and in truth, she didn't mind that regardless of what she said, the gypsy would likely expect some money afterward. "Yes, okay, why not?"

The woman motioned for her to sit beside her on the wall, then she picked up the well-worn, thick deck of cards. "While I shuffle and cut these, I want you to think of the most important question you have in your mind at this moment." Jordan watched as she expertly shuffled the large cards, cut the deck and placed the bottom half over the top. Then she fanned the cards out across a colorful silk cloth she had draped over a section of the wall where they sat. As instructed, Jordan tried to focus on just one of the many questions that just minutes ago had swirled through her head.

"Now, while thinking of your question, please run your fingers over the cards and pick one that speaks to you. Feel free to take your time." Slowly, Jordan let her fingers travel across the cards. They were slightly sticky from use, but at the same time they felt cool and soothing to the touch. Inexplicably, her hand stopped, and she pulled a card from the fan.

"Each card you choose," the woman explained, "represents your present position, your present desires, the unexpected, and finally, your immediate future and outcome."

We can probably rule out the unexpected, Jordan thought. I think I've pretty well got that covered.

Then, as if sensing what Jordan was thinking, the woman said, "Let's start with only one card today." She motioned for her to turn over the card she'd chosen. An image of two beautiful upside-down intertwined hearts revealed itself. "Ah, I see you are a woman who cuts straight to the matter at hand." She smiled, and her voice tinkled with a mirthful laugh. "You have chosen the Lovers Reversed, a very revealing card."

"How so?" Although still skeptical, Jordan relaxed and was quite enjoying sitting in the late afternoon sun with this lovely woman who radiated a sense of calm and peace.

"Even when the hearts are upside-down, this is a very positive omen. It is associated with the sign of Gemini. The twins. It is, of course, symbolic of romantic relationships, but it also can relate to all the relationships in your life. Were you perhaps thinking of a particular one that you are questioning?"

A lump formed in Jordan's throat and she could feel the sting of tears. Not trusting herself to speak, she nodded.

Lightly, the woman put her hand on Jordan's wrist. "It is all right," she assured her. "The cards often bring emotions to the surface. When the hearts on this card appear in reverse, you may be feeling confused or torn about a relationship or a situation you are experiencing. I urge you to pay attention to your heart. What you are feeling is more important than what your mind thinks about it. Don't ignore your heart. It is the center of all things. Does that make sense?" she asked quietly.

"Yes, it does," Jordan admitted. "I have always been one to analyze things and make my decisions based on facts." She couldn't believe she was telling this to a perfect stranger.

The woman nodded sagely. "I understand, but intertwined hearts are a positive omen for your love life even though they are reversed. The card you have chosen indicates the relationship is already in place. It is very immediate. In the here and now. However, it indicates there may be a delay in you feeling as deeply as the other person does. Perhaps there is another, standing in the way. Could that be true?"

Jordan swallowed hard and nodded again. "Thank you, you have been most helpful. This has been lovely." And she sincerely meant it. Perhaps meeting this woman and her sweet little dog was exactly the reason she was meant to come to the cape today. She reached into her bag for her wallet. "But I'd like to pay you. Please excuse my rudeness earlier."

The woman waved off her gesture. "No, please, I felt when I first saw you I needed to give you this gift. I am very glad you were open to receiving it."

"That's very kind of you." She put her wallet back in her purse. "Well, I suppose I should be heading back to Tropea." She ruffled the puppy's ears and wished its mistress goodbye. Then, as an afterthought she turned back. "I'm sorry, I don't even know your name. I'm Jordan."

The woman stood up and again, Jordan was struck by not only her beauty, but the intensity of her deep brown eyes. "It is a pleasure to know you. My name is Arabella. I hope we will see each other again." She handed Jordan a card and touched her lightly on the arm. "I am always available if you should have more questions you need answered." Her smile turned serious. "And not just about affairs of the heart. Your life holds many challenges at this moment."

Chapter Fifty-Four

Jordan awakened to the delicious feeling of the sun streaming through her bedroom window, the rays warm against her face. Or perhaps it was the quiet chatter of people meandering down the lane to begin the rituals of their day. Whatever had awakened her, she was ready to shower, dress, and join whoever might be in the square for coffee.

As overwhelmed as she had felt the day before, for some reason—perhaps her meeting with Arabella—she felt lighter, more alive today. She still smarted when she thought of Ash's betrayal. At the same time, she missed him, but at least now she knew the truth. With each new answer she was able to provide Quinn for the police investigation, a little of the burden she'd been carrying alone was lifted from her shoulders. Simon had his contact in the Carabinieri searching for any signs of her father, and although they had made little progress, he kept her in the loop on a regular basis. With nothing else she could do at the moment, she had a brand-new day ahead of her and she intended to make the most of it.

Dressed in white shorts and a black tee shirt,

Jordan stepped into the inner courtyard, and locked the door of the apartment behind her. Spying the family of turtles outside the owner's vacant apartment adjoined to hers, she tilted a container of food into her hand and threw a few pinches into their tank. As usual, the big shy one stayed behind its rock, but the little ones surfaced quickly, each nibbling furiously at their breakfast. Things were far from perfect, but today, she was determined, would be good.

The solid metal door that led from the inner courtyard onto the lane was the original gate from 1720 when the apartment building had been a palace for one of the privileged families of Tropea. Though rusted, the bolt turned easily in her hand as she pushed open the outer door to the street. But something on the other side blocked it from opening all the way. She leaned her shoulder in and pushed harder. The damned garbage workers, Jordan thought, they must have left the bins in front of the gate again. But they should be empty, so why was she having such difficulty? With one final push, she managed to open the gate wide enough to stick her head through the gap and look out onto the street.

A scream lodged in her throat. The bloodied face and body of a man was splayed across the dew-covered cobblestones. Before she could get her wits about her, the gate was ripped from her hand and someone bolted in through the opening, taking her with him. The gate slammed shut, and a meaty hand covered her mouth as she literally was swept off her feet and dragged back toward her apartment door. With all her might, Jordan kicked and clawed at her captor's face, but against his strength it had no effect except to further enrage him.

"Where is the key?" he growled. "Open it!"

Heart pounding, she tried to reply. But with his hand over her mouth, only a muffled sound came out.

"Give me the key," he commanded as he loosened his grip. "I swear to god, if you scream, it will be the last breath you take."

With numb fingers, Jordan fished frantically in her small, cross-body purse. She felt the cold metal of her apartment keys and pulled them from the bag. If only she had the can of pepper spray she always carried in her purse in Vancouver.

"Open it," he ordered, covering her mouth again.

Her hands shook so badly she couldn't get the key into the lock. His other massive fist grabbed hers, pushed it in, and turned it until it clicked. He dragged her roughly across the threshold, kicking the door closed behind them. Once inside, he threw her onto a chair where for the first time, she saw his face. Her eyes widened. The pulse thundered in her ears. She was looking into the icy steel gray eyes of Salvatore Castellano.

Tied to the kitchen chair, she sat rigidly upright, watching him circle her like a vulture, shouting a string of profanities. She closed her eyes and prayed, trying hard to focus on the meditation she'd used in the bunker. *Breathing in, I know I'm breathing in. Breathing out, I know I'm breathing out.* How many hundred times had she chanted the mantra silently to herself?

"Open your eyes," he demanded. "I want you to see exactly what I'm going to do to you. Just like I had to watch Constantine burn. Only your death is going to be *much* slower." He wiped some spittle from his bottom lip. "I should have killed you when I had the chance."

Jordan's stomach lurched, and she gulped for air. "Why are you doing this? I wasn't responsible for Constantine's death. The sharpshooters closed in on him and *he* was the one who started the barn fire. I was just another of his victims, like my parents. *Please*," she heard herself beg.

"It was *your* father who betrayed Constantine. And Constantine's own son, Giancarlo Vicente, who tipped off the Carabinieri's shooters. He traded your life for his father's. You will both pay for this. First you, then once I find him, Vicente. B*astardo*."

Giancarlo is still alive! Riveted, she watched as Castellano rounded the kitchen counter and yanked out each drawer in succession. What was he looking for?

He grabbed something out of the drawer by the stove. A box of matches. Then he fetched the backpack he'd dropped inside the door. From it he pulled out what looked like a wad of long, thick string and slowly, methodically, laid it out on the floor. Jordan's nose prickled as she detected the smell of gasoline.

Dear god! He was making a wick.

When he finished unraveling the string, he tied one end to the heavy, gas stove burner cover. Next, he slowly fed the line down the stove and across the floor. The end of his homemade wick he tied around Jordan's ankle, his hands sliding up her bare leg. She shuddered and closed her eyes as he turned back toward the kitchen. He was going to switch on the stove and run. *This place will go up like an inferno and I'll be...*

Suddenly, there was an almighty crash. She leapt from her chair, which toppled over taking her with it. She screamed as several uniformed men exploded through the apartment's front door.

"*Non muoverti o ti sparo!* Don't move or we will shoot!" one of them shouted.

Castellano's back was to the police. Jordan saw the almost imperceptible turn of his wrist. She held her breath as she waited for the click. And the flames that would soon snake menacingly across the floor toward her. But the click didn't come. Instead, in the nanosecond of a heartbeat, he reached into his breast pocket, pulled out a gun, and spun to face the sharpshooters.

A series of shots rang out. Jordan screamed, and still lying on her side attached to the chair, tried to roll out of the way. She watched aghast as the bullets found their target and catapulted Castellano off his feet and into the air. He landed heavily on the kitchen floor with a sickening thud. Heavily armed officers instantly spread out and Simon emerged from behind their protective shield.

"How? How did you..." she tried to ask, but her voice failed her.

"Never mind that now. I'll explain it all to you later." Simon righted the chair and quickly untied her hands and feet. "For now, let's just get you out of here, shall we?"

As vehemently as Simon insisted, Jordan stubbornly

refused to go to the hospital for observation. Two hospital stays in recent months were more than enough, thank you very much. He finally had no choice but to acquiesce.

"But I still don't understand how you knew Castellano had me. And how in the world did you get into my apartment?"

"Someone called in a tip that there was a man lying dead on the road in front of your gate."

Had a neighbor heard her scream? "Who?"

He shook his head. "The voice was distorted but our sound people said it was definitely a woman. We called the officer on duty outside your apartment and when he didn't answer I dispatched my team immediately. We still lost an officer but thank god for whoever called it in."

"I know. I'm so sorry Simon." Jordan shook her head. "I feel responsible."

"Not your fault, love. I'm just glad we didn't lose you too. If we'd gained access a split second later, Castellano would have set the whole place on fire."

"But how did you get in?"

He leaned in so only she could hear. "This isn't for public consumption," he said, "but after what my men went through to rescue you the last time, I acquired a key to your outside gate."

Hey eyes widened. "Let's just keep that as our little secret." He winked, then turned serious. "Jordan, it's over. Castellano is dead."

"My parents. Any word?" She desperately wanted to ask about Giancarlo.

"Why don't we take that one step at a time?" he replied. "Perhaps, now that we've got Castellano and

I don't have your safety to worry about I can push the Sicilian police a bit harder." A glimmer of a smile lit up his face again.

Was it all in Jordan's imagination or was he wistful and stalling for time? "That sounds like a plan," she replied. Maybe she could use the time to find Giancarlo, she thought guiltily.

Chapter Fifty-Five

As much as Jordan was nervous about venturing outside her apartment again, she knew if she didn't, she would be giving in to her fears, which is exactly what the likes of Castellano would have wanted. But he was dead and no longer a threat. So, she locked her apartment door behind her and headed across the inner courtyard. As soon as she pulled open the gate she was startled to see the young woman who had read her Tarot cards at Capo Vaticano. "Arabella. What are you doing here?"

Arabella's eyes darted up and down the laneway, then she put her hand lightly on Jordan's arm. "I don't want to alarm you, but I must speak with you."

Instantly, Jordan's hackles went up. "How did you know where I lived?" Fear registered on the woman's face.

"I can explain. Please, just give me a chance." She looked furtively in both directions again. "Could we perhaps go inside?"

"No, we cannot go inside." When she told Simon about her time with Arabella, he'd warned her about the gypsies who were always coming into town to beg, and sometimes steal from tourists. She pulled her cell phone from her pocket. "If you don't leave this instant, I'm calling the police."

Arabella stepped back as if she'd been slapped. "When you left the cape after I read your cards that day, a woman came up to me and started asking questions about you."

"What kind of questions?" Jordan slammed the iron gate behind her, forcing Arabella off the step and into the road.

"She said she thought you looked familiar and she wondered if she might know you. She asked if I knew your name and where you lived."

"What did you tell her?" Jordan started down the street away from the apartment. Arabella hurried to keep up.

"Why, the truth of course. That we had just met and I didn't know anything about you."

Jordan stopped in the cobblestone street and turned to look at the woman. "So how *did* you find out where I lived? Arabella, I don't know what you are up to, but I can assure you I will report you to the police if you come here again."

"I sometimes do readings at the place around the corner and I saw her again. I didn't think she recognized me, so I followed her out of the café. She was looking at the names on the doorbell outside your gate. I followed her several times. The last time, she was standing in the entrance of the building across the road from your apartment. As if she were waiting for you to come out."

"When was this?"

"Yesterday. She was about to cross the road to your building, but a man came along and stopped at your gate. The woman disappeared into the other building. When she didn't come out I left."

Jordan's skin tingled. Whoever this woman who Arabella had seen had been outside her apartment just before Jordan opened her gate and Castellano attacked her. "What did this woman look like?"

"She was very pretty, and tall, like you. Dark hair. She was tanned, so she must not have been from around here. We have not had that much sun yet."

Tall and tanned. "Arabella, I need you to tell this to the police." Jordan started to dial Simon's number on her mobile.

An expression of terror crossed the young woman's face. "Please, no police."

Jordan shook her head, frustrated. "You haven't done anything wrong. I'm sorry I treated you so badly a few minutes ago, but I need you to give this information to the police. It's very—"

But before she could finish, Arabella stammered something of an apology, bolted across the square, and disappeared.

Damn!

Chapter Fifty-Six

Jordan was at her usual table in Cannon Square, wishing Giancarlo were with her as the sun was about to make its final descent. Just as the waiter strode toward her with a glass of white wine, the sun disappeared into the sea, and darkness dropped like a shroud over Tropea. But it was only temporary. With so many people out enjoying the remnants of another stunningly beautiful day, lights soon came on all around town. The majestic Santa Maria dell'Isola monastery, which stood 800 meters across the water from where she sat, was bathed in a warm amber glow. As she sipped her wine and reveled in the astounding beauty of her surroundings, part of her was grateful to be alone. The other part thought back to the picnic she and Simon had shared at the top of the monastery. She was confused about her feelings for Giancarlo versus what she felt for Simon. One of them was here, and she suspected, was totally available to her. The other left a void in her heart when he simply disappeared from her life. *Why, Giancarlo? What couldn't you tell me?*

As she considered her conflicted feelings,

something in her peripheral vision caught her attention. At first, she thought it was her imagination playing tricks on her. No, it couldn't have been. A light blinked at the top of the monastery. It blinked twice more, paused, and blinked once. Positive it was Giancarlo using their secret signal, she left her wine on the table and raced down the hundred steps to the base of the monastery below the square. Tearing across the gravel parking lot, she reached the bottom of the steps where she squeezed her way between the iron posts of the closed security gate.

"Giancarlo?" Out of breath, Jordan called out as she made it to the top. "Are you here?" But no reply came from the void beyond. She moved from the highest elevation near the front of the monastery and backtracked down the last few stairs she'd just ascended. It was eerily quiet as she approached the area between the two wooden doors she and Simon had laughed about following their picnic. When a figure emerged from the shadows she thought her heart would burst from her chest.

"Not who you were expecting, is it, Jordan?" asked a female voice. "Too bad you'll never see your precious Giancarlo again. I guess your little romance just wasn't meant to be. He was too good for you, anyway." A woman, roughly Jordan's height and build, held a flashlight upwards, illuminating her own face, giving it a ghoulish incandescence against the dark backdrop of the night sky. Jordan's heart pounded as she wracked her brain, trying to recall where she'd seen the face that sneered at her so contemptuously. Then it hit her. It was the woman who had been with Castellano at the café in

Taormina. The attractive tanned brunette in the white linen dress. This woman had lured her here, making her think it was Giancarlo signaling with a flashlight. But how could she have known about their unique way of letting each other know to meet at the top of the cliff? *Oh my god.* Jordan's stomach lurched. The only person she'd told was Simon.

Simon! Why?

"I've been waiting for this moment for a very long time, Jordan." The woman's husky voice jolted her back to the present. "We were so close on that island, you and me. We could have had a drink together, just the two of us talking about our dysfunctional little families. Of course, I wasn't staying in the fancy house you call a cabin. No, I was in a shitty little lean-to. Watching. And waiting. Too bad your P.I. friend interrupted my plans. Now it's come to this."

Jordan felt the blood drain from her face. "I don't even know you," she stammered. "I've never seen you before that day in Taormina."

With the flash of her hand, the woman reached up and ripped off an auburn wig. Underneath, her blond hair was plastered to her head. The face turned grotesque, its charcoal eyes and tight grimace contorted with rage. The voice rose an octave, tight and shrill. "Now do you know who I am?" she screamed. "You've passed me dozens of times, but you never gave me a moment's notice," she hissed. "No, not you, a spoiled rich girl with everything given to her. Everything that should have been mine."

With stunned disbelief, Jordan recognized Callie, the waitress from the restaurant beneath their office.

Her rants and accusations ricocheted around in Jordan's brain, only to land in a jumbled mess. As confused as she was, the thought that this maniac could have been stalking her on Annabelle Island was overshadowed by a sudden surge of adrenaline that coursed through her body. While she desperately wanted to turn and run down the stairs, there was no way she was going to turn her back on this deranged creature. She was mentally calculating what it would take to overpower her when she heard a click. She had heard that sound before. Then she saw a glint of light reflect off something shiny. Instantly, she knew: it was her attacker on the seawall.

In one quick motion, the woman raised her hand. In it she held a knife.

"And that doddering old fool, Ash Courtland. He knew your mother had an affair with *my* father!" She made a figure eight in the dark with the blade and took a step forward. "She was pregnant with me and when the great Gavin Stone found out, he tried to force her into having an abortion."

"You're insane," Jordan shouted. "My mother couldn't have children of her own, and my father would never have done that."

"She could, and he did," she spat. "But Ash wouldn't let her have an abortion. He must have had a spine back then," she snickered. "So, she had me and Ash brokered a private adoption. Then along *you* came two years later. But you, *you* were good enough to keep and she didn't even give birth to you," she hissed, taking another menacing step closer. "She could have kept me, her own flesh and blood. But instead, she gave me away like an unwanted toy."

Jordan tried furiously to piece it all together, but nothing made sense. Her father had entrusted Ash with her trust account when he and Kathryn went into the Witness Protection Program. Why would he be loyal to a man who knew his first wife had had an affair? Logic aside, it didn't change the fact that Jordan was facing down a lunatic with a knife.

"Would you like to know what my life was like while you were living in Canada like a princess?" She stabbed the knife in the air between them as if to punctuate her question. Jordan jumped back.

"Well I'm going to tell you—thanks to Ash Courtland, I was adopted by a thug and his twenty-year-old plaything wife," she sneered. "Only I was the consolation prize because she couldn't have a kid of her own. When she left us, he didn't know what to do with me, so the bastard would lock me in a closet for days at a time. Just like you were, in that bunker." She took a step forward, holding the knife inches from Jordan's face. "He told me every day what a worthless piece of garbage I was—that my mother should have aborted me. *Your* mother!" Her eyes turned wild. "The useless piece of shit who adopted me. Salvatore Castellano."

Castellano was Callie's father! Jordan felt the force of the woman's breath as her rant escalated.

"I should have let him kill you when he had the chance. Now, that honor belongs to *me*. My call to the police is the only reason you're still alive."

Without turning her head, Jordan's eyes darted from side to side as again, she considered her options. But from the narrow ledge of the stone steps where they stood, there was no escape. To one side were two wooden doors she knew from her visit with Simon were locked. To the other, was a sheer drop to the black expanse of the Aegean Sea below. In mere seconds, she knew she would face the third and most terrifying option.

The quiet dark of night suddenly crackled with a series of flashes. It sounded like multiple camera lights all being switched on at once. Circles of white-blue light flooded the ground around them. Startled, her attacker squinted away from the glare, looking over Jordan's shoulder toward the mainland two hundred feet above. Forgetting about the knife, Jordan half-turned to see what she was looking at. Behind her, the area of Canon Square was lit up like a Christmas scene, illuminated by floodlights and the flashing lights of police vehicles. Over the quiet lapping of the waves below, they heard a man shout from a megaphone. "You are surrounded. Both of you, put your hands in the air and walk down the steps. First one, then the other."

Neither woman moved.

A crowd had gathered in the square. Onlookers froze, speaking in hushed tones as they watched the two figures teeter on the side of the cliff. A sniper crouched beside Simon, his assault rifle aimed at the monastery. "Which one do you want me to take out?" he asked quietly.

"I don't know," Simon hissed through clenched teeth. Even with high-powered military binoculars, he couldn't distinguish which one of the two on the cliff was Jordan. He could tell the other was a woman, but they were both about the same size and build.

Where the hell was the sniper's spotter? This wasn't his area of expertise, but he couldn't risk waiting. His phone rang. "What!" he shouted into his earpiece. It was Quinn, who instantly had Simon's attention. He listened carefully, acutely aware of the tension emanating from the taut body of the shooter beside him. "Okay, stay on the line with me in case I need more information," he commanded Quinn.

He picked up the megaphone. "Jordan," he yelled, "open the wooden door and run! Get into the tunnel." His words echoed off the limestone cliff. "It's tight, you'll have to crawl on your hands and knees, but you can do it." He took a deep breath and yelled as loud as he could. "You can do this, Jordan! Do you hear me?"

Time seemed to stand still. One of the women moved forward, only to hesitate and back away from the entrance to the tunnel. The other grabbed for the door closest to her as if she were going to open it.

"The one on the left," Simon whispered to the sniper."

"Are you sure? How do you know?"

"Just fucking—"

The crowd collectively gasped, then watched fixated, as one of the women plunged over the cliff and hurtled two hundred feet down to the black abyss of the sea below.

Jordan's legs had turned to jelly. She could see the line of police cars snaking their way down the sharp switchbacks of the hill leading to the monastery, but she could only lean weakly against the side of the cliff, her thoughts suspended in disbelief. As the circulation slowly returned to her limbs she squinted into the glare of the floodlights still emanating from Canon Square. As she allowed the tears to come, she wondered if she would ever sit there again, her glass raised to Giancarlo's, toasting the end of a spectacular day as the sun dipped magically into the sea.

This time, there was no discussion about going to the hospital. While she was physically drained, Jordan felt mentally stronger than she had in months. Flummoxed, paramedics stood beside one of the ambulances that idled at the foot of the monastery, their vehicle empty. Simon just shrugged. She later learned he had dispatched two emergency vehicles, so she wouldn't have to be transported with her attacker. Now, as she adamantly refused to go to the hospital, it occurred to her there probably would be no need for the second medical van. Instead, it would be rescue boats navigating the rocks below. It could be days, if ever, before searchers would find the body of the woman who had flown past her and hurtled off the cliff.

With the rush of adrenalin finally winding down, Jordan's eyes felt like lead. She could fight the overwhelming sense of fatigue no longer. As Simon put his jacket around her shoulders and led her to his car, she pushed aside the question she dare not ask. That, and others, would just have to wait.

Chapter Fifty-Seven

How do you ask a man who is responsible for saving your life, how he could have betrayed you? All night, the question had been weighing heavily, like an elephant sitting on her chest.

Jordan made coffee. Simon was bringing pastry from the bakery down the road from her apartment. She paced. She second-guessed herself. She even considered whether it was something she really needed to know.

Now, as they sat across from each other, having breakfast in her sun-filled living room, she took such a deep breath she thought her chest might explode. She was still praying there was some other explanation.

"Simon, how did you know I was at the monastery?"

To her surprise, he didn't hesitate. He didn't even look alarmed. "Why, Sebastian, of course." Sebastian was the owner of the Ristorante Al Cannone, the sunset bar. He was also a close friend of Giancarlo's.

"If it wasn't for Sebastian, we would never have known you'd run out of the bar last night and gone up there."

"He told you?"

Simon met her eyes. "Jordan, what are you saying? Sebastian called me because he knew it couldn't have been Giancarlo on the cliff. He had just spoken to him, and he was in Rome. He was concerned for your safety."

As Jordan poured them both more coffee, she could only hope Simon hadn't realized the true meaning behind her question. She leaned forward on the couch while he propped extra pillows behind her. "How did you know which one of us to shoot?" No use wasting time on small talk, she thought. "You couldn't tell which one was me on the cliff, even with the binoculars."

He took his time before he answered. "The truth is, I didn't."

"Then how? Please don't tell me my fate was left to a lucky guess."

"Thankfully not," Simon said wryly. "It was Quinn."

She raised herself off the cushion. "Quinn? Please tell me he's not here in Tropea."

"No, but it was Quinn who figured it out."

"What, that this woman was stalking me?" Jordan puzzled. "But how would he have known who else was on the cliff that night?"

"Thankfully," Simon replied, "her psychologist broke doctor-patient privilege by reporting her to the police. Of course, Quinn got involved and she was able to relay one critical detail to him about her treatment of Callie."

"And that was?" Jordan fixed Simon with an

expectant look, at the same time not sure she wanted to hear the answer.

"That Callie Rousseau was severely claustrophobic. Apparently, it was so debilitating she couldn't even get into an elevator." Simon shook his head, his lips set in a tight line. "But I couldn't be sure, after what you'd gone through in that bunker, that *you* weren't as well."

"Claustrophobic?"

"Well yes. I know I would have been." Their eyes met and neither spoke for a few seconds. "Anyway, it was still a huge gamble, but under the circumstances we didn't have much of a choice."

"But you knew the door to the tunnel was locked. Both were. Why did you shout for me to open it and go in?"

Simon's eyes bored into hers. "Because Quinn believed in you." His voice was barely audible. "When he called me, he insisted you had the mettle to go into that tunnel. And Callie didn't. All I needed to see was which one of you would go for the door."

Jordan's throat ached as she tried to suppress her tears.

"So, after shouting to me through the megaphone and seeing one of us move to open the door, you told the sniper which one to shoot. I would like to thank him. Your officer who shot her before she came at me with that knife."

Simon's eyes held hers. For a moment, it was as if neither of them breathed.

He knew.

Chapter Fifty-Eight

Simon moved the vase of flowers he'd brought, from the kitchen table to the windowsill of the living room where she could see them. He went back into the kitchen to unpack some fresh food he'd picked up at the market.

"They're beautiful, thank you," she called out.

"I thought you could use something colorful to cheer you up."

"You're sweet, but you don't need to do all this fussing over me. It's time I started going out to do my own shopping. I feel well. I think I've fully recovered."

"Excellent," he conceded. "But it doesn't mean you're all right. Besides, I like fussing over you."

She hesitated to ask. "Simon, when can I go back to Vancouver?" Was it her imagination or did he look crestfallen?

"What's the hurry? Do you have something you need to do?"

"Nothing major. I'd just like to get my parents out of witness protection, and get on with the rest of my life, that's all." As soon as the words left her lips, she felt bad. "I'm sorry, I didn't mean to be sarcastic. I'm so grateful for everything you've done for me. Most especially for saving my life."

"No apologies needed." Simon's smile momentarily faded. "And no thanks, either. But could I ask you to stay here just a few days longer, until everything is cleared up in Vancouver?"

"I guess," she nodded. "But what is there to clear up? The police have confirmed that Castellano was behind my abduction. He most certainly hired the guy who kept me captive. Thank god they finally have him in custody." Jordan shivered as she thought of the revolting creature with thin, greasy hair. A complete nobody; just a perverted leach on society who happened to be in the right place at the right time.

Simon told her that before Callie and Castellano started competing for who could get to her first, Callie had hired this creep to "babysit" her until she could figure out her next move. That hadn't ended well. He was also likely behind her informant's disappearance. She wondered whatever had happened to poor Mickey after he'd been used to lure her out to the valley that night. With the myriad of equally dreadful possibilities, she pulled the blanket Simon had covered her with a little higher.

"Castellano told me," Jordan said to Simon, "while he held me captive in my apartment, that he had blackmailed both Ash and me. Quinn said it's likely he was Ash's killer. They're just awaiting the results of DNA tests, which should be in any day now."

It was surreal, how detached she felt. It was as if she had tied everything up into a neat little package.

Got the animal who held her prisoner in an underground bunker for two weeks: check. Killed the gangster who blackmailed and subsequently tried to kill her: check. Watched as her deranged stalker hurtled off a cliff before she plunged a knife into her prey's heart: check.

But something about Simon's expression made her pause her mental checklist. He caught her watching him and turned away, ostensibly to rearrange the flowers.

"What?" she asked to his back. "What aren't you telling me? It's about Ash's murder, isn't it?"

"You must be getting tired." He turned around. "Why don't we talk about this tomorrow?"

Now she knew for sure he was evading her question. She reached out and clasped his wrist. "Please, Simon, don't do this. After what I've been through, I deserve to know everything."

He nodded and pulled up a chair beside her, studying her intently. "You're going to hear this sooner or later, so I may as well tell you." He reached over to take Jordan's hand. "The therapist who reported Callie to the authorities?"

"Yes."

He took a deep breath. "There's no easy way to tell you this. It was Dr. Danforth."

Her heart lurched, and she snatched her hand from Simon's. "*Dr. Danforth?*"

"When she came out of surgery she was able to tell the authorities who attacked her. She had been treating the woman who was stalking you at the same time as you were seeing her. That's how we figured out who was threatening you up at the monastery."

"Simon, that woman was deranged. Delusional. She tried to tell me Cynthia Stone, my adoptive mother, had an affair with Castellano, and Ash arranged for him to adopt her. It's ridiculous. She is…*was* a lunatic."

This time he didn't look away and locked eyes with hers. "That is all true," he said barely above a whisper. "What she told you, not the delusional part, although some may beg to differ."

He might as well have slammed a two by four into her midsection. "You can't be serious." *Will this ever be over?*

"I'm afraid I am." He took both of her hands in his. She tried to pull them away, but he held on tight. "I had hoped to wait a few days before telling you all this." The smile was gone for good now, and his brows knitted together in a deep furrow. "Although the woman who was stalking you went by the name of Callie Rousseau, she used several surnames but as you now know, her legal one was Castellano.

"She was telling the truth when she told you she was adopted. But it was Vittorio Constantine who brokered the private adoption for his key foot soldier, Salvatore Castellano and his-then wife. As you well know, there were no limits to the power Constantine wielded back then."

Simon paused, searching Jordan's face, presumably wondering how she was handling these revelations. She felt sick. "Go on," she commanded.

"Like her father, Callie set out to weave her way into every aspect of your life. In fact, she and Castellano ended up in competition for who would get you first. She had been stalking you for at least a year, maybe longer. Then, she started seeing your therapist, Dr. Danforth."

Jordan's hand went to her chest.

"I know," Simon nodded. "I'm sorry. Would you like a drink of water?" he asked as he rose from the chair.

"No, tell me the rest."

He sighed, then sat down and resumed his story. "Apparently, Callie had been Dr. Danforth's patient since shortly after your rescue. She was being treated for something called intermittent explosive disorder, as well as severe claustrophobia. Presumably, she suffered the latter from being beaten repeatedly and locked in dark closets by Castellano. Before Dr. Danforth was attacked, she started to connect the dots and realized that it was *you* who Callie was obsessed with. Her counseling sessions were starting to mirror things that you had confided in your therapy."

Upon noticing Jordan's reaction, he put his hands in a gesture of surrender. "No, your therapist didn't divulge anything of your discussions to us, nor anyone else that I'm aware of."

Jordan quashed a sigh of relief, but inside her muddled brain she desperately tried to put the timeline together. How many weeks ago had she seen Castellano and this Rousseau woman at the café in Taormina? That would mean she would have had to go to Vancouver, attack Dr. Danforth and then return to Italy. It seemed far-fetched, and she told Simon so.

"It was definitely her," he said of the therapist's would-be killer.

"How can they be so sure? You said someone saw a woman fleeing the doctor's office. It could have been someone other than Callie."

Simon seemed to consider that for a moment. "Jordan, was Dr. Danforth in the habit of putting a sticky note on your file after your session was over?"

She gasped. How could he have known that? "Yes, why?"

"She must have done that with all her patients. She didn't have Callie's file on her desk the day of the attack. Callie must have just dropped in without an appointment. But Dr. Danforth did make notes, so she must have had a session with her. In any event, she had written *Must warn Jordan* on the note she put in her out basket."

"So, Dr. Danforth knew *then*," Jordan said.

"Yes, and Callie knew she knew. On that sticky note, over top of Danforth's scribble, and in the doctor's own blood, Callie wrote, *Too late, bitch!*

Jordan suddenly felt light-headed and chilled to the bone. Simon tucked the blanket around and under her feet. "How's that, better?"

"Thank you. But that's still circumstantial, isn't it? That Callie stabbed her, I mean."

"It might have been," Simon agreed. "However, while testing the DNA from the considerable amount of blood at the scene of your therapist's attack, they got a hit on another unsolved murder."

"She'd killed before?" It took so long for Simon to answer that she thought perhaps he hadn't heard her.

"Ashton Courtland," he said, barely above a whisper.

"Oh god, I thought Castellano killed him."

"We did too," Simon nodded. "But Ash must

have put up quite a fight. Besides his blood at the scene, there was another donor. Callie had drunk from a water glass in Dr. Danforth's office, from which they lifted both prints and saliva. Saliva doesn't always provide a reliable comparison with blood, especially if it's been degraded with age. However, as bright as Callie was, she made a very simple mistake by drinking water in her impromptu session, then leaving the bottle behind. Forensics was able to match the DNA from both crime scenes."

"Don't you think that's odd, given how devious she was?" Jordan asked.

Simon rubbed the stubble of his two-day beard. "That's the beauty of my business. It's usually the small things criminals do that provide us the biggest results."

"So that's it, then." Jordan shuddered. "Callie Rousseau, a.k.a Castellano definitely killed Ash. It still gives me the creeps to think she was on Annabelle Island. Just the two of us."

Silently, she thanked Quinn for dropping in unexpectedly and being such a pain in the ass that day.

Chapter Fifty-Nine

Simon insisted on making Jordan something before he left. She sensed he wanted to stay, but after she'd forced down some scalding hot tea, she graciously bid him goodbye at the door. "I'm so grateful to you, Simon." She gave him a hug. "I really am, but I just need to be alone with my thoughts. Then I think I'm going to sleep all day. You were right, I *am* exhausted."

He returned the embrace, perhaps hanging on a few seconds too long. "I understand completely. But call me if you should need anything. *Anything*," he emphasized. "I'll call you tonight just to check up on you."

Jordan wondered if she should have invited him to stay. Even though the central heat was on, the living room felt cold and inhospitable. She couldn't look at the kitchen without seeing Castellano laying out his homemade wick that nearly led to her incineration.

She jumped when her cell phone rang. Maybe Simon had had second thoughts as well. But it was

Quinn. A quick glance at the clock told her it was midnight Vancouver time.

"Quinn?"

"Hey, how are you doing? I called Simon first, expecting you'd be in the hospital, but he said he'd just left your place."

"I'm okay," she lied. "What are you doing up so late?" With some sadness, it dawned on her that she really had no idea what Quinn's nocturnal habits were. Or any others for that matter. She knew little about his personal life other than the tragedy of losing his wife and young son. She made a vow to remedy that when she returned home.

"What time *is* it?" Quinn sounded distracted. She could imagine him squinting, trying to read his watch because he stubbornly refused to give in to reading glasses.

She told him it was early morning and assured him he wasn't keeping her from resting. "I'm grateful for the distraction actually. Simon said you're a hundred percent certain that Callie murdered Ash. I still can't believe she tried to kill Dr. Danforth as well. And very nearly succeeded. How is she doing, by the way?"

Quinn told her the therapist had a long way to go but the doctors were pleased with her progress. He answered a few more of Jordan's questions, but seemed in a rush to get the small talk over with, and she found herself wondering about the real reason for his call.

"Simon told me everything you've found out about Callie. I can't believe what Castellano subjected her to as a child. I can't feel sorry for her, but it's no wonder she had mental problems." She felt a little disingenuous, as she herself had been seeing Dr. Danforth for post-traumatic stress issues following her abduction. "I can't understand what possessed Ash to get tangled up with her in the first place. I feel so stupid that I never saw any of this coming."

"That's actually why I'm calling. Not about you being stupid," he quickly added. "But, I thought you might like some *good* news for a change. Two things actually."

Jordan couldn't imagine what good news could possibly have come out of all this grief, but skeptically told Quinn, "Bring it on."

"Okay. First, your blackmail situation. Remember those photos that you received before you left Vancouver?"

How could she forget? "Oh, god, Quinn, do we have to go there now? Really?"

He jumped in immediately. "It wasn't you, Jordan. In those pictures. Callie Rousseau orchestrated the entire thing. Seems she was pretty adept with video equipment, not to mention other things."

"Jesus, Quinn, can you just get to the point?" The thought of those photos made her want to vomit.

"She videotaped herself in that hotel in Seattle. In a suite exactly like the one you stayed in."

"She *what?* With whom? She didn't do what I saw in those photos by herself, Quinn." She'd prayed he hadn't seen them, at the same time knowing that was highly unlikely.

"Turns out it was some bar-hopping schmuck she'd picked up in the lounge the night she was there stalking you. He thought he'd hit the jackpot until she threatened him with a knife if he didn't make himself scarce right after their little fling. With you staying in a suite just down the hall, she apparently had more important things on her mind than to give her latest mark breakfast in bed."

That's why the images were so grainy. So that Jordan wouldn't realize the photos weren't of her. She'd just assumed the worst, when she saw the background and recognized the suite.

The safety latch on the door that she had forgotten to engage. Should she mention the awful hangover? "Please tell me she wasn't in my room, Quinn."

"That I can guarantee. If she was, we would not be having this conversation, kiddo. You wouldn't be here to tell the tale, if you know what I mean."

"Oh."

"Having said that, you're still damned lucky. They found a substantial amount of Rohypnol among her possessions."

"The date rape drug?" She had written a four-part series on it, years ago.

"One and the same. She was in the bar at the same time you were. At any time, could you have left your drink alone?"

Oh my god, she had gone to the bathroom while still on her first glass of wine!

After answering Quinn's final questions about the night in Seattle and feeling somewhat relieved that she hadn't passed out and engaged in God knows what, Jordan asked what the second part of Quinn's news was.

"You said you had more information about Callie. No offense, but I think Simon already beat you to it. He was here and explained everything to me just before you called."

"What Simon told you was based on old information." Instead of gloating, Jordan heard Quinn suck in his breath and then exhale loudly. She wondered if he was smoking again. "Callie definitely murdered Courtland and attacked the doctor. But what Simon told you about her motive—that your mother had an affair with Castellano and Ash knew about it—isn't true. Additional lab results have just come in. I hope you're sitting down. As I recall you saying to me recently, this is going to take a while."

It was a lot to digest as Quinn filled her in on the additional tests the Integrated Homicide Unit had done from the scene of Ash's murder. With her knowledge of criminal investigations, she was familiar with some of what he explained. The last piece, however, was completely beyond her comprehension and she asked him to dumb it down for her. "Just get to the point, J.J.," she pleaded. "What does this all have to do with Callie Rousseau and Uncle Ash?"

After a pared-down version of advanced DNA, specifically blood analysis, Quinn finally made his point. "Castellano couldn't have been her father, Jordan. Simon's forensics team ran his blood type after they shot him. And Cynthia Stone isn't her mother, either. None of what Callie told you is true except that she was adopted by Castellano."

"How can you be so sure?"

"Because Callie's blood type was AB negative. Quite rare, actually. Only one percent of Caucasians have that type. She would have had a difficult time finding a blood donor if she ever needed one."

As if anyone should care, Jordan thought.

"But here's the kicker. We got your mother's— Sorry, Cynthia Stone's blood type from her prison records." Jordan detected another long inhale on the other end of the telephone.

"There's not a snowball's chance in hell that those two could have produced a child with AB blood. Setting aside the rarity of Callie being AB negative, it's genetically impossible."

The sudden revelation that Ash had been murdered for nothing, hit her like a sledgehammer. That lunatic set out to take everything from her: money, her freedom, and then Ash. And almost Dr. Danforth. *All for nothing.* The dam broke, and tears coursed down her face. "I want to come home, J.J. I *need* to come home."

Quinn didn't say anything, but she knew he was still on the line, this time patiently waiting.

She took in a ragged breath and held her hand to her chest. "I *hurt*," she said with a strangled sob.

"I know you do," he said quietly.

"Even though I know what Uncle Ash did was despicable, it ripped my heart out when he was murdered. For nothing. And it was all because of me."

"No, not because of you, Jordan."

"This grief is overwhelming, J.J. I don't think I will ever get over it."

"As difficult as it is to imagine now, you *will* eventually get over it. Or at least the pain will be a little less in time."

She wanted to ask him if it had lessened for him, if nothing else but for the perverse satisfaction of hearing him say "no." Some obtuse business guru the newspaper's department heads brought in once, had tried to teach journalists never to ask a question to which they already knew the answer. In all her years of investigative reporting, she vowed never to heed that advice. It was by asking the questions of both victims and criminals, from petty thieves to parents of children mutilated and killed by serial killers, that the most illuminating answers came. If she had assumed she knew their answers, she would never have been privy to the revelations that came out of their mouths.

"Has it gotten easier for you with Karyn and Tyler?" She held her breath.

There was a deathly hush on the other end of the line. Not only had she asked Quinn about his wife and child, but she'd referred to them by name.

She was berating herself for crossing the line when she heard him clear his throat. His words sounded tight, as if they were being squeezed from his throat against their will. "Always know in your heart that you are far bigger than anything that can happen to you, Jordan. It's the only thing that has saved me from diving into a hole and taking the hole in after me."

"I'm sorry, J.J. I...I just wanted someone else to feel my pain."

He let out a tortured sigh. "I do, kiddo. More than you know. Why don't you come home and maybe we can fight this one together? No, not *fight*," he corrected himself. "Unfortunately, we both belong to an exclusive club. One whose members have had people they love, murdered. We can't change what's happened, but we *can* have our hands at each other's backs. I know it's not much to offer but I always keep my promises."

Jordan wiped her eyes and exhaled. "I know you do, J.J. I know you do."

But, she couldn't leave Italy now. She still had one more thing to do. She rang off, then made her next call.

Chapter Sixty

Giancarlo Vicente parked his car and walked the few blocks to the restaurant. Furtively, he looked around, feeling strangely out of place after his self-imposed exile. He arrived about ten minutes to six, just in time to see Jordan walking into the square outside the restaurant. *Their* restaurant.

Weeks ago, word had reached him in Rome that she was in Tropea, but fearing for her safety, he had stayed away. Now actually seeing her, he thought his heart would leap from his chest. Unable to move, he remained across the street and watched as the proprietor, his old chum from childhood, seated her at their usual table by the railing, overlooking the majestic Santa Maria dell'Isola. It was hard to believe that just last night, a Carabinieri commander and his SWAT team had transformed their romantic spot into a police scene. He had watched it all unfolding on the news. Now, on this beautiful evening, there was nothing in the historic square but quiet conversations and the tinkle of laughter as patrons enjoyed the warm ambiance.

Having finally plucked up his courage, he was about to cross the road, when from the opposite direction he saw a blond-haired man, casually but impeccably dressed, stride confidently into the square. He shook hands with the proprietor, who pointed him toward Jordan's table. She was reading a menu and casually looked up to see who was standing in the last remnants of her sun. A megawatt smile, the one that had drawn him to her like a magnet, illuminated her face. He didn't need a photograph to tell him the man she was smiling at was Interpol agent, Simon Grenville.

Heart pounding and feeling like a voyeur watching from across the street, he wanted to run. But something kept him glued to the spot. He watched transfixed as Jordan put down the menu, stood up, and wrapped her arms around Grenville's neck. A smile broke across the man's face and he enveloped her in a long embrace while he tenderly stroked her hair. They fit together as if one was divinely created for the other.

He wasn't sure how long he had been standing there; it seemed like an eternity. After embracing, the couple sat down and gazed fondly at each other across the table. A waiter deposited a glass of wine in front of Grenville, who, without taking his eyes off Jordan's face, nodded his thanks.

Giancarlo looked out across the sparkling water that surrounded the monastery, the special place where she had stolen his heart almost a year ago to the day. Just in time, he thought. At the stroke of six, his last memory, as he turned and walked away, was of Jordan, and Simon Grenville toasting each other as the sun, like his heart, slipped silently into the sea.

Chapter Sixty-One

The sun had performed its dramatic flamenco curtsy, and Jordan sat at a candle-lit table as she had done so many times with Giancarlo. For reasons she couldn't surmise, just minutes before Simon arrived at Cannone Square, she realized the hole in her heart was less gaping. In its place was anticipation: the excitement of something new. She'd taken up that dance again. Now, it was Simon who held both her hands nestled in his and gazed into her eyes. Etta James' *At Last* played softly in the background. At the last minute, she'd changed from the red linen dress she'd thrown into her suitcase before leaving Vancouver. In its place, she wore black pants and a sleeveless green silk blouse, cut in at the shoulders.

"So, can we agree this is a real date?" Simon teased. His eyes crinkled at the corners. "You look beautiful. The emerald green brings out your eyes."

"Thank you. And yes, this is a real date," she assured him. "But I have something I need to tell you first." She paused, searching his eyes, hoping to find a lifeline. But she knew the answer lay within herself. If this relationship was to have any chance at a future it could only be if she was completely honest with him. And herself.

Despite the warm air, she felt a little shiver run down her spine.

Simon pursed his lips and nodded.

"I need to tell you this as Special Agent Grenville. Not as Simon, my date." Her voice broke and she worried her face might crumple at any moment. "It's about what happened that night up on the cliff. The night Callie Rousseau fell to her death."

He reached over and put his thumb gently on her lips. "We don't need to have this conversation, Jordan," he whispered. "It's over. Things turned out the way they should have."

She started to reply, but he shook his head. "It doesn't matter at whose hands. Either way, she'd be dead."

"You *knew*." Why hadn't she been interviewed, or even worse, arrested?

"Of course, I knew. But what's the difference whether she was killed by my sniper, or—"

"Or, because I pushed her," Jordan finished his sentence. She choked back tears. "My conscience." She took a ragged breath. "That's what makes the difference, Simon." A disobedient tear ran down her cheek. "I will have to live with what I did for the rest of my life. I'm not sure I can bear that."

He nodded sagely. For one agonizing moment, she thought he was going to accept her confession. Then he reached for her hand again. "That night, I wasn't sure I could bear the thought of not having you here with me."

"So, the end justifies the means?" she whispered.

"Men judge generally more by the eye than by the hand, for everyone can see and few can feel. Everyone sees what you appear to be, few really know what you are."

"Machiavelli," Jordan said. "Is my life, with all my flaws, more important than Callie Rousseau's?" Her eyes searched his. "There but for the grace of God, go I."

"...For that reason, let a prince have the credit of conquering and holding his state." Simon squeezed her hand. "Or a *princess*."

EPILOGUE

Two blocks away, Giancarlo stopped and leaned his head through the open window of the unmarked Carabinieri police car. "I have confirmed she's there," he said to the officer behind the wheel.

He looked at the anxious couple waiting in the back seat. "Your daughter, she is with Interpol Special Agent, Simon Grenville in the square. You must go to her now."

Gavin Stone looked stunned. "You're not coming with us?" Giancarlo saw him reach for his wife's hand. The couple looked tired, their faces strained. They looked older than when they'd entered witness protection only a year ago.

"Giancarlo, without you, none of this would be possible," Kathryn Stone said. "Jordan will want to see you. Please, you must come."

He leaned further into the car and forced a sad smile. "Without Agent Grenville, your daughter would not be alive. I betrayed her by vanishing. Even though it was for her own good, I do not wish to inflict that pain again." His voice broke and he looked away, embarrassed the officer could hear.

"I cannot risk her safety another time." His eyes pleaded with them both. "Please understand. I cannot."

"Will we see you again?" Kathryn asked. "Before we leave for Canada, I mean."

"It would be too hurtful." For him or for Jordan? he wondered. "It is your time to be together and to heal. Go now, be with your daughter."

"Thank you, Giancarlo, for everything you've done for us," Kathryn said.

Though she'd aged, he was struck by the lingering beauty she had passed on to her daughter. Knowing he would never see Jordan again, he tried to memorize every line and the curve of her mother's face. This moment would have to last him a lifetime.

"She never gave up hope that you were alive," he said. "It is my greatest honor to return you to her."

Wrestling with grief so bare and raw, he forced himself to turn and walk away, and to not look back.

Seconds later, the bomb went off.

More books coming soon.
You can sign up to be notified of new releases, giveaways and pre-release specials—plus, get a free book!

www.karendodd.com/free-book

If you loved the book and have a moment to spare, I would be so grateful if you would write a short review on the page where you bought the book. Your review helps spread the word about the Stone Suspense series and gets my books into new readers' hands. Thank you, in advance!

A WORD FROM KAREN

Thank you for reading SCARE AWAY THE DARK. If you enjoyed the story, and you'd like to follow the rest of Jordan's adventures, I'd recommend DEADLY SWITCH the *first* book in the Stone Suspense series.

From the gruesome discovery in an exclusive enclave of West Vancouver, British Columbia, DEADLY SWITCH takes you on a wild ride from Italy's Amalfi coast to the idyllic seaside town of Carmel, California. Gavin Stone's tormented daughter, Jordan searches frantically for her missing father, matching wits with devious criminals. With demons of her own to fight, she shouldn't care about proving him innocent of murder and embezzlement, but she does.

Murder…intrigue…a romance built on a house of cards: this thriller will satisfy your thirst for the adrenaline rush this intricately plotted story delivers. A delicious stay-up-all-nighter, DEADLY SWITCH stuns with its heart-pounding conclusion. You will not see it coming.

Here's what reviewers are saying about Karen Dodd's stunning debut thriller:

"A riveting read; engrossing, entertaining, and clever. Extremely satisfying!"

"I had to force myself to put it down!"

ABOUT THE AUTHOR

Karen Dodd is the author of the critically acclaimed debut thriller, DEADLY SWITCH as well as SCARE AWAY THE DARK, the second book in the Stone Suspense series. She lives on the west coast of Canada with her husband, Glen and laid-back Ragdoll cat, Bello.

A note from Karen:

Building relationships with my readers is the most rewarding part of writing. I *love* doing book clubs, either in person, or by video!

I occasionally send newsletters with details on new releases, exclusive offers and other bits of news relating to the Stone Suspense series.

Sign up here for my newsletter to be the *first* in the know AND receive a free e-book!
www.KarenDodd.com

You can also find me on:

Facebook: karendodd.author
Instagram: @authorkarendodd
Twitter: @authorkarendodd

ACKNOWLEDGEMENTS

Although at times, writing can be lonely, producing a story worthy of keeping readers entertained and engaged for hours is never a journey taken alone. This book is no exception. SCARE AWAY THE DARK has been made infinitely better by some very special people.

First, heart-felt thanks to my steadfast and loyal critique partners, Penny McDonald, and Cathy Scrimshaw. These wise women have been with me since the inception of my first book, DEADLY SWITCH. They have given generously of their time, their wisdom, and on occasion, their shoulders to cry on. We have been together for four novels collectively, and one about to be birthed. I bow to you for your wisdom and unparalleled support.

A second group of staunch supporters who deserve my sincere appreciation, consists of my advance reader team. These individuals enthusiastically leapt at my offer to receive early copies of the book in exchange for spotting any remaining errors and offering honest reviews: Pat Smith, Roxanne Thornton, Angela Greville, Linda LeQuesne, Karrie Converse-Jones, Bonnie Hutchinson, Diana Stevan, Trudi Luethy, Karen Sanderson, Greg King, Bernadette Woit, Neil Abramson, Barb Heard, Francine Legault, Gail Muise, Lucy Traini, Eric Lidemark, Briar Ballou, Gaby Brencher, Mimi Matthews, Doug and Mariette MacLeod, and Leslie Nolin. By the time you read this, I pray that I have done you justice in providing a read worth your dedication and time. You are, after all, the best representation of my ideal reader. I humbly thank you.

I would be remiss in not acknowledging my good friend and fellow author, Rod Baker. He and his partner, Anna Axerio, saved me from colossal embarrassment by correcting everything from boats, birds, and mental health, to my Italian. And thank you Rod for assembling the shelves that *your* books reside on in my writing studio.

I must thank my editor, Joëlle Anthony, with whom I have a love-hate relationship. I loved her for her brilliance; I hated myself for not seeing plot holes big enough to drive a semi through! Thank you for your remarkable insights and hard work, Joëlle. And for teaching me how to get the two little dots above your name! Any remaining errors are mine.

My spectacular cover designer, Sharon Brownlie of Aspire Book Covers, deserves kudos beyond the usual acknowledgments. Half-way around the world and in opposite time zones, Sharon shared my tendency toward obsessiveness, exceeding my deadlines and unreasonable expectations, while remaining gracious and calm. The result is an amazingly beautiful book cover of which I'm very proud. If you need a talented graphic designer who listens and offers sage advice, contact Sharon at: www.aspirecovers.com. Sharon, I'm afraid you're stuck with me for life!

As may be evidenced by the four years between books, writing *SCARE AWAY THE DARK* was so much more challenging than my first book. However, it has caused me to grow and to be much more engaged as a writer; I was like a dog with a bone: I couldn't let go! I thought about my characters and their predicaments every waking hour, and often while asleep. When an author experiences the inevitable frustrations of overcoming obstacles that appear to be insurmountable, there is always one special person who makes you feel it is all worthwhile. For me, that person was the best-selling author of the Dylan Hunter Justice Thrillers series, Robert Bidinotto. I had reached out to congratulate him on the release of his third book and acknowledged how challenging each one can be to complete. A few days later, when I was feeling lower than low, I opened my emails to find a personal reply. Robert had taken the time to validate my struggle and to empathize in a way that I knew I had been deeply listened to. As I toiled day after day to finish the book, I would re-read his email, and literally, I coasted to the end on the wave of his encouragement. Robert, my writing life has been enriched immeasurably by your strength and integrity. Thank you!

Finally, to my husband and soul mate, Glen: I thank you for your unwavering support and your compassionate heart. For your patience when I was off cavorting with my cast of characters, often at the expense of not having a hot meal when you dragged yourself home from doing what you do better than anyone I know. You are the rudder of my boat and my shelter from the storms. I love you.

— Karen Dodd
February 2018